The Baby Jazz

Gregory Papadoyiannis

Translation from Greek: Andriana Minou

Fomite
Burlington, VT

ISBN-978-1-942515-69-2

Library of Congress Control Number: 2016961040

Fomite

58 Peru Street

Burlington, VT 05401

www.fomitepress.com

Cover painting: Jasmine Papadoyiannis

SUMMER

1. Summer in your own words

Jazz does not want to learn any more words. She believes she already knows enough.

Jazz can say three or four of our own words clearly. Not long ago she could say more.

There used to be three of us.
Now we are left on our own, just her and me.
That may also be of some significance.

Jazz, however, has got her own words. Over the last months, she has acquired the habit of reconstructing the same words in order to say more things. She refuses to learn more words. She says words beginning with her favorite syllables, *ya, ma, ku, ta*. These dissolve and recompose in her mind, like playdoh, so that they mean several different things. Thus, ya-i means pacifier, while ya-a means glasses (my glasses), or grandma (the one from the fairy tales, there is no actual grandma nearby), or even cat.

Ma is a hard syllable – for me. Every time I hear it I wonder if she's going to continue; if she's going to say it twice. She doesn't do it often.

I don't lose hope; I constantly talk to her about everything that is happening around us. I enunciate the words. I try to teach her new ones or correct her own. I explain over and over again, that the pacifier is called pacifier and a cat is called cat .

Words are necessary, I tell her. What would we do without words? We have to learn them.

Jazz listens to me carefully; maybe she believes that all my sentences are the beginning of a fairy tale, but eventually she insists on her own thing.

She has, however, a variety of exclamations. She makes a special *aaah*, when she sees the cat, our cat, Smooch, as well as shorter versions of it for every other animal, whether it is a cat on the street or an elephant on TV. She is not particularly fond of dogs, whenever she finds a small one, though, she fearlessly pulls its muzzle.

She doesn't seem to understand insects. I always talk to her and I point at the animals in a huge story book that someone has brought her. She likes listening to me but she never repeats what I say.

Every day, she tears a page or a half from that book. I don't blame her, it is a horrible book for any age; it has, however, many animals in it. The book uses that usual name rhyming, Jen the hen, Claus the mouse, and so on.

But the stories in it lack any meaning, consistency or even a trace of beauty. It is a thoroughly idiotic book. I tell her off when she tears it, but she is right. I should buy her something better.

Why are fairy tales so stupid? I'm going through a phase of frustration with all fairy tales, in general. Jazz, of course, doesn't understand the story plots, her attention is only attracted by familiar stuff – a baby, a cat, a tiger (the animal story book is our best fairy tale these days), but I do understand them, I rediscover them actually and I feel disappointed. I find Andersen depressing, the Grimm brothers unnecessarily complicated, Charles Perrault, certainly more likeable (but I always omit the wolf's murder in *Little Red Riding Hood*) and I am generally irritated by the excess of kings, the silly princesses who are always waiting for the best boyfriend, the lads who will be princes, but in the meantime suffer from delusions of grandeur.

Even Puss in Boots is nothing but his boss' lapdog and an outrageous impostor. Tom Thumb is nice, I have to say, but what about the giant who is craving human flesh? And don't get me started on parents who abandon their children in the woods!

Well, that happens in the city as well.

As for Hansel and Gretel, yes, I admit that there is a good part, where they nibble on the gingerbread house but in the end they push the old witch in the oven. How can you say that to a child? Of course I skip it. Just as the Big Bad Wolf, she simply goes away in the end.

There must be wholesome fairy tales somewhere that you can narrate to a child, from beginning to end. But where?

In the beginning, I would do something stupid: I would tell her a story. It was the same story, I would just invent a new variation each time. It went like this:

Mum is gone…but if we are good and if we are not noisy and if we drink all our milk every day and if…

From this point on the improvisations started, depending on the day. But the story always ended like this:

So if we do all these, mum will come back…

It may take a while but she will come back.

Then I stopped telling this story. It was bad for both of us.

2. When the Giant Squirrel gets angry

The giant squirrel climbed on a half-eaten piece of cheese. From there, he could easily see his big enemy, the duck that went quaa. *Mother mouse gathered her babies, as she could see a storm brewing. The youngest one, always used to slipping away, deftly slunk in a little field of cat rissoles and crammed under a newspaper insert. The frog, who believed he would become a prince, was suddenly left alone in the green meadow. He nearly lost his eye last time. He tried to concentrate. You cannot afford to daydream when the giant squirrel gets angry. He will ask you three questions. If you do not answer correctly, he will eat you. And then what will become of you, frog? Not a prince, that's for sure.*

Who is Donald Duck's girlfriend?
A. Minnie
B. Clarabelle
C. Daisy

It's a huge rectangular room. In the middle there's a large dark table and opaque windows covered with curtains all around — nobody comes here to see the view, harsh lighting and an invisible secretary, who has placed notepads and pens in front of us — not even a laptop — for four people. Four empty glasses and a bottle of mineral water complete the decor of the table. We have been here since nine o'clock sharp. That was some time ago. We are expecting the *big heads*. Nobody bothers to tell us when exactly they are coming. We are supposed to be having a small meeting, in order to get ready to answer their questions. But that's exactly what we have been doing for the past two months. We almost can't bear looking at each other anymore. To people close to us, if we have any, we talk with a certain pride about our work, always prepared to remember or invent stories about someone famous whom we happened to meet. But here, we are nothing but patient yes-sir--employees. We will wait for as long as necessary. The big heads will at some point come, ask questions and we will respond. This is our job. We live by asking questions. Nothing existential. We are something like luxury porters of showbiz.

What color was Marilyn Monroe's hair?
A. Blonde
B. Black
C. Red

Our job does not seem to require big brains, does it? Sometimes, not even the little bit we have.

— What if somebody answers that she had red hair in a such and such film? the director asks me.

He enjoys entering my territory. We are friends, as friendly as two people who work on TV can be (i.e. not much) and especially on the same production (i.e. hardly), but we have known each other for years. He was the one who suggested I quit the publishing house and the novel editing and introduced me to TV. This happened several years ago. The director was a guest at my wedding party two years ago. Sometimes we have lunch together (near the office) or, after working on TV, we go for a quick coffee, and we talk about TV and work.

— She never had red hair, not that I know of.

There is actually some hesitation in my voice. I don't know that much about Marilyn. Just at this moment my imagination brings forward an image of her with red hair. Is it just my silly imagination? Such questions can cost you your job on TV. The manager is perhaps using this as a pretext to enter the conversation.

— We must check it.

This is his magic sentence. He never checks anything himself. His job is to check the rest of us. To my understanding, he has neither friends, nor something like a family. He always stays out late in the evenings and spends quite a lot. He tells us himself, in quite an unnecessary detail.

I try to remember what her hair was like in *Misfits*. I love that movie. It's black and white. I'm not sure, but I think that her platinum hair has a darker shade there. Maybe it's just the contrast of the film.

— Imagine someone proving to us that she was a redhead in some porn she shot before she got famous. Can you imagine that?

He makes his favorite gesture. The cutthroat.

— She never shot porn, I say bluntly.

— How do you know? I've heard…

He has heard everything about everybody. In reality, though, he hardly knows what color his own hair is. But that's what his job is about. He ought to seem like he knows everything; for other people.

— Anyway, we'll check it, the director says. We don't have a fucking laptop…is there an internet connection in here?

Nobody answers.

— These are obviously questions for the stupid, he continues. Tell us a couple of the others.

We have had this conversation a thousand times over the last two months. Questions for the stupid. Questions for the very stupid. Questions for the average ones. Questions that don't win any money. Every producer's favorites. Questions that send the players home empty-handed.

How ugly the giant squirrel was! Nobody loved him but everybody feared him. They had to be afraid of him so that he would let them live. So was the frog who would become a prince. He used to hang out with Barbie but lately they have drifted apart. She must have made the first step, we belong in different worlds, she told him. He hasn't seen her since. Only in his dreams sometimes. Or on TV on Saturday mornings.

Snow White suddenly woke up in panic. She wasn't going to wait for the prince any more. No dwarves were near her; they were long gone. She would never see the entire big picture. A happy home and a set table. Nothing is left now but some empty chairs, sparse smiles, red noses and cakes on the table. And pictures galore. Snow-White wondered where that would lead to. She had made up her mind; she would start her life over. So will I, pondered the frog. He had no desire to become a prince any more.

3. A Fennec on Treasure Island

In which continent does the fennec live?

    A. Asia

    B. Africa

    C. Australia

They quietly stare at me for a while. Obviously they do not enjoy little animal stories.

— Sounds like bullshit, the manager says.

Yet, when I last read it out, a couple of days ago, he said it was OK. The difference is that now he is scared. The judgment day is here and he doesn't feel safe.

— It's bullshit, the director agrees. Who cares about fucking animals? People don't like that kind of stuff.

— It's one of the difficult ones, I say, trying to save the fennec.

— We told you to find difficult ones that are fucking funny, the manager insists. Anyway, now it's too late.

— We'll go through them all tomorrow, says the consultant. Today we'll have a general discussion and we're going to tell them that we aren't ready yet.

Which is loosely translated into: *You* are not ready yet and *I* will cover for you, but not for long.

Do you have any idea what the fennec is? It is a timid and cunning little animal that lives in the deserts of North Africa. It looks like a fox. It spends most of its time hiding.

A bit like us. The people behind the bright lights of a television show. Four little fennecs in the desert of Goldbeast TV production company. That is precisely the spirit. Goldbeast has offices in ten countries on four different continents and provides entertainment for people watching television shows (usually quiz shows) in fifty-seven countries around the globe. From Uzbekistan to Chile and from North Africa to the icy Antarctic, Goldbeast offers entertainment. The big heads are located at the organization headquarters in New York. This year, they have decided to launch the Treasure Island Quiz Show in England where I've been living for the past ten years, since I was offered this job. I am originally from Greece, but I feel I belong neither there nor here in London.

How to win a million dollars? It's very simple: by answering the questions we have created. My job is to make these templates. With me are the director of the series, the executive manager and the game consultant (what a great job —if only it really existed). The folders with our proposals are placed before us, scattered on the desk.

The other three have pretty much secured their heads, that is, their posts in the production, at least until the first ratings come in. I haven't — not particularly. Yet, I have been doing this job for ten years. The atmosphere is highly charged. The money is big, a failure means that heads will roll. In these jobs, rise and fall are matters of chance. Just like quiz shows.

I wonder how interested I am in the whole thing. Not as much as I should be. It helps to think that you have no other way of making money. But it's not enough. My mind is wandering to something completely unrelated to the quiz or the questions.

— What's up, the director asks me. Everything OK at home?

I know he hasn't the slightest interest in what happens at home. He just wants to say something to dispel the silence.

No, everything is not OK at home. The house is not mine anymore. Once, not long ago, we were like a family there. A small family, surely. Maybe it was all in my head, though. Now, I return to a different house every evening, consistently worse than the one I left. There is nothing like a family there. Only a creature that destroys everything and furthermore requires love, attention and devotion. I have no idea how all this happened. And even if I know, I do not want to remember.

— Everything is fine, I reply trying to look cool.

— New dad, aren't you? The production manager adds.

It's high time he showed interest for something other than the questions. There are obvious traces of an (let's call it friendly) irony in the way he picks his words; I'm not exactly at the usual age for having children. I was thirty eight when she was born and I will be forty next February.

I try to forget that. The executive manager is a young man, at least five years younger than me. Nevertheless, I have to treat him with respect. That's the hierarchy in this job. It is re-shaped with each new project. Those ending up above you, demand respect. That's why I smile innocently at his ironic mood.

The game consultant smiles. Or at least she tries to. She finds the capacity of a new father for a forty-year-old rather amusing. She does not smile frequently though. You immediately understand this. She does not belong with us. She is here rather to check what exactly we intend to do. She is one of us now, but she will be the first to pull the rug under our feet if something goes wrong. That's her job.

— Everything is under control, I say and it sounds somewhat irrelevant. It doesn't matter. The conversation ends there.

Everything is fine, apart from the fact that for the last couple of months I've been alone. Alone with her. And I don't know what exactly I should do. And every day my anxiety grows because I feel I am making things worse. A huge question mark waits for me at home. But that's not something I should be thinking about here. We are here to offer entertainment.

The meeting with the big heads was short. They came in suddenly; three men in their forties and a secretary or something. Her cold beauty caught our eyes for a while. Then the producer handed out the folders we had prepared to the heads. Most of the contents had already been e-mailed to them. They were not particularly concerned with the questions. They probably believe that they can be altered in a few hours. I can't imagine any of them going through that process — I mean writing something. Big heads are born as such. We lowered our own little heads over the papers, waiting. We were rewarded with a modest smile. After that, they talked with the producer about the dates. That's their big problem. Then, they said their goodbyes and left as suddenly as they came.

The director takes a deep breath.

— Let's go for a coffee, he says, in his friendliest tone.

— I have to go home, I replied.

— OK, see you tomorrow then.

I left them there to continue the discussion. The rule is not to ever miss a discussion that concerns you, even indirectly. The situation can turn against you in a split second. But I wanted to get out in the fresh and slightly icy air of the street. I walked a little. I wasn't in a hurry to get home. I just wanted to get out of there. But the situation at home, well, that was another story. I feel guilty that I do not want to rush back. But it that's the way it is. I walk aimlessly on the wet streets simply delaying my return. No, things are not OK at home.

4. My father came from Hollywood

It is still summer. A difficult summer. The weather is quite hot. For some reason I believe that everything will be better when the temperature drops. I don't know why I believe this. You could say I'm searching for shelter in the chill of the autumn. Until recently, I was dreaming of the moment she would be born, the moment I would have my own child to tuck in. You know the picture. There is nothing more beautiful and Hollywood-inspired than a father putting a colorful, soft blanket over his child with a goodnight kiss. Then, he turns off the animal-decorated lamp and a joyful day comes to an end.

When Jazz started walking, I thought it was the right time for me to become the perfect Hollywood father. Her mother had to tell me several times: we don't cover babies with blankets. It is dangerous. They have a sleeping pouch instead. A sleeping pouch. The baby gets in and that's the end of the day. Lamps, animal-decorated or not, are also dangerous. And to make matters worse, Jazz does not seem to appreciate the value of her father's kiss. She just accepts it. It is one of the things-I-do-to-feel-better-about-myself. I never embraced the dangerous-blanket theory. I have watched lots of movies and I have identified (here is the real danger) happiness in life with happiness according to the directions of the best American scriptwriters. Now, some time later, I'm just waiting for her to grow up. When she's three, she will be ready for our Hollywood goodnight-scene. Although after everything that has happened since, this is the least I am missing...

This is a city you cannot love easily. It took me a while to get used to the weird weather. And I can't really say I'm entirely used to is, to be honest. Here, however, on the sixth floor of an ancient block of flats in East London, one can feel the summer refusing to fade. A warm breeze is coming through the window. Smooch has been perching on the windowsill for hours. I never understood whether he likes the summer or not. Probably not. Cats love the sun but they do not like summertime. I think Smooch loves the winter sun. I am standing next to him and I am looking at the last shapes of the day dissolving. This here has been a strange summer, completely different from what I had become used to. It was the first summer with the child. It had nothing to do with the previous summer with the baby, immersed in its stroller. Summer for children; what I considered alone, when I was a child, I can now feel lost in the depths of time.

But through her eyes, I may find it again someday. Such poetic thoughts occur to me only when she's asleep. Maybe that's when I can love her a bit more. Maybe because it's easier to love a tiny creature wrapped up in a pink bunny sleeping pouch or whatever that thing is called. Jazz is sleeping peacefully in the room upstairs, a loft just inches bigger than her tiny bed. In the absolute silence, I can hear her breath and the hollow thumps she makes when she changes position and her body touches the wooden partitions of the bed. It is a crib with a wooden railing; she would not stay in there otherwise. She would soon stand up and cry her way downstairs.

The quiz got approved at last. Shooting starts in about a month. The show is scheduled to come out just before Christmas. I will have to spend many hours at the studio every day. What am I to do with Jazz? I must convince the woman that takes care of her in the mornings to come in the afternoons, and as for the mornings, I am going to need daycare. I do not like it but I have no other choice.

Do I not like it? Let's be honest here. I will be freed from a burden. But is that what a child is? A burden? Am I that cruel?

I search online. I don't know what else to do. I could ask at a nursery from what age they accept them. But this is easier. I google the phrase: appropriate age for kindergarten. I find an article. It says that children who go to preschool early, gain precedence over the others. It says that children who start preschool at the age of two tend to be better at Math and English than the rest. Good. This is not what I was looking for, but it suits me for now. I keep reading. It goes on to say that children who attend daycare before the age of two may acquire antisocial habits. This I don't like. I shall wait until she is two years old. In two months. For how long? For as long as it takes. I don't search for any more articles. Does that make me a fraud? Maybe not. A man selfishly set in his ways? Definitely. Yet I have a feeling that I will miss her.

At least for a while. The shooting will last for a few months if all goes well. If something goes wrong, I will return home. There are a million reasons for a show to get canceled. I think up a few unintentionally, I almost want it to happen. But why am I thinking about it? In any case, I have trouble with the hours I spend with her. I don't think I help her enjoy herself. Later on, when we'll be able to talk, when she'll be able to understand me, I'm sure I will do better. But until then, we have a long time ahead of us.

What is my problem? 'My problem is not the fact that I am alone.' I remember an old comic book; the hero is a desperate lonely guy who sends letters to God asking for help for this and that. He has a problem with everything, just like me. His wife has abandoned him. At least he lives alone. 'I don't mind the loneliness' the comic guy says, 'my problem is that I have nobody to talk about it with'.

In reality though, I'm not alone. Nobody can be alone when there is Jazz. I'm just someone who has been abandoned. Someone left behind. But I do not panic. It's just that I have nobody with whom I can talk about it. Or about Jazz. That's probably why I started writing.

5. The rules of the game

Jazz doesn't tear everything up anymore. A few months ago, especially ever since she has started walking, she used to tear up any kind of paper she would get her hands on and mainly newspapers. She has shown a strange respect to books, however. She has never torn up one. Or hardly ever. She has slightly torn up the one I'm reading now, but mostly out of excitement, because I let her leaf through it.

The shooting for the quiz show will start soon. Yesterday, the director and I visited the set to take a look at the setting. For the time being, it is a vast forest of scaffolding. I have seen similar ones, but this time I found it particularly repulsive. Maybe that's because I have been moody lately. During the whole ride, I was trying to estimate how long it would to take for me to commute here and back. The scheduled rehearsals, the trial shooting will take a month. Then, we'll go into the studio for the actual shooting. In the meantime, more than ten people, scattered all over the hierarchy ladder will be fumbling around my questions, trying to justify their posts. They will be free to correct, alter or erase my questions. In a quiz show, the person who writes the questions is just a cog in the machine. I won't be the only one writing them; there are ten external collaborators for this job, poorly paid and only for the questions that will 'play' on the show. They haven't figured that out yet, they are led to believe that everything they write will be useful. The best case scenario is, however, that only one out of the twenty questions each of them creates will pass. There's a huge supply of young people who think of it as an easy job, as well as older collaborators who want to supplement their meager income. In a time of financial austerity, the supply is enormous. That gives them the liberty to 'hire' — no strings attached — too many and retain very few. And I will have to decide who stays. Good stuff. That, along with the questions I create myself, will be my job. Of course, I will have to be at the set during the shooting. To ambush and finish off dangerous players. Something like word safari.

I try to teach her to avoid some things, to stop messing with the garden hose, not to touch the socket, not to eat the flowers. Also, not to scoop the dirt out of the flower pots; she loves playing with dirt. She has stopped eating dirt though. The last time she did it was when we went to that deserted beach in January. She ate some sand and she bit on a pebble. It was not the first time but I guess she was finally convinced that it was inedible. I also try to explain to her that she shouldn't climb on the coffee table in front of the TV. Of course, she shouldn't watch TV. However, she quiets down when she watches TV. This is mostly my own concern. I must learn not to find shelter in television. It is a shelter though. And a few precious minutes of truce.

I imagine that this can be destructive. I find comfort in the thought that it could always be worse. Parents who let their babies get hypnotized for hours in front of the TV. I'm glad I'm not one of them. But when I despair, I turn on the TV.

She doesn't watch everything. She doesn't pay attention to the news. On the contrary, at about that time, right in the middle of the eight o'clock news, it is the time for the greatest destruction. It is the final act of a day's war. The war that Jazz has declared against the normal environment of the house – sadly, something like this does not exist anymore; I can't even remember what it used to look like. She has never lost a battle, since she has clumsily started walking. There were three consecutive steps. Then she leaned back and I had to keep her from falling on the floor. But there were three whole steps. That was nearly four months ago, at the end of the winter. She was about one and a half year old. She was a late walker. She is generally late in doing some things. I don't believe it matters. Now she's almost two. She should be able to talk more. There's always a 'should' based usually on the example of other people. I'm no expert on children's upbringing, but I feel that behind every 'should' there are simply adult weaknesses to be found.

I have no idea how to raise a child. What I mean is that I have no clue what somebody ought to do to raise a child properly. Alone. Of course there are books. There are friends willing to advise you. There are magazines for parents, filled with lengthy, colorful articles, tributes to the terrible twos, or threes, or fours. But nobody can actually help you when Jazz wakes up crying and you can't understand what she wants and she doesn't know what she wants and she can't tell you what it is or give you the chance to talk about it. There are no rules. I have to invent them. But why me? Why should I know how it's done? It's very likely that I'm making countless mistakes. What do other people do? Do they learn the rules from books? Do they improvise like I do? Other people, however, are not on their own.

I write with a tiny font, as if I'm afraid somebody will read what I write. I'm probably more frightened that I will read it and I get scared of myself reading it and getting disappointed. That's a nasty game. I feel the need to write and then I think I write nonsense. I'm so worthless that I can't even describe what I feel — what is happening to me. Why am I doing it then? Because every single day I need to feel that I do something to get my mind off things. Maybe because I want to talk to somebody and nobody is around. Writing releases a part of me. I'm afraid I'm being melodramatic, cliché, ordinary, shallow, silly and boring. But who cares since nobody is going to read all this? After all, everything is pointless. Nothing matters.

I wonder if I suffer from some form of depression. Who knows? I don't have the luxury to look into it, even if it is so; even if I reach a point when I won't be able to take care of myself, I ought to be able to take care of her. You don't need to look for the meaning of life when you have Jazz. She simply exists and since she exists, she is the meaning. Luckily, she doesn't understand any of this. I sometimes envy her.

P.S. Who can be such a jerk to call their child Jazz? I don't know, it came naturally. Her

English name is Jasmine, so after a pile of nicknames, I ended up calling her Jazz and I got used to it. And she doesn't seem to find it odd. After all, I love jazz. When she gets older, I will stop it. Yes, but what if I have already traumatized her until then? I have no other answer: I love jazz.

6. Guilt and baby swear words

Jazz throws everything down, she opens drawers and cupboards and hurls everything she finds in them — the truth is that there's hardly anything left — she climbs on any surface she can and wherever she does not climb, she stretches her arms and throws down anything she can reach. She doesn't need to see what it is. She just throws it down.

In the beginning of the summer (when she started walking with ease), I supposedly fashioned the big room, where we spend most of the day, into a fortress, making it inaccessible to creatures less than one meter tall. However, as a Gulliver in the land of the dwarves, I failed miserably. My fortification is full of gaps. She is less than 70 centimeters tall, but when it comes to destruction she is masterful in using her hands. She is also extremely inventive in finding ways to increase her height using just about everything as a stepping stone; even me, when I get on the floor to get closer to her world. I become one more stepping stone for her exploratory frenzy. Otherwise, she uses cushions, boxes, books, the printer, a bag of fruit forgotten on the floor, everything. There are, also, some things that you can't always keep in distance; and there are other things you can find in every household. Though they seem like peaceful, innocent, useful things, they turn into frightful weapons of destruction when Jazz gets her hands on them. Coffee tables had to be removed. Then, chairs proved to be as dangerous, because she can climb on them and reach the table. That is where the Holy Grail of her world must be. The place where I have randomly accumulated everything that had to be rescued from devastation. Naturally, shortly after this, the drawers from the furniture had to be removed and, eventually, the entirety of the furniture followed.

Now we live in a vast field with green artificial turf in the middle. A rectangular plastic mat suitable for playgrounds. So the child can play quietly. But Jazz detests borders and restrictions. So, she is constantly out of the green area or she uses the entire green mat as a shield by lifting it and enjoying herself with the dreadful noise created by the things that happened to be on it. Some of them are never to be seen again, or when they do re-appear, it won't matter; they will always be lost in the world of a-feral-child-was-here.

Lately, she has demonstrated an uncontrollable desire to operate the remote control. When she trips and falls after a risky mission, there is only one way to calm her down: give her the remote control. In order for the solace to work, though, the TV is supposed to be on. She quickly realized that this is the only time it is valuable. Consequently, I only turn the TV on and off from the switch now. But she knows well where to find the remote control and she knows pretty well that its use is to change channels. The remote control calms her down. So does the cell phone. But I am determined to draw the line at the latter. Someday, somebody will teach her how to use it — but not me.

I am gradually finding some ways of dealing with her impetuosity. But I'm not giving her the cell phone. I only do it to calm her when she stumbles and hurts herself. She has fallen several times. Almost every day she slips or loses her balance when walking and she falls. Or she will try to climb up the staircase – she hardly ever falls there, of course, but there's another million ways for her to fall. She falls quite often. Sometimes she just gets tangled up at my feet, and then, I feel guilty for my clumsiness. But the greatest guilt I feel is when I tell her off and yell at her.

When I suddenly scream at her, she jerks. Usually, that is followed by tears; more yelling is mostly followed by more tears, creating a never-ending loop which will stop only if I find a way to soothe her. There are also punishments, of course, which usually include time-out in her playpen. I occasionally grab her forcefully and put her there. I feel so much guilt I often apologize to her. Fortunately, she seems to get over it quickly. Sometimes I swear at her. I aim at child — friendly variations of swearing (hoggle-zwiggy and blorging-floo are some of them; I wonder whether other people have thought of this too or perhaps I am some kind of genius when it comes to child anger management). But sometimes it's plain swearing. Some people say that it harms her, that she's going to remember it. I feel hopeless. But I also feel hopeless when she won't stop her shenanigans, like dropping the lamp that is above the sofa — she has to climb for it, but she's getting better and better at it — or dropping the, supposedly well protected, phone next to the lamp. She usually doesn't throw the phone down. It's an old-fashioned wired telephone — I read somewhere that wireless phones are harmful. Actually, I have purposefully placed a phone in her playpen; a regular telephone just not plugged in. She looked at it for a while in the beginning, and then she let it drop. Since then, she has never paid any attention to it again. It must be the tone she hears from the real phone that enchants her, when she picks up the handset. She puts it against her ear and says mama. She doesn't stop saying mama with the handset against her ear. Then, I feel hopeless again but I don't tell her off. Or maybe I do occasionally, when I'm having a bad day.

I keep wondering if I have the right to yell at her. The easy excuse is that I must protect her. I definitely have to protect her. I can't let her fall down the stairs, I must yell at her, so she doesn't climb them. I could of course spend some money and have a baby gate made for her. But I can't afford it; which is not her fault. Even worse, there are times when I scream at her because she does something that simply bothers me. Then I keep saying to myself that I do not have that right — I can't do that to a twenty-two- month-old. On the other hand, I think that she is cunning enough to learn anything inconvenient for her.

But then again, why am I thinking of this? Perhaps because it is inconvenient for me when she doesn't learn things she should learn? In any case, I'm a goner — a loser, in a way. What I mean is that the paradise of doing- as-I-like doesn't exist for me, I don't know if it ever existed. When I think about my parents, I really doubt it did. I don't owe them a favor for this, though. On the contrary, I get angry thinking that I might have been kicked out of that paradise much too soon. And now I do exactly the same.

Who is interested in what I write? Only I am, I guess, or somebody just like me who goes through the same situation. So, practically nobody. But it calms me a little. Now and then I feel slightly repulsed at myself, when I write. I don't know exactly why; because I don't do it well is one thought. It comes and goes, though. I can't see the point of it, but since it is only my concern, it doesn't do any harm, does it?

Jazz, however, forgets easily, or at least it seems like she does. She is easily distracted by a cookie, or the remote control, or even a screwdriver, which has to be quickly retracted from her because it is dangerous, and here we go, all over again. For the time being, she's sitting on the dresser, throwing the remote control directly at my head. Can't help but utter a baby swear.

The Jazz war

piece of mother-mouse ear, cookie crumbs, traces of tomato and squashed banana piece, orange and blue building blocks, more building blocks, large intact squirrel, small frog that goes *fshhh*, torn magazines, torn newspapers, shredded literary insert from Sunday's newspaper, half-eaten pink geraniums, small squirrel with bitten tail, vest — probably clean, one sock, some other sock, TV remote control, DVD player remote control — broken. Filofax, papers, hat, one shoe, one clean diaper, ointment for back pain, torn stool cover, lid of food container, another food container without lid, CD without sleeve, unpaid electricity bill, accountant dossier — open, vanished contents, cookie crumbs, half-eaten piece of cheese, traces of milk, baby bottle with some water in it, empty coffee cup, filofax pages, squeaky duck, duck that goes quaa quaa, non- singing frog — no batteries included, mismatched building blocks, Snow-White jigsaw puzzle piece, camera pouch, one pad from a pressure device, CD without sleeve, sleeve from some other CD, unidentified recordable CD. Cat rissoles, harlequin shoe, pink scoop, children's size Sherlock Holmes hat, book in mint condition, slightly crushed cover from another book, cereal, undamaged peanuts, father's sneaker, sphygmomanometer.

This used to be a regular room. Then, the Jazz war started.

7. Ukiyo–e: a floating world

Sometimes I feel ashamed of the job I do. It's not exactly the fact that you deceive people (no modern-world deception easily admits its mechanism), but it is definitely the way you give them doubtful — or even false — dreams. My job is to create a simple image of happiness, when the quiz begins with the easy first questions, and then to prevent those dreams from coming true. With some help from the Fennec, the Marmot, the Lizard with the thousand faces, the Triassic period (right before the Jurassic), the town Funafuti (capital of the Tuvalu islands), the nationality of the litterateur Ilkan Tarush (Turkish), the Shofar (trumpet from ancient Israel – the other options are: rodent from Eastern Asia and cold vegetable dish from Central America) and *which fruit is considered the healthiest according to the International Food Matrices: apricots, apples or grapes?* It's option number one, but you must be a sick genius — to say the least —to positively know the answers to all the above. The bosses always prefer something better. Here is something they like: *Who was not awarded a Nobel Peace Prize?* Winston Churchill, Henry Kissinger, Mahatma Gandhi. The third one is the correct answer. That's the kind of questions they like. But practically everybody can guess that. So if the player does guess it, one person is to blame for trying to be a wise guy; the person in charge of the questions. Of course it's not an easy job. The bosses always have an opinion (usually a catastrophic one) and the worst part is that there are people who occupy themselves with all this information. More people than you think. They learn all the possible-impossible answers. They read the books that

I read, they search the Internet the way I search the Internet and — just like in crime films — I, the murderer (of their dreams), must be always one step ahead. My mind must follow the insane paths of their research — and annihilate them with even-more-unlikely-questions.

Every now and then, I have to admit, especially when I know for a fact that one of those professionals is on the set and about to play (even though there is often a red alert for them during the draw — we have those quiz vultures flagged and we make sure they never reach the player's cubicle), a desire for the cat-mouse chase is awakened in me — until you actually win, though, there's a good chance that you are the mouse — and from the control room, next to the director, I steer the game in a way that all their hopes get crashed on the rocks. The system allows you to change the questions until the last minute; and there are questions that simply cannot-be-answered. Maybe the first one, yes, or even one more but never all of them. I rely on these questions; it's the only way that my head can remain in the TV industry. And I enjoy it when they lose. We cheer when we see them break down in disappointment. We know we have saved the company's money and, more importantly, our heads. Later, when the lights dim, a feeling of shame and disgust for what I do reappears. It is inevitable.

Jazz doesn't watch TV quizzes. Jazz likes old black-and-white movies and Mr. Bean. Also, she somehow can distinguish the satirical shows and seems interested in them, as well as in cartoons. But they usually suck; aliens and guns and childish super heroes, a total disgrace. I look forward to the day when we will be able to watch *Finding Nemo* or *Lion King* or *Ice Age* or even Buster Keaton movies, although I'm afraid that at the moment they would encourage her destructive tendency. There is definitely plenty of time until all this happens. We are still in the midst of an incomprehension desert, with a few oases of… love. Love? I'm not sure if what she feels for me has anything to do with love. Her feelings, in general, are a floating world — that is what Japanese artists called their woodcuts in the 17th century: ukiyo–e: a floating world.

I sometimes entertain her when I lift her up in the air, I lift her high enough for her to reach the rice paper ball we have for a lamp shade and shake it with her little hand. Or when I lift her upside-down, holding her from her feet and I gently let het put her little hand down on the floor first so that she can stand up. She likes it when I do this; she laughs and makes these little happy sounds. Lately, since the 20th month, she puts her little head on my lap and I stroke her, I softly massage her, I rub her back and even this isn't love.

Tonight for the first time, I softly put my head on her shoulder. She was quite calm. There are surges of restlessness alternating with calm moments. I gently leaned on her; I basically let my head touch her shoulder while we were watching TV. She didn't show any crazy enthusiasm; how could she after all? But I think I saw her smiling and she kept watching TV and I knew and she knew that this was something like love, something like tenderness, as if a small part of everything I have been giving for so long was given back to me. It was nice. Is it possible that she somehow understands that I will take her to the nursery? Can she be sensing something like this? Smooch always knew when I was leaving and he would start giving me the cold shoulder from the night before. He often climbed on my suitcase and wouldn't get down. When I returned, he wouldn't come near me for hours. He still does it. Cats don't like to travel; but they don't like it when you travel, either. When it comes to babies and cats, the answer to the question of love is never given to you. You may believe whatever you want. There is, however, another thought I like. Children, like cats, accept you for what you are. No cat will turn its back to you because you put on weight, or because you are losing your hair or because you drink. Not even if you leave and be gone for a while. Not even then. Perhaps not even if you decide that you should spend some time apart.

It is a little silly to think about that. I feel guilt — this isn't news — that's why I think like this. It will be just for a few hours. But it will be just the beginning. Little by little, the world will come between us. Pretty melodramatic; I should be writing a soap opera.
What would happen if we stayed together forever? How long would forever last? Not to imprison a child, but to keep them with you. Teach them the things they are supposed to learn before going to school; stay together until then. I have heard of people who do this. They keep their children at home. They teach them things there. Even instead of school. What kind of bullshit am I thinking? I can't even stay with her for half a day… It will be great at the nursery. A welcome change for everybody.

AUTUMN

1. A game of words

When Jazz was born, we used to buy baby magazines. I would joyfully go and pick one, depending on the free gift it came with and I would then read it cover to cover. But I don't think I learned anything I didn't know already. The same goes for baby.com which started appearing in my email account, god knows how; maybe through the hospital, the doctor or the baby food I buy – but then again, I don't remember giving my email to anyone, I don't know how they figure it out. I'd rather not think about it.

I believe though, it's about time I learned more things. I ought to learn what exactly one should do to bring up a child properly. Of course I've read a couple of books since she was born; some of them were quite amusing. You know, stuff like, *How to put your child to sleep* (back then, we thought it was very important), *How to bring up happy children*, even books like *It is a foetus' world*. One of them, by Professor Alfred A. Tomatis was really excellent. I haven't studied anything consistently though; but have I ever done anything consistently in my life, in any case? (That's a scary question). Meanwhile, it's rather late now that the child is already two years old; but one has to start some time. Maybe there's still time to fix some things. Starting tomorrow, there will be consistent studying. I will find out what I have to do. I have to. But I don't have time of course.

They don't like my questions. They don't say it to me straight, but they find them old-fashioned. If you are pushing 40, you are too old for TV. If you haven't reached an important post until then, you are at fate's mercy. And your fate wants you out of the game.

Every day I try hard to come up with as stupid questions as it gets; questions that make me sick of what I do. It's a bit like inventing a questionable drug — just to keep my job. Isn't that what everybody does? People don't want to listen to questions about authors, books or art. People don't read. They may listlessly flip through what TV indicated as the latest best seller but that's all. People don't want to watch history questions. People find history boring. People find boring anything that looks difficult. People find boring anything that makes them think. People don't want to think. They just want to suck images through the shiny glass screen; watch pictures and get hypnotized. So that they don't have to think. That's what we all do here. That's what I do.

Who discovered penicillin? People don't care about penicillin. They have modern antibiotics.

When was the first photograph developed? People couldn't care less about the first photograph. They have cell phone cameras.

When was the first postage stamp released? People only send emails now.

When was the first gasoline-powered car put in circulation? People don't give a damn about the gasoline-powered car.

Give us something else. Give us something interesting. Tell us something that-won't-make-us-die-of-fucking-boredom!

What is Lady Gaga's star sign?

Until what age was Britney Spears a virgin?

How many lovers does Rihanna currently have?

Nice try, but they still want something more pleasant.

Which cartoon is also the surname of a US president?

Garfield, Snoopy or Droopy? The correct answer is the first:

James Garfield, 20th President of the USA

History again? Do you or don't you want this job already?

I feel like an idiot because I can't write questions for complete idiots.

Carl-Friedrich Benz constructed the first gasoline-powered car in 1886. It had three wheels and reached 16 kilometers per hour. This man, who lost his father when he was two years old and loved bicycles, had a dream: to build the first vehicle without horses. He and his wife Bertha, had been involved with the invention of the automobile ever since they were engaged. When they got married, Bertha became legally unable to reserve the rights to an invention. Only her husband had this privilege now. But when he failed to proceed with the refinement of the invention, she, without his permission, carried out the first car trip ever made. It was August 5, 1888. Bertha was the driver and the passengers were two of her children. I try to imagine them speeding in the August sunshine; she wearing goggles (when did we start wearing sunglasses? Here's a question they might like) and the children shouting, mad with excitement, standing on their seats and sticking their tongues out to terrified passers-by. Bertha took detailed notes of everything that happened on this trip. When she returned, after having travelled 106 km, on the Mannheim—Pforzheim route, they could finally perfect the first car in history and begin mass production. They kept making cars until the end of their lives.

Who cares?

Now she sounds as if she talks to herself, but with words only she understands. It sounds a bit like a song or like she's having a conversation with herself. When it comes to having a conversation with me, she doesn't show any progress; but when I tell her something, she seems to understand. I wonder if she understands more than she shows; like some prisoners in war films, who know the language but don't speak. Sometimes she gives it away though. Then again, maybe the things I tell her are too obvious. She likes drinking her milk on her own now, when the bottle is half empty and light enough for her to carry it around and sip it slowly. I told her to drink the milk and stop fooling around or else she would go straight to bed and she seemed to understand it; she stopped fooling around and drank it.

2. My mistakes are better than yours

It was a nice little bar in Shoreditch, full of old-fashioned black-andwhite movie stills. It wasn't far from the office. It was quiet, and stayed open late. The director went straight to the point before even the drinks arrived.

— We have a problem with the questions.

— It figures. Every copy I send comes back with more notes than questions.

— Look, I get that you have done a lot of work, but you know how it is…

— They're scared.

— They're scared. That's it. It is a huge project. Too much money, huge production…

— They want to give me the sack?

— Nobody said anything like this, not in my face. But…

— …they want better questions.

— They're not happy.

— They never are. That's their job.

— That's true, buddy. But we have to play along. Can't you change your style a little bit?

— I'm doing my best.

— I know you are.

I wondered if he was actually worried about my job or mostly about his status. I had been his choice, we had been working together for years; he had always been the frontman, the PR man. It was his domain. I was in his shadow. I was the man chosen by the director. So, if I wasn't suitable for the job, he would also be in trouble.

— I will try to change my style. I understand the problem. Alright, man.

— Do try to play along. That's the whole point. If the show launches and goes well, we're ok. But until then…

— We do what we're told. OK. I'll make an effort.

— Good, forget about it now. Everything ok at home?

— Everything is OK. No problem. As always.

— The kid?

— The kid is growing up.

A thought crossed my mind: had he forgotten if it was a boy or a girl? He always asked about the 'kid'.

— You should come with us one night. A night out with the guys from the office. You can get a night off, right?

Even the thought of it was exhausting.

— Of course I can. Just tell me when and I'll be there.

We had our drinks, watching the rain through the bar windows. It's always demeaning when you lose a job. But I would be free. Free to do what? I have no idea.

What was it I didn't like my parents to do to me? What were the problems they caused me? What was my worst fear? How did they do me wrong? And: (the-million-dollar-question) Which of these mistakes am I repeating?

Let's see: I didn't like going to bed early. I didn't want to be lied to. I didn't want to watch them fight. (Ok, at least Jazz won't suffer from that — after all, I realized this only when I was much older)

But how consciously could I understand when I was her age? How can I know for sure since I don't remember any of it? My first memories are after

I was three years old. My very first memory — it feels more like a photo, pinned on my mind: a lady with two little dogs, a white one and a black one; later it dawned on me that it was probably an old lady from the balcony across the street.

Let me continue: I didn't like much of the food they gave me. And I didn't like being forced to eat it. Jazz doesn't have that problem either: she eats everything. There's only food she likes and food she really likes. Easy-going kid.

Later on, I didn't like the get-togethers of grown-ups. They talked about things I didn't understand, they didn't pay attention to me and they showed a general disinterest in my presence; as if they didn't want me there. Also: I didn't like being treated like a baby. But there is still time for that.

What problems did they cause me? I'll make you a list. I'm insecure. I'm timid. I'm shy around women. I'm moody. I'm odd. I'm (still) a fussy eater. I'm more sad than happy (not just now, I've always been like this). Also: I talk to myself. I don't trust people (this gets worse as years go by). I'm scared of death. I'm scared of old age. I'm scared of the possibility that there is nothing beyond this life. At the same time, I'm scared of the punishment for what I'll do in this life. There's more of course, but I'd better stop. But am I sure that *they* caused all these? No, I'm not.

I used to be whooped. By both parents. Nothing terrible but it did happen. Sometimes it wasn't even my fault. But when exactly is it a child's fault?

Also: they weren't honest with me — one more thing I realized much later.

My worst fear was, of course, punishment. Punishment meant isolation. The feeling that you have done something wrong. The agonizing feeling (they actually told me this) that I would always be bad since I was a bad kid. Darkness certainly terrified me. Older kids terrified me. Especially the ones who bullied me. I was a shy, bespectacled boy, not particularly tall, rather average; at everything. Thankfully, back then I didn't know the meaning of the word 'average'. I was a normal kid. What is a normal kid? A sitting duck. Is it normal when other kids beat you up?

Apparently it was, according to our teacher.

But let me go back to parents. I was also afraid of the idea that I would be left alone without them — that was always one part of the punishment. We will leave you on your own. My father often threatened to throw me out of the car, when I was being naughty during family trips. I was also afraid of the idea that they would take my toys away – that was a classic threat. Sometimes they did take them away; they broke them or threw them away, I don't remember exactly. Also: the idea that God would punish me. This must have been the worst.

Did I experience a living hell? Did I experience more or less the same as everyone else born in a Greek provincial town during the 70's? I don't know. I can't find all the others and ask them. But I do know that kids my age were being beaten by their parents. Some were poorer than me. Some lived in very poor homes and had no toys. And that was also a way for them to remind me that I needed to be better. Later on, I learned how to read and I started talking to myself. How many mistakes did they make? How many mistakes do you see in the cryptic image of my carefree childhood?

Which mistakes am I repeating? I don't know. Maybe I just make my own mistakes.

I feel a little tired, doctor. Can we continue next time?

3. Just pretending underneath the hollow moon

There is now a second woman in our lives. The first one is the strict and burly, middle-aged lady who comes once a week to help with the housework, tidying, and ironing that I've always hated. But even when she's at home, it's like she isn't. I don't know how she does it, maybe it's a gift. The second one however, the girl who will babysit Jazz when I'm away, is a rather chubby young girl, cheerful and always smiling. She wears her hair in dreadlocks, she wears loose-fitting clothes, you would call her cool I guess, and she studies eastern philosophies — I didn't even know you could study this around here. I like her style, but it seems like she belongs in a completely different world — maybe it's just me. I feel rather awkward near her but Jazz seems to approve of her, unenthusiastically though. Would it satisfy me deep-down if she cried and asked for her daddy? Maybe. She doesn't do it anyway. So, until the evening shooting begins, the situation will remain as it is. I'll be getting back home at around six or seven and the time I'll have with her will be minimal. Isn't that what I wanted?

Jazz pretends to be asleep. She shuts her eyes tightly. But she can't keep it up for long. She opens one eye and peeks at me to see if I fell for it. She keeps smiling during the entire performance. But she can't see that. I don't complain — she loves sleeping. But now, she pretends she's asleep, in order to avoid sleeping. She reminds me of those dreams we have of being awake, so we can sleep a little more. I've always loved sleep. I think that I chose this line of work, editor, because I could at least sleep more. When I was very young, I wanted to become an author. Back then, my father still found this amusing. When I repeated it at the age of fourteen, my father went through my things, found something like a short story and started reading out loud the parts he considered funniest. I don't quite remember what it was, definitely something dramatic. It ended with a death, I think. I do remember the glazed door between us, though, so that I didn't hear him. But I did. I remember his shadow behind the door and his voice mockingly repeating: "He wants to be an auuuthooor". My father did the right thing. What he thought was right. I never repeated the word. I stopped writing for myself. I think that this must be the first time I write something for me, after the millions of words I've written or corrected for others, for almost twenty years. But now I write about Jazz. She is my alibi. Does this make me an author? I don't think so. What I believe about Jazz is that I will let her do what she wants. It sounds vague but I prefer it this way.

She is sleeping, actually sleeping now. Every now and then, I can hear her in the night talking her own words. Even more rarely, she suddenly starts crying, but softly, calmly. I call it discussion crying. She cries what she wants to say. She cries the same way as you and I would talk. Maybe there isn't much difference. I go near her, I talk to her for a while, mainly gibberish, and she immediately goes back to sleep. Alternatively, I change her pacifier — we have four similar ones — or I give her milk, if there is any left in her bedtime bottle.

The days are still long. When I get back in the evening, we go for a walk with the stroller. I like talking to her. I tell her stories about my day at work, old stories I remember, stories I make up on the spot. While we cross streets to reach the park, I show her things and I explain to her what everything is. She seems to enjoy all this. When she feels like it, she looks around and points at things, talking her strange talk. I guess she also wants to explain things to me, in her own way. Sometimes we use the same words, but when I ask her to repeat something, she gives me a sly smile and says nothing. It's a game. But she can tell the buses from the cars. She likes staring at trees and when I let her run free, she picks flowers and brings them back to me. The playground is full of water puddles due to the recent rain. I toss small pebbles in the puddles. So does she. When it gets dark, she can tell that night is coming. She doesn't say it like that, but I understand her. She has also learned the moon, the only thing she learned this month. I ask her where the moon is, she raises her finger, looks up and points at the moon. She says: oooh. That's what she says when she sees it rising: oooh. It's like she discovers it for the first time every night and she welcomes it.

She utters words as if she's asking questions. She says: Mom? The truth is that I have cut down on stories about moms. She says it anyway. Of course, if I ask her to repeat it, she says nothing at all or something completely incomprehensible, like the songs she sings to herself the rare mornings she wakes up in a good mood and not crying her eyes out. She almost always wakes up crying. I used to think that she's having dreams from other worlds, from past lives perhaps, and she gets startled when she wakes up in 'this' one again, so she starts crying. Luckily, she gets over it quickly. Yesterday, though, she woke up in the middle of the night because she hadn't digested properly. I had given her a bunch of different stuff, sweets and salty snacks and she devoured everything too fast and of course I am the one to blame for this.

I have found a game for us to play, but I guess it isn't particularly clever. We pretend we're hitting each other. It goes without saying that she hits me and I try to fend off her blows and her tiny fists. My slaps begin sharply but land on her cheek like strokes. Her blows however become quite strong. I also make sure I make the sound effects. I imitate the noise an actual blow would make. *Boom!, bang!, pow!, clank!,* anything I can remember from cartoons. Jazz gets overly excited and she hits hard and shouts like a maniac. It's nice to see her enjoying it but this raises two issues: One, if you're not careful you can be seriously injured and two, when you want to stop, she doesn't. She yells even louder and then you have to pamper her or promise her something better before she gets really pissed off. In the meantime, she bursts into tears, which is always an easy solution.

I already said so — it's a stupid game. I wonder if there are other people who are being so idiotic with their children. In the movies, I often see dads fake 'fighting' with their sons. But Jazz is not a boy. The truth is that until it goes too far, I really enjoy it. Am I being a complete asshole? What am I teaching my child? Beating others up?

Jazz has no problem with daily rituals like bathing and feeding. She just enhances them. She wants a pacifier in the bath and she wants to drink her milk on her own. When she gets bored with food, she tosses it but never before then. There is, however, food — like potato chips — that she never gets bored of, and therefore never gets tossed. Very often, when we are sitting on the balcony during daytime, she points at the sky and says oooh. I have no idea what this means. She might be looking for the moon in the morning sky. She might be wondering where it has gone. It makes sense.

4. Small betrayals while the fever rises

This was her first day in daycare. I was told that crying is natural at this stage. *She'll get used to it. She has to get used to it.*

I can't shake off a feeling of betrayal that has been following me since I turned my back and left her there. I was told that I shouldn't look back at her as I walk away. This is also natural.

The try-outs have already begun. There's nothing particular for me to do but I'm supposed to be there. Like most of us, I am obliged to wait for hours just to check something on the computer or to see somebody on the character generator or to give my opinion on the question tests. These tests are done on technicians or players that are mere fry-brains, who will never get to play, but they don't know it. My questions have been totally butchered, of course. Very few have remained as I wrote them. Some people, higher up the ladder, have joined the game and started writing their own questions. For the time being they are enjoying themselves, but when they'll have to do it permanently they will remember that there is somebody who is getting paid for this job. Then probably they'll decide to replace him with somebody else.

The group life at the shooting does not thrill me at all. All those indifferent discussions to pass the time, the inevitable useless socializing, the hurried cigarette smoking outside the security door in an abandoned yard, the group meal once a day with food packed in cardboard boxes…

I never particularly liked it but now I find it unbearable. It is unbelievable that there are so many people around and I don't have the slightest desire to actually talk to anyone. I think that everyone else in there feels the same. So, our contact is as mechanical and prepacked as our meals.

The incessant afternoon crying causes complete hopelessness. Red alert. All the available presents were given — even the ones for older children, all the free magazine gifts were opened. The heavy weapon is always something sweet.

I had decided, or I should say we had, not to give her any sugar until she was two. The doctor was more conciliatory. I can give her controlled doses. So, the sweets quarantine was terminated in late summer with a real ice cream. There was enthusiasm galore — for my part. She looked at it with curiosity and perhaps a little fear, for a while, until it began to melt. Then I yelled at her; I was afraid my festive mood would start fading. The result was her pouting and the ice-cream melting some more. Finally, she deigned to eat two spoonfuls. I ate the rest. That was our first ice cream. Now that I'm writing about it, I think it says a lot about our relationship. More guilt. But it doesn't make me better.

Something sweet usually erases tears. But this time the crying resumed, as soon as the chocolate finished. She finally got quiet with potato chips. Somewhere in the building, I can hear sex screams. A woman, not old, in her early thirties, I guess. Then they stopped abruptly. The only thing that mattered to me was whether they would wake up Jazz.

I try to imagine her. She must be young, not even in her thirties. They met at a concert. He is slightly older than her. He is unemployed and willing to remain so. She paints, but she feels that the city smothers her inspiration and dreams of travelling. He dreams of becoming a writer, but he can never concentrate for more than half an hour. He writes provocative stories like *The Fairy's wet dream* and asks her to read them. She always asks what happens next and this annoys him. He throws the pages in the garbage bin. He constantly fiddles with a script, in which she has the lead part, of course. Meanwhile they live off what she earns doing all kinds of odd jobs. He accepts money from his parents, every now and then, but he is too embarrassed to tell her. In the evenings, they go for long walks, talking about life, drinking cheap drinks in forgotten bars. They often argue about silly things, but then they make up and make love ceaselessly. Which of the above do I envy? Not even the last one.

I don't have time to think about it, the crying has started again. This time I finally realized that she was ill. She was feverish all night, not too high a temperature luckily, but she wakes up, she cries non-stop, she shouts something unintelligible and whatever you give her is not what she wants. Maybe she is complaining about the heat, her fever, a tooth coming out, maybe she is just irritated. Anyway, she just won't stop.

I get that familiar panic that she is never going to stop.

In the morning, I put on her shoes the wrong way again. Will he never learn?
    Usually, a parent would say that. Jazz would say it to me now, if she spoke. She is coughing. Should or shouldn't she go to the nursery? My personal interest tells me that she should. The doctor, whom I am beginning to trust less and less, says that we should let the fever develop. I find it absurd. I make chamomile tea and put it in her milk. It's the only thing I remember from my mother. The result is her not drinking the milk. I probably underestimated her — once again. When I leave her behind the familiar gate, I realise that I'm afraid they may give her back. I must go to the shooting and at the same time I am deeply worried. And of course I feel guilty. As usual.

How many mistakes do I make on a daily basis? Which one is a big one? Which one is serious? Which one may scar her for life? Aren't our mistakes necessary, since our children will grow up to live in our own world? Is this a good thing? Is this what I should want? Her living in the same world as me? Is there anything else I can do? Do we all repeat the same mistakes over and over again, so the world remains the same when it could be…what? In this country, maybe in others too, when you catch someone doing something wrong, the most common thing you hear is: Will I fix the world? The answer is obvious. Nobody will fix the world. We will leave it be.

'Let her get used to it. She has to get used to it.'

How many things have we gotten used to, even though we shouldn't?

How many things have we mistakenly gotten used to?

And what can we do about it?

5. Bird stories

Jazz doesn't like: the sea, doctors and bald people. The doctor is bald and this makes things worse.

I don't like him either. He is an elderly but modern guy (I'm not sure if that's the best combination) and he looks like a slender bird. He has some sort of earphones hanging over his blouse instead of ears. He puts them on Jazz's body and the least one could say is that she doesn't like this. She is constantly in tears when we are at the doctor's. Tears are interrupted only when he feeds her some kind of tiny healthy biscuits, but this doesn't last long. He doesn't have much to say. The temperature is something common, nothing to worry about. She has been growing properly, nothing below average, but only her head is a bit larger than average. Then the doctor gives us a photocopy where everything we need to know or we should anticipate regarding her age has been written down. While we're leaving, once again I feel disappointed with myself for not managing to learn anything extra about the child. I'm not quite sure how to ask though.

At the end of the summer we went to the beach and I noticed that she had started being less scared of the sea. She generally likes water but only from the hose or the tap. She behaves quite nicely towards others: she waves at babies and, when she's in a good mood, she tries to greet everyone, she puts her hand over her heart to say thank you, but after the pause she starts sulking.

She sulks at least three times a day. She allows me to feed her but she gradually gets more confident and she doesn't accept any directions regarding the use of the spoon, which she tends to hold tight until the moment it reaches her mouth; this is when she suddenly turns it upside down and its contents end up on the floor. She dances according to her own rhythm, and — no matter how incredible it sounds — she tries some sort of dance moves with her feet.

She insists on holding her bottle of milk, the organic milk recommended by the doctor, because she has figured out that as long as she keeps holding it she won't have to go to bed, but she doesn't drink. She even says "no, no." She wouldn't say no, no till now; she usually let the milk, or whatever, drop on the floor. Now she keeps hold of it. Yet, feeding her with the milk bottle used to be one of the few things I used to enjoy immensely. When she realises she's in a bit of a tight spot, she starts drinking. Tonight I let her hold it for as long as she liked just to see what she would do. After a while I turned the TV on, although I generally avoid this, but she still hadn't even taken a sip. She even asked for the "bob" (the ball), which she simply throws down softly and waits for someone, that is, me, to catch it. But as this couldn't happen, we forgot about it. She was cheerful though and pinched my arm a little.

She sees "bob" everywhere; in the TV, on my T- shirt, anywhere. Bob is also what she calls the sun, the moon and the record printed on the T-shirt I was wearing this morning, the pink one I only wear at home.

I presume that it's not easy for a man to desire her, but there must be someone out there who would. I'm referring to the burly lady who comes once a week to tidy up the chaos in our apartment. We hardly talk to each other. She's a foreigner but she speaks our language quite well anyway. I would like to ask her about her life but her cold gaze and her strict movements prevent me from actually trying every time I think of it. She is not pretty, that's for sure, but not too ugly either. But she looks like she comes from a world with no emotions. She must have her reasons of course; she must be sharing emotions with some people. Not with us though. She doesn't pay any attention to Jazz, it's not her job of course, but the way she ignores her bothers me. Jazz makes some effort to approach her in her a primitive way, but it's always in vain. It always bothers me when

people ignore her. Actually, Jazz is also a way for me to show off, a reason
to be proud.

Look what I've done; a baby. It's mine. Feel free to show your excitement. I need it.

There's finally something useful on TV; a documentary about birds, the birds-
-of-paradise in New Guinea. Eight out of the forty-two species of paradise
birds live only there. We watch some birds with a spectacular orange plumage,
and later on, the natives snatching the feathers and using them to dress up
for their dances and rituals and then again the birds – the females sitting
back and watching the males plucking all the leaves off a tree to show off,
something between dancing and martial arts. The female will pick the one
who impresses her most and will mate with him. We also watched the mating.
The male was a bit clumsy but the female seemed to be yielding to her fate,
since she had had her choice. She stayed still, waiting for the male to fulfil
his duty. Of course – once more – I started wondering whether she was
supposed to watch this, but then there was a break for ads, and we avoided
a rather violent movie and ended up watching a music video. She likes them,
especially when there's dancing involved. But half of the music videos are
simply seminars for strippers. In most of them there's some sort of pole used
by the singer for pole dancing. Jazz gets really excited sometimes; she stands
up and tries to dance, she makes some moves that I find cute, then she pauses
and stares at me, waiting for some kind of approval. I applaud of course. Am
I undermining myself with all those poles? Am I becoming too conservative?
I turn the TV off. Jazz starts sulking. I turn it back on. One more song, I tell
her. Just one. We watch a music video with a singer touching herself in the
bathtub. She is surrounded by floating flowers. I try to be patient until it's
over. No more music videos for tonight.

*I don't feel like going on with this. I think I need some kind of emotional reward up front
in order to keep writing. Today I will only make plans. It will be some sort of detective
story. There are always happy and unhappy ones, that is, with a happy ending, where Jazz
will make a smooth landing in the reality of children, or the world around us, while an
unhappy ending would be the opposite. As in all good detective stories, you are never sure*

whether the bad guys are actually bad, the characters are a bit grey, in the end we also like the bad guys. I'm some kind of detective who tries to help her find the solution but the main hero is Jazz.

And what if I am the bad guy?

6. You must leave the fish at home

The potential victims started arriving in the early afternoon. Shooting will start at eight. We already know there's not going to be any shooting tonight, but they don't. It's one of those tests they need to pass. They get them to come to the studio and then they let them wait for hours. Endlessly. The waiting feels endless because absolutely nothing happens for two or three hours. Then they suddenly start yelling, blinding spotlights shine in our eyes and all the little pets of the production go back to their nests. Some run to the control room, others get on the players' platform, they disappear in the make-up room, they sit on the generator, they get crammed in the sound cabin, they climb on the scaffolding, some must even squeeze in the basement, where the fake money safe is. This only lasts very few minutes. Then the void resumes. We go through the questions again and again. My assistant has never worked in television before. She is impressed with everything, although I think she is mostly terrified. She keeps reminding me of the production orders. There is no doubt whose side she will be on should something go wrong. When I tell her something she listens to me quite pensively and I always wonder if she really got it. She receives orders from the producer himself anyway. Time passes aimlessly and there's always a technical issue which is impossible to solve, it is a sort of ritual. People who hold the lower posts swear at each other, but not violently, it is a bit of a routine, they just try to wind each other up. Once someone senior appears, the swearing stops and the issue is soon resolved; once they leave, another issue appears.

I keep an eye on our prey. When they first come in the studio they are excited, especially the women. The men are usually a bit more reserved, or at least that's how they try to look. (However, they very often get furious with each other when they lose the money because of one question only. They don't know that there's also us, behind the glass, wasting our lives looking for this one question that will trap them).

As the hours go by without anything happening, their enthusiasm grows fainter. They sit at the audience platform, gazing at the players' glass cage. They dream of getting in there. But they are simply expendable. We have called them merely in order to examine their reactions. After all, the orders are crystal clear. Only one player will win the first three shows. In other words; twenty-minus-one losers. They will go home empty handed. Then we can relax a little and let some more win.

They told me I should bring her to nursery earlier in the morning. This way she will get used to it sooner. But this won't be so easy. She doesn't like staying in and by now the weather has become too chilly for the little ones to go outside on the lawn. In the morning she snatched Soprano's fish; that's how I call the stupid fish that moves its head to and fro, while there's music that sounds mostly like noise. I call it like this because it reminds me of a *Sopranos* episode, in which somebody gives this fish to Tony as a present. I remember this is how the episode ends. We were mad about the *Sopranos* the summer before Jazz was born. I wanted to stay at home all the time; I watched old *Seinfeld* episodes in the afternoon and the *Sopranos* in the evening. We watched them together. She wasn't crazy about this at first but she gradually got into it. It was our sole entertainment while waiting for the baby to come. I didn't let Jazz take it. She burst into tears of course, but when we went out in the street it was OK. When we went through the nursery door, she started crying again. I left her in her teacher's hands, turned my back and left and felt guilty of course. but it's supposed to happen this way, this is one of the many supposed-to-happen-this-ways. I feel guilt for all the supposed-to-happens that suit me; that buy me more time to spend on myself. For some reason "Good Thing" by the Fine Young Cannibals pops to my head. I always loved that song. I wonder what happened with Ronald Gift.

I wonder if we all become like this because some other people before us didn't have time and let their child's first years pass with all those supposed-to-happens-that-suit-us. They say that the first three years are the most crucial ones. Some even believe that when a child becomes two it's already too late; their character has already been formed. That's why I feel guilty.

How is it possible to write and to find what I write disgusting, and still, to keep writing? It definitely isn't something I can do well, since I feel this way. So why do I keep doing it? My vanity is much stronger than my mistakes, I guess. What could I achieve this way? Why do I insist? Who cares?

WINTER

1. The terrible twos

She starts crying again at the nursery entrance. Until we arrived here she seemed happy. She has been away only for three days because of the fever. But this seems to be making her feel like a stranger again. *Does she feel like a stranger in here or does she feel like this world is a stranger? I can't be sure about this. But I realise these are two immensely different things.*

I don't blame her. I wouldn't like to spend my day in here either. Although the "nursery" I spend it at is much worse.

Why do I leave her here then? Why do I not take her out from here right away, before it's too late…?

She stretches her arms towards me and she makes me feel guilty about turning my back on her again. The nursery is the first station where responsibilities may alight. More of them are coming up. On my way out I feel like I am a child again and that I've done something wrong. And I know I'll get caught.

I've already given a name to this change I've noticed: furious Jazz. It's something that has been happening lately. She gets really wild suddenly. As if she has the need to do something "bad" at all costs. Her eyes start rolling all around, looking for the right way to make mischief. It doesn't make any difference if I manage to prevent her or if I yell at her afterwards; she will burst into tears either way. Is this attention seeking? But she's already got my attention anyway. I'm fully occupied with her as long as she is awake.

I was talking with an old classmate who lives in New York, and this was when I first heard the term; "Oh, it's the terrible twos" he said in this accent that reminds me he's been living there for twenty years already. And he explained it to me. He doesn't have children though. Then I googled it too. The terrible twos is a stage in a child's life, sometime between two and three. It is a type of infantile adolescence, which is quite similar to standard adolescence. Children have outbursts of anger or sadness, they are unable to communicate, they're irritable, they tend to become even more insecure and they generally make their parents' lives hard. This lasts for a few months and of course demands some extra understanding and attention.

What I've noticed is that sometimes, usually after a meal, or when bed time is approaching, she's seized by some sort of mania and does exactly what she is "not supposed to do", mischiefs and little disasters — a familiar behaviour, of course — but more urgent and fast than it used to be. For as long as these fits last, it's as if she cannot communicate at all, as if she doesn't want any contact with me whatsoever.

She woke up at 6 in the morning, maybe because of the light or the heat, the milk soothed her a bit only for fifteen minutes and she kept going with a combination of crying, singing, "conversation", mumbling, and some even more intense crying every time, until, after a full hour of trying, I got up and tried to find ways to calm her down. Is this what the terrible twos are? A futile effort to communicate with your child? How will I manage what's coming when she's a teenager?

But it's too early for this. This is the time when I make the mistakes that I'll have to pay for later. What an elegant way of talking about raising a child…

Is she actually growing up? She doesn't learn new words, she doesn't run steadier, she doesn't do anything smarter than what she did last month. I can't even tell if she's getting taller or not. She must be getting taller. Not much. I don't know why, but I was under the impression that children grow every month. But that was vegetables, not children. Raising a child is the most important thing in the life of a grown-up. Do you agree up to now? However, it is the only thing about which nobody bothers to attend any training. On the contrary, everyone believes that it is so simple they must know already. I've never met anyone who would admit that they have no clue how to raise a child. I admit it but I have nobody to admit it to. And what's worse is that I'm constantly growing up too. That's for sure.

I often remember that scene from Yasujiro Ozu's *Tokyo Story*. The grandmother is visiting her son's house and she's trying to tame her restless grandchild. They're out on a hill on the same level as the roof of a house. There's only grass all around and a bridge at the far end. The little boy must be three or four years old maximum. He's plucking the grass, not paying any attention to his grandmother. She asks him "what will you be when you grow up? Will you be a doctor, like your dad" The boy doesn't bother to reply, he keeps playing and she is wondering: "where will I be when you will be a doctor, will I still be here?" It's a really simple scene, lasting less than two minutes and that's why it is so shattering.

Where will I be when she grows up? I'm not a child. I'm approaching forty. She probably came into my life too late. How long will I manage to be fine and stand by her? How many things will happen to her and I'll never see? How many things will I never find out?

The Japanese director's black-and-white films from the 40's to early 60's must have influenced me heavily. I managed to download them, along with other Japanese films — I'm a bit obsessed with Japanese cinema as well as with prints.

One of the last times we talked she told me, *"you always wanted to have an affair with a Japanese woman anyway"*. I found this tragicomic later on.

When will I stop being near her? How soon or how late? What will I have achieved by then? How much good or how much harm will I have done to her? These thoughts are not helping me at all.

Yasujiro Ozu never had any children. He actually never had a family at all.

He spent almost his entire life with his mother as his sole company and on his tombstone — at his beloved city, Kitakamakura, in the province of Kanagawa, near Tokyo, the setting for most of his films — there is only one character; mu, which stands for "nothing".

2. Music for Jazz

I read a bit about the terrible twos before I leave for work.

The book is all right. I picked it at random of course but the writer seems to be well informed. She is a woman with children and a happy marriage, and I find this reassuring. Who would trust a book written by someone like me? I don't write about what I know; I only write about what I don't know. Some of the things I read sound a bit familiar nevertheless, as if I already know them somehow. Maybe from magazines. Maybe I've known them all the time. Well, yes, I must trust the child. I must be patient. The terrible twos are a crucial phase in the child's life; perhaps the most significant one before adolescence. The child is not a child yet. The child is still a baby exploring the world of children. And this is slightly terrifying. (Especially for me). The child is encountering something unknown. There are many possibilities but they are all uncontrollable. The child doesn't know who or what it is. The child is discovering his/her own limits.

All the above could have easily have been referring to me as well. Poor Jazz. It is terrible that you only have me to take you by the hand and lead you to the adult world. How about not going anywhere? At least not yet. I wonder, is this why she has stopped learning new words? Is she afraid that words will gradually lead her to the wild world out there?

There's something terrible about this job, too. Getting into this world exhausts me so. It feels like a ghost train ride. It's as noisy and the setting is equally fake. But the realness of the monsters around here is unreal. There are moments when anyone who has the right to shout does so. You must constantly pretend this is none of your business. Their swearing is very well calculated of course. They swear about indefinite stuff. They never refer to you personally. Well, almost never. The lowest ranks (office boys, handy-men, cleaners, assistants to electricians and cameramen) have no such privilege. The swearing they listen to is specifically directed at them. Swears bear their names — nobody bothers about their surnames. What's worse is when you start wondering why this happens, why so many people are behaving so badly for a lie, an optical illusion of happiness (that no one can touch), for a mirage of success (that almost no one ever reaches). But the money earned by the production is real. And it is what makes the world go round. There are good moments of course. When the game starts, when the lights are turned on and you can hear nothing apart from the presenter's screeching voice. Or when someone loses; there's a sigh of relief echoing from the basement to the top of this miserable building. Another one bites the dust. No need to worry now.

She's eating quite a lot, because she is enjoying a game. She rarely eats because she's hungry. Food is a delight and a game, a discovery, and lately hunger has been turning into a game. She shows me things she wants to eat. She has a unique talent in discovering things she is not supposed to eat in every corner of the house. But since eating is an art that intrigues her, she easily learns that she must eat something new. That's what she did with baby food and also when I replaced it with her first solid meals; the first fruit, the first pieces of bread, meat and all this. I enjoyed teaching her this whole process. It was always very easy. I had to show her only once.

I'm at my computer; she comes closer and wants to pull the mouse pad towards her. So I take the mouse pad and put it on her head. She doesn't mind this "punishment" at all and after a while she manages to pull it and put it on her head herself, checking whether I liked the new game.

In the evening we watched music videos again. It has become something like a pre-bedtime ritual. I kept testing her reactions. At first it was Kesha's

Tik Tok, that is, rap style. I was hoping she wouldn't get into it but she clearly liked it, she moved her free hand and then the milk bottle in time. Then, it was *Bad Romance* by Lady Gaga. She seemed impressed but didn't follow the rhythm this time, only in the beginning, when it actually sounds a bit like a nursery song, and then she climbed on the sofa.

I handed her the teddy bear shaped bottle to hold (the one that always touches its nose ceremoniously, as if it's trying to make sure that it is still the same) after I emptied the milk and filled it with water. For some reason I believe she must sleep with something, is she going to become more emotional this way? Even if that is so, is it a good thing? Who knows? More of my nonsense. I am actually following the advice of another book (I've bought two more and I've ordered a few). I find the following passage from that book really impressive:

"Children are compelled to live in a nightmare. They find themselves in an unknown world, surrounded by creatures speaking an unknown language, making them do things for reasons they cannot grasp. And then nocturnal darkness comes. It is natural for children to be afraid. The objects they hold close to them in the dark are a shield that comforts their fears".

After reading this I am ready to accept anything she would like to keep with her in bed. Even if she asked for the fridge I would carry it in to her.

If I am managing to write the truth, this must be obvious through what I'm writing, right? It must be obvious when something contains its own truth.

It's embarrassing to admit, but no matter how much sympathy I feel for the downtrodden, the immigrants, the homeless, when I hear the slightest noise around us I instantly think kidnappers and organ trade. I'm scared. Of course it's over the top, but I'm scared. I'm afraid that someone is lurking in the park. I'm afraid that someone will sneak in the house at night or snatch the child at the nursery when the teachers are not attentive enough. How can someone do this job? How can someone snatch children? Do these people have children themselves? Are they afraid someone might snatch their children from them?

It's Sunday. For the first time in my life, I realise that I don't know what the results of the games are. Still, I had almost nothing to do today. There was no walk in Victoria Park, the weather is bad. The antidote is a small square piece of sweet.

I finished the first book about the terrible twos. I read it quite fast. I only omitted two chapters. One of them was entitled: *What to do now that your baby has siblings.*

The other one: *Sharing housekeeping duties.*

I believe I will not be needing these.

Her smile is enchanting. I wonder if Mowgli grew up with any restrictions. Did anyone tell him what to do? Superman, he must have been rather restricted. When did he arrive from planet Krypton? Was he young? Older than two years old? What kind of nurseries did they have there? Did his teacher tell him off because he liked flying in the play room and kept bumping his little head on the ceiling? Spock must have gone through a lot as well. I prefer not to know how nurseries were in planet Vulcan. Full of stern women like the one who helps me at home? But he was programmed to endure this. He had to learn how to hide his emotions. No matter how much I like him, I really don't want her to resemble him. I resemble him enough myself already.

I want to get out of this city.

3. When I grow up I want to be Squidward.

The teacher at the nursery says that Jazz was naughty once again. She talks about the boundaries that need to be set. This keeps troubling me. I listen to her and agree that boundaries must be set. She talks about "home" in general, probably trying to be polite. She says, "the child must be taught at home that there are some limits. There's still time for this to be done".

There's still time? Does this mean that it will soon be late? There's still time for whom? Me and her?

(She's not bad-looking, perhaps a bit too formal, but I suppose she's not like that all the time. She's young. She probably has someone waiting for her at home every night. Perhaps even a child. Perhaps she is alone, desperately looking for someone. Perhaps she can't have children for some reason and that's why she chose this job. That's why she's desperately looking for someone who already has a child; preferably a little girl).

Now she's looking at me inquisitively. Of course not; she doesn't mean "me and her." Me and the invisible "her" who should have been at home. The teacher must be wondering why she never appears.

What she suggests sounds very childish; she says I should buy a short stool, a children's chair and when she is naughty I should make her sit there for two minutes. Two minutes because she's two years old. When she's three it will be three minutes, then four and so on. I promise I will take care of it but I keep wondering whether this way I am becoming an accomplice to a small (or big?)... crime? Not exactly, let's not be so melodramatic... at least an act of coercion. I cannot help thinking of this image from the future, my daughter is twenty, the little chair has now become an armchair and I insist that she must sit there for exactly twenty minutes. I grin. The teacher stares at me, puzzled. She probably doesn't trust me, she thinks I won't manage. "At the end of the month I would like to see both of you," she says, referring to her mother. Then she walks away and leaves me with Jazz.

At the end of the month. I would like this too.

She cries her heart out for almost no reason at all. And then, as unexpectedly as she started, she stops, and her cute little face lights up like a hospitable sky. We return home. I haven't got much time. If I manage to put her to sleep I will have a few hours of peace before I go to the shooting. It's going to be a difficult night tonight. The chubby girl will come to keep Jazz some company. I will work overnight again. I won't see her to sleep, I won't kiss her goodnight. I'm not sure at all if she actually needs all this of course. What if a complete stranger came along, and did precisely the same things? Would she notice the difference? Would she miss me? Would she cry for me? The girl says she doesn't cry at all. I bet they're watching music videos on TV the whole time. And that's the best case scenario.

The following day is a Saturday. We go for a walk in the garden, it's actually a large park, and I'm always a bit nervous we might get lost. We're both startled by the guy who appears behind her. He was wearing old, but not dirty, clothes. He didn't seem to be going anywhere in specific. Maybe he lives here. Quite a few people have lost their jobs lately and things are probably getting worse. He followed us for a while and then vanished in the park. For some reason this brought to mind *Zoo Story*, the play by Edward Albee. We left a wrecked truck behind us, I don't know if it was supposed to be in here, but it definitely wasn't a pretty sight. We pass through a grim zoo. Most cages are empty. It wouldn't surprise me if I found out that most birds had actually been snatched by the guards themselves. There even used to be a lion here. A miserable lion, but it was a real one. Now there are only a few ducks swimming in the filthy water. We saw a couple of ponies further down the road. She was not particularly impressed by any of the above.

Is it right for her to see only beautiful images? What about the world she will live in? Should I present it to her a bit prettier than what it really is or should I offer little glimpses of what awaits her? I think I've been choosing the former until now, but I don't know what I'll do when she gets older.

We're finally at the playground; Jazz doesn't know what losing my way means, so she will never accuse me of it. She has a peculiar expression, as if she has never seen children before. She might be annoyed by the lack of free swings. Some children are sitting in a circle, singing a song about a granny who keeps animals in her yard. I find this depressing. At last, there's a free swing, and she really likes this. It takes two to seesaw; there was a little boy nearby, but he looked a bit fierce. I put her on the seesaw and went on the other side, moving it up and down, slower and faster. Jazz didn't want to leave, but this game exhausted me so I took her to the slide, where she tried to climb facing backwards. She didn't manage. She was rather tired after this. Of course we had the baby buggy to return.

We watch SpongeBob SquarePants on TV. This is something we watch together. The whole thing started because I wanted to find something we would watch together. I had no idea who SpongeBob was. I had watched a bit of the film and it pissed me off. I found it too "grown-up". Kids should watch something suitable for kids, I thought to myself. Not something that is about adult problems, disguised as cartoons. Why should a child see that Mr Krabs' dream is to earn as much money as possible? But the time it was broadcast was convenient, so we started watching it. Jazz was really excited at first but her excitement soon faded away. The truth is she can understand very few of the funny things happening. I try to get in her frame of mind. The only thing that's fun is all those fishes and starfish and other sea creatures she sees. But they're all weirdoes. How can she understand that Patrick is a total moron and that SpongeBob is just a naïve idiot? How can she grasp Squidward Tentacles' terrible loneliness? The only thing she finds entertaining about him is the fact that he has four feet. The truth is that after watching a few shows I started suspecting that she is merely watching it out of politeness. Of course Jazz doesn't know what politeness means, but I think she likes seeing that I like something. Something which is a bit "hers" too, because it is a mickey-mouse (we call all cartoons mickey-mouse). When she sees that I'm having fun she pretends she is having fun too, even if she doesn't get the jokes. On the other hand, I totally identify with Squidward Tentacles and I almost suffer every time these two morons, Patrick and Bob ruin his peace and quiet (they sometimes destroy his house entirely). Of course I'm supposedly watching this for her sake. But there's been a slight role reversal. In reality it is Jazz who makes me watch cartoons every Saturday morning, at eleven o clock sharp. I'm ashamed to confess, but I have postponed or refused to do loads of jobs or meetings who happened to be at the specific time on Saturday. When one of my few acquaintances hears that I cannot make it at that time because I am watching cartoons with my daughter, I imagine that he admires me, he might even think of me as an eccentric doting father. But of course nobody can suspect the truth. Entrenched in his rock, usually with his earplugs on, sinking in his favourite armchair or in his bed Squidward is reading a book, playing the clarinet or simply enjoying his solitude. All he needs from others is to leave him alone. Just like in *I am a rock*, an old song by Paul Simon, he doesn't need anyone. I would very much like to be like him, but I have Jazz.

For at least twenty or thirty years I will have to take care of her. Then, I hope, she will take care of me. Isn't that how it works?

4. One mistake is enough, goodbye Treasure Island

It was just a usual show. That day we must have shot two or three sets. Everyone had lost. The control room was bursting with enthusiasm. A couple of friends played against each other at the last set. They knew very few answers, but luck had helped them a lot. They managed to get to just three steps before the end. But one of the best traps I had prepared for that evening's menu was waiting for them there. It was one of the few times I went upstairs in the control room to explain how they should set the trap. An elementary question. But I could see right through them. Just like in a wrestling fight, when you have to pick the right moment to finish someone off. You must spot their weak point. I knew that it would only take a simple blow to send them back home empty handed; a simple question that would make my triumph even more entertaining for the audience. The spectator is as much of a sadist as we are. He just loves watching them lose. And he wants to watch them lose because of a question that he is sure (in the safety of his cosy flat of course) he would have got right. This is when he enjoys it even more.

And that's exactly what happened. They were positive they had found the correct answer. So they placed all their remaining (virtual) money on the circle with the number of the question. And they lost. And then the croaking sound effect for defeat was heard, our favourite sound, and it was deafening. The players lost the ground under their feet for a while and by the time they came round they were already in a taxi back home.

Empty handed. Mission accomplished; one more successful evening for the production budget.

The show is broadcast live. The studio manager who had taken over the production insisted on this; he thought it would earn us time and money. Also, it gave the show a touch of the arena vibrancy — this was exactly how he had put it. The first phone-call came very few seconds after the big stage spotlights were turned off. The presenter's make up was already being taken off.

"It's wrong. The answer you took as correct was wrong!" The girl who picks up the phone didn't pay much attention to the first call. Just like many others apart from her, she was convinced that "our" (it soon became "my") question and answer were correct. It couldn't be otherwise. It was wrong nonetheless. It dawned on me suddenly, when they started coming in the small computer room, our nest, one after the other. We were already smoking our second cigarette. It was generally forbidden, but not when we had won. We had won. That's what we thought. But we were wrong. The mistake was mine. There wasn't even one correct answer. That was meant to be my last night in the show, and perhaps even my last one in television in general.

What was the name of the Chinese emperor who met with Marco Polo?
A. Chenghis Khan
B. Kublai Khan
C. Tamerlane

It was Kublai Khan, ok! But none of them was Chinese! All of them were Mongols. So all answers were wrong. How could I have made such a silly mistake? I wondered about this so many times over the following months. I didn't manage to find the answer either then or ever. How could I have written three wrong answers to one question when I was supposed to be checking (and not just me) all the answers dozens of times before they were transferred into the computer of the show? Technically, it was that chubby girl's fault, the one who was supposed to be my assistant. She was the one who copied the questions in the computer and this was when they went on air. But she was just an assistant. The person who had to lose his job was the one in charge of the questions. And that was me. But why had I made such a childish mistake? There is no right answer — not here either.

The mistake is a mischievous and strange little animal. Sometimes it hides in incredible places. Its biggest weapon is the fact that it can — like a chameleon — stay still in the same place for hours and remain unseen. And although it is right there, in front of your eyes, it is impossible to see it. It is perfectly camouflaged between the foliage of correctness and your absentmindedness. I had thought of this when I still had enough time to think of nonsense. But it was true. The mistake, in this job at least, is often rather resistant to checks. Even though it might seem easy to spot — it is literally before your very eyes — if you don't notice it at first, it manages to remain unseen all the rest of the times you will read through it mechanically. Fine, then. I didn't see it. There were at least ten people who had copies of the questions that evening. Why didn't anybody else notice? Well, because they didn't actually care at all and because no-making-mistakes- was-my-job. Unless they saw it and they let this happen. So that they could get rid of me with some spectacular publicity — it didn't matter if it was about a mistake, it was still publicity — for the show.

It is unbelievable how many people bothered to call in order to tell us. When it was already too late of course. This is precisely the advantage of a live show. Everything happens within seconds before the eyes of the spectator, the sadist I mentioned above. The spectator and the players experience the process simultaneously. And that's fun.

What is even more unbelievable is the whole fuss about this incident. It was broadcast on the news, along with an apology by the production and an announcement that the person responsible had already been sacked. It was repeated on all the morning shows of other channels, in the appropriate malicious tone of course. It spread like wildfire on the internet accompanied by the mocking comments about the entire show and its contributors; there were even some conspiracy theories that it was all on purpose so that the show's mediocre ratings would improve. This was even written in two evening papers – it was actually a headline at the front page of one of them. I presume that the only clever thing I did that night was resigning with an email I sent to all the collaborators of the show, the moment I arrived home. I was just trying to get there before them. Television was finished for me anyway. Later on I thought that the only comforting thing about this whole story was the fact that Jazz is still young. She would never find out how stupid her dad was. By the time she grows up, the tragedy of the question-guy of *Treasure Island* will be forgotten. Or at least I hope so.

These are strange, empty days. It doesn't matter if you like what you do or not. You are in full swing now and you have learned how to regulate your life according to specific rules. Suddenly I am floating in the air like a child's balloon that escaped from a pair of reckless hands. I am suspended in a void of hours I do not know how to fill.

The only mail I receive from work, my "old job" I mean, are some formal messages of consolation that end abruptly and a dry phone-call from the finance office, letting me know that I will receive my fee in about two months. That's all. I feel a bit shamefaced. The way I left work, no matter if I resigned, was humiliating. But I must get over it. This job is over. So is the TV season, generally, for me. If something new comes along, it will only be next spring. And that's not very likely to happen.

Now I must take care of the house and myself.
I have so much time in my hands. Isn't this what I wanted?
But I don't feel like taking care of either.

5. We've gotta get out of this place

I have to go somewhere and I take the baby with me. She really is a baby, she is much smaller, she has no hair, there's only fluff on her tiny head and she's wearing a floral dress like the ones they dress bunnies with in fairy-tale illustrations. The dress is a bit too large for her and it looks like I've put her in a potato sack. So I take her on my back and I start the motorbike. Suddenly I stop because I feel that something is wrong. The child should normally be behind me, in a carrycot, but there's nothing behind me. Of course I get terrified something has happened to her, I freeze the motorbike in the middle of the road, a dirty avenue full of cars and a filthy gutter, next to the river. I turn around and try to make way, stopping the cars. I move upstream but I still cannot find any trace of her. My anguish grows of course and my fear, my panic, my guilt, the more I proceed without finding anything. Until I hear a voice — I don't know where it comes from — which says "the TV is here to take interviews". I go towards there, already certain that something nasty is happening. Near the gutter, on my left, I see the remains of something like a grey shirt, I hope it's garbage. I keep going towards the reporters, terrified, panicking and I wake up.

Do I want to leave her somewhere?

Am I afraid I might lose her?

Then another dream, it's also something like nightmare, a bit milder and subtler though. This time I'm travelling with my mother. We stop at a deserted place. Another miserable place, like the one before. Something like a swamp. I say, we must leave our suitcase here. My mother stops the car and I go out to throw it away. I know my mother doesn't like this, but her disapproval is silent, as always. You only need to look at her and you immediately understand she doesn't like what I'm about to do. I leave the suitcase and return to the car. I'm not sure at all whether I've done the right thing. We don't speak; we don't exchange a single word. We sit there in the wilderness and we don't start the car. I feel bad but I know we must go on.

Doesn't my mother want to leave?

Don't I want to leave?

If I leave will I leave something precious behind? Like…? Like this awful job? But this job has already left me first.

We're leaving this city as soon as possible. I've put the house in Athens up for sale. I'm still not quite sure whether leaving this city is for the best. I guess I'll start realising what it is I want as soon as the estate agent starts calling about prospective buyers.

Getting her dressed exhausts me. To be precise, it irritates me; that's why it exhausts me. I have divided the clothes in matching categories, so we wear a specific ensemble every day. If a piece of the ensemble is missing, I start panicking. The same happens when I can't find something after the laundry or after ironing. The truth is she makes my life hard with socks and shoes, especially socks. Perhaps she should have learned how to put those on herself. The only thing she has actually learned in the past months is how to spread her little arms uncomplainingly so that I put her top or her jacket on. I like lifting her in the air the moment I put her trousers on. I grab it from the dangling edges, before I button it, and I lift her up. She enjoys it but not as much as I do. Bathing her is almost never a tiring procedure. I let her throw her squeaky duck in the water. But she usually gets bored of it and prefers other toys that are not meant for the bath. I give ground in this case. I also give ground when it comes to clothes. I am not too strict with letting her wear clothes that are slightly dirty. Every piece of clothing she wears gets a bit dirty within two or three hours. But I overlook this. I am content when I can postpone the laundry routine for a bit later. Sometimes I even get her to wear a sock from the laundry basket. This doesn't make me a bad father, a bit careless perhaps. Who will find out?

Her hair is not much yet. I'm not sure if I comb it right. I'm trying though. She doesn't mind, for the time being. Hairclips are a bit of a problem, however. They never stay in one place. Not to mention ponytails, when they will be needed. She will be the only girl who will not have a ponytail, because of her useless dad. She likes herself as she is though; she enjoys it a lot when she climbs on the toilet seat and looks at herself in the corner of the mirror. She likes me as I am too, I guess. She will never call me ugly or fat (I have gained some weight since the summer). She accepts me the way I am. I am simply her dad.

My mother was very strict when I was young; maybe not strict as much as stubborn. My father was the same of course but I didn't get to see him much. What I found impressive, although I couldn't describe it yet, was the fact that they always agreed. They didn't have to be together in order to decide on something. It was as if one would finish a sentence the other had started. They rarely disagreed or changed views on any matter, but my mother sometimes — not always — would protect me from my father's outbursts of anger. The only difference was their manner, not the essence. They had lots of problems as a couple, also something I realised later, but not much later. But when it came to their behavior towards me, they seemed like one person. My father died relatively young and my mother stayed alone for the remaining twenty years of her life. Therefore — I was also getting older, after all — her manner started changing, naturally. She stopped being so strict and the only weapon of influence she kept was her silent disapproval. She wasn't able to impose her will through shouting or punishments, but she did her best with her silence and the sorrow revealed on her face. I don't know if it was better that way. Probably not. There were times when I could not react and I preferred to give in or to hide something from her. In reality, I learned how to hide almost everything from her, and we only talked about harmless stuff. But even then, she seized the opportunity, through an exceptionally advanced mechanism I could not help admiring, in spite of the fact that it made my life hard. I kept seeing her and loving her and hiding things from her until the end. Towards the end, she had become so weak that she didn't even need to show me what she wanted in order to be content with me. I was the one trying to discover what it was that she would have wanted me to do. I don't think that was an enviable relationship. I wouldn't like it to be this way with my child. But if I had to keep something, this would be one emotion that covered all the rest; my mother always gave me this impression, without saying it with words; "I'm here for you, whatever you do. There's loads of things I don't like about your life, but whatever you do I will love you all the same". This I'll try to keep. Not the rest.

I don't like thinking of it, I don't like writing about it (although nobody ever reads what I write and I don't know if this will ever happen) but since I lost my job I've been going through a phase of mild depression that follows me everywhere. I don't want it, I try not to think about it, but this little animal whispering in my ear that nothing has any meaning and none of the things I do matter, is constantly with me. It stops only when I am with Jazz. Then it lowers its head and goes away but I know it is never too far. I can feel it spying on me from somewhere but I know it cannot deal with Jazz. It can't mess with Jazz.

Why am I writing this stuff? I definitely don't have any special talent. It's not an inspiration springing out from inside. I find it difficult, and I push myself, especially these days, to write, even just a little. What I write is not exciting; it's not about murders or love— affairs. Even when I go back and read what I've written I'm afraid it seems totally uninteresting. There are no heroes – I am no such thing myself at least. Why do I believe it might interest anyone? Best case scenario is it would only interest someone like me. But how many are there out there? How many are there like me?

6. Did you know we are leaving?

I haven't managed to sell the house in Athens yet. I don't feel any denial in me; I feel a little sad but not sad enough to change my mind. I haven't actually spent much time there. My mother spent the last twenty years of her life in that house, although she had taken care of transferring it in my name. I don't have particularly happy memories from that house. My mother passed away about a year ago. At least she managed to see the baby.

There is no other woman in our lives any more. I'm referring to the chubby girl who was baby-sitting for us of course. From now on I'll be the only one to keep her company. Either I like it or not. There's only this sullen shadow of a woman who helps at home.

Soon, we will have to get rid of her as well. I might have to learn how to do everything myself. My payments will be two or three months late. I still have some money to live on but I must start thinking of the future. If we leave this city I will have to sell the house. I'm not sad at all. Where shall we go though? That's not difficult to decide. The only place in the world where I have something is a tiny house on a big island. I don't believe we can stay there; it's a half- built house near the coast, at the Libyan sea. It's the Greek island of Crete. I don't feel like Crete is our homeland; the only thing I know well is that house, which is not even situated in an inhabited area. The nearest village is twelve kilometres away. It would be too great a decision to stay there. Some time ago I used to flirt with the idea of living like a hermit, I felt like a hermit for two or three days during my short visits to that place, but this was just an impression that would help me feel better. All these years, the purpose of these trips was this: to feel that there's always the possibility for me to abandon everything and live close to the sea forever. I would have the luxury to be as romantic as I liked if I were on my own, but there's two of us now. Even if I managed to tackle various practical issues, such a decision would be too defining for Jazz. And too cruel perhaps. No, I'm not that strong or that desperate. But we will have the option to visit the place often.

I am realising that since I've lost my job I have started thinking in plural more and more. We've been spending many hours together and it might be my impression but it doesn't feel like sharing the house is too difficult after all. She has calmed down a bit. Who knows if she realises the difference. Now I'm all hers when she gets back from the nursery. Our daily routine definitely contains a stroll in the buggy, weather permitting. It's not bad at all. She sits quietly in there, lost in her own thoughts, watching the world and I get lost in my own thoughts pushing the stroller. Sometimes we stay out for quite a few hours. I don't go out much; I haven't been out on my own in the last three weeks. I guess my business with this city is finished already. It was a good deal for as long as it lasted. I never really loved it. And it didn't do much for me either. Now I must invent a new homeland; for me and Jazz.

I go and pick her up from the nursery. I enter the room without her noticing me. She's sitting down on the carpet, moving her arms, not mechanically though, like children are taught to move them; it's as if she's conducting an orchestra. At least that's how it looks like to me. She's grounded again, the teacher explains. Three or four little girls are sitting by the CD player. She's sitting at the far end of the room. She was punished because she wanted to take the CD out of the player and mess with the buttons. But she ate her whole lunch as usual and the teacher mentions that she likes acting frilly; she flutters her eyelashes and gets you to do whatever she likes. I know this too well. When we get home, she starts looking for mom. This is not very usual. Maybe it's somehow related to what happened in the nursery. Maybe she needs more care and protection. I suppose that she hears other children talk about their mums. I suppose she sees other mums bring their children there. I'm insufficient. Maybe she has started feeling the lack of her mother. Is this absence going to leave any marks? How much can her life be affected by something like this? There's nothing I can do. Nothing. I can't even explain the reason why there's nothing I can do. I give her a tangerine. I try to take all the pips out but I'm not careful enough. She goes to the couch, where she loves eating and after a while I see her take the chewed tangerine out of her mouth. I'm about to get angry but she spits a pip out and puts the tangerine back in her mouth. I'm astonished. Did you actually do this? I ask her. *Do you know how to do this?* She smiles. I dress her hastily and carry her to bed. She complains as usual but she soon calms down and falls asleep.

How is Greece nowadays? Probably worse than ever. The country is sinking in a financial crisis spreading all over Southern Europe. In Greece, where everything happens in a rather exaggerated manner, because of the sun perhaps, but for other reasons as well, things are worse than everywhere else. In reality, the financial crisis has not started now; this is when it became too obvious for people to keep denying it. Greece has been in a subtle kind of crisis for ages, perhaps forever. It's not as apparent in the rest of the country as it is in the capital. Athens is a sad city full of homeless people, beggars and immigrants, the latter living even worse than the former. It's a city full of empty shops, ugly streets and miserable ruins. Violence in those streets is a frequent phenomenon, and also — nearly always — pointless. The violence of politicians, who blindly obey a corrupt system that bred them is much more relentless and aims only at one thing; things to remain as they are. The protesters demonstrating against all this are people of all kinds, shouting desperately and in vain for justice under this terrible sun. But Athens is a dark city. The sun in Greece makes sense only in the islands where millions of tourists swarm the beaches hoping they will live their Greek dream, ignoring the crisis of course. Greece is a country that is still surviving thanks to artificial dreams.

I must tell her about the trip. It's not just a trip, after all. It's a new house, a new space, a new city, I dare say, a new country. It's not easy. How is she going to take it? Who am I kidding? Even if she could object, how seriously would I consider it? Would she make me change my mind or something? Of course not. But at least I have to prepare her. How well can you prepare a two year old for such dramatic changes? Maybe all this doesn't matter anyway. We are used to saying that whatever we do is for our children's benefit, after all. But, now really, how much did "her own good" influence my decision? Do I really want this? I don't know. Since I lost my job I've also lost most of my confidence in everything. I just feel sad, I let my grief for all the things I haven't got close in on me, and I keep living.

7. Observing Jazz

She has a tendency to challenge danger; perhaps she enjoys attracting my attention this way. She also pushes my hand away when I try to caress her and this gets on my nerves. But I think she has a more sophisticated sense of humour than me. I gradually realised that this is something that could develop into a game.

Her eyes are so big and clear…

When do our eyes start becoming miserable? When do they stop being so clear? When are we broken?

I have to check if the eyes of other babies are equally clear. I doubt it. After all, Jazz is the most beautiful baby in the world to me.

I believe she has a particular personality and this is obvious in every move she makes. This might change of course. But for the time being she's a very specific type; jokey, cunning, stubborn, jolly, but also irritable and of course a cry-baby when it suits her, that is, all the time. Furthermore, she has invented her own words in order to avoid learning how to speak properly; therefore she's also an idler. Today she threw away the green pacifier again, the good one, the one with the little elephant on it; she threw it on the street because she got fed up of waiting for the ice cream I had promised her.

She was really good when we went to the trattoria with a friendly couple. She didn't try to walk around, and made an effort to attract attention, but – apart from an elderly Italian lady and two young girls who showed some interest – she didn't achieve much. She gave an impressive performance though. The girl who had joined us (a friend of the couple; perhaps an attempt at setting me up with her? — Nah, she's too young. No reason for her to get involved with me — or Jazz) taught her how to clink her glass and say "sheers". Every now and then she would get off her chair in order to offer her food to people — this would be out of the question some time ago— smiling and greeting anyone who would pay some attention to her.

She eats almost everything. But she follows some kind of hierarchy with eating. If you start feeding her something she likes, it will be quite hard to go back to something she likes less. If you start with French fries she won't go back to tomatoes. Yesterday we sat on the couch and ate tangerine and then a few leftover paprika crisps and then tangerine again – I know that's not right. It was lots of fun but of course she stained the couch. The stains won't go away, even though I rubbed them with the dish sponge.

In the afternoon she was really cruel towards the plants though. She wouldn't stop uprooting them, especially the flowers, and tasting a bit of soil. I thought this is some kind of cruelty; it might just be ignorance of course, but I suppose all children her age are like this.

I wonder if I'm right to push her to learn things. She probably knows that the moment she starts communicating the game will be lost. Are we the executioners of children's real happiness? What would happen to her if I let her do whatever she liked? All right, I would just prevent her from falling over. She doesn't like falling over either, after all. I think I'm merely protecting myself when I forbid her everything because I can't be bothered to deal with her. But I have rights too. In any case, whatever happens, it won't be as bad as what I went through.

Her behaviour towards strangers is always much nicer than her behaviour towards me; we have discovered only one activity we can share, that is, watching TV while playing with the milk bottle, but then again, this is convenient mostly for me. She's much more open to learning from other people. *She's already getting bored of me.*

In the morning we watched some children's music videos. Some of them are all right but they're all perfect for pedophiles. All those little girls playing sexy and the fake childhood love affairs are nauseating. Maybe it's because we both had a temperature — hers was higher, and this always lowers her spirits.

At the "school" show, she's just wearing a hat, but she's constantly observing the rest of the children who are dressed as angels, elves, fairies and Santas. She causes trouble — well, I wouldn't exactly call it trouble — only when she calls the teachers by their first names but they don't pay any attention to her, as they're fully occupied with the show. She doesn't hesitate at all to walk on stage even just for a little while during the photo-shoot. I suppose she will be ready by next year. Crowds don't seem to bother her at all. I was terrified by them as far as I remember. I still am. But I hide it.

She knows we're up to something illegal. She takes the cold water bottle and drinks. The icy water brings tears to her eyes but she insists. When she gets over it, I see her marvellous little conspiracy laugh, the one that appears in the shape of two small wrinkles under her eyes. And then she starts all over again. Of course I'm telling her it's wrong, but I am not preventing her. I like watching her. She also enjoys throwing garbage from the balcony. She has started throwing everything, and not just garbage though.

She's definitely pretentious when it comes to photographs. This smile is totally artificial. In the Christmas photos, she faked smiling or laughing but I didn't like this much. There's this song by the Bee Gees I used to enjoy terribly, the one about the Christmas tree that says we were small and Christmas trees were tall. Now we're tall … I've got to find it.

I don't know why it's called the *First of May*; to me it's a song about the Christmas tree, about Christmas. I will teach it to her one day. But what could the Bee Gees be to her by that time? Something like what Perry Como or Nat King Cole is to me.

I took more photos of her by the tree, just like last year. This year the tree is not even a real tree; the decoration is in a flower pot surrounded with fairy lights and her toys are lying below it. We'll spend the Christmas holidays together full time. This sounds very melancholic.

She wasn't enthusiastic at all at the visit of a little three-month old baby. I realise I have nearly forgotten that time, although I miss it somehow. I miss her image as a baby drinking milk, leaning on her mother's arm, relaxing little by little or trying to touch the toys hanging over her cradle. She insisted on touching not only the baby's shoes, but everything, especially the baby's head and I wasn't quite sure she wouldn't give the baby a small punch too, well, we didn't let her anyway. Later on she chewed a bit of clay. She might have been faking but how could one tell for sure? It's our last day at the nursery and our buggy is the only one parked at the yard. I'm the only one who brings her on foot. I've only got one job now; and that's Jazz.

8. Big journey to the small city

It's a long journey. It begins early in the morning in a taxi that will take us to the airplane leaving for our homeland. Unlike me, she seems quite cheerful. I don't know if she has actually realised what a journey means; last time we travelled she was still too young. She's very obedient though. No trouble with getting her dressed. She will be holding her Hello Kitty handbag and Pom the Hippo. He has become her favourite lately. The problem is that she has no free hand for me to hold. I finally convince her to put Pom to sleep in the handbag. He'll get tired, I tell her, better if he sleeps in there and we'll wake him up later.

She seemed at home in the plane. She played with the stickers kindly given to us by the airhostess almost the whole time, not caring about anything. The weather in Athens is dull. It's not always sunny there, no matter what they say. I'm not in the mood to see or show her anything. Some other time.

I'm taking care of the details regarding our new house in the small town.

We get on the boat two days later. She liked the sea a lot but not as much as people and especially babies, as long as they can walk of course. She has started looking down on very young babies, but children interest her a lot. She shows a slight preference to little boys but this might just be my impression. She was quite quiet on the street, in the really busy city. She drank water from her little glass and spat it out as a game, so before I realised it her dress got really wet. I decided to ignore it. I just hoped she wouldn't catch a cold because of this.

Funnily enough, although she slept for quite a while on the boat, she was rather intolerable the whole time during our trip in the rented car — and that was a long way to be honest. She was constantly asking for something — like Pom, whom she would let fall down and then cry about it, or her pacifier or the water bottle, which she would throw down immediately and then ask for again. She doesn't know what she wants.

She wants my attention.
She wants to understand what the point is of all this. She wants us to take a break because she's bored. She wants some meaning in her life. How do you talk about all this when you are just over two?

On the boat — for as long as she was awake — she gave an entire performance when everyone started pushing each other, waiting for their turn to get off. This has always been a process that lasted too long. Nothing has changed. She finally got the audience she craves for there. She performed the entire set of tricks. Two children, the girl was 7 or 8 and the boy was 10, were so bored with the journey that they took this as a lifesaver. The boy pretended that he couldn't understand why a baby would act like this; why she's not responding, acting weird, not obeying and so forth, and he kept asking details about my laptop and my cell-phone. The girl immediately asked whether we had no cabin because we were poor. That's not exactly the case. Things are not that bad, even though the house hasn't been sold yet, but I decided to get the day— boat to Crete precisely for this reason; to avoid getting into a cabin. I always found them depressing. Maybe I also get a bit claustrophobic in there. The little girl helped though; she liked holding the buggy. Another child appeared through the crowd and got obsessed with Jazz. Her name was Stavy or something. She wouldn't let go of Jazz, cuddling her and tolerating her slaps. She didn't want to go, she started crying when they pulled her away, but Jazz was much cooler. Another thing she really liked on the boat was having lunch. Although she nearly had a rice— shower while playing with her food, she was exceptionally sensible.

Late in the evening, we are already at our new house.

I'm on an island. It's not summer, the weather is grey, grim. It's windy, people stay at home. She's here too, I know it. We didn't come together, I've only just arrived. However, I know where she is; I can see her. She's at a house with friends. Innocent friends. Or at least, that's what I think. Will I get to see her? Yes, when she's not too busy. It's good that she wants to see me, but the fact that she doesn't come here immediately makes me feel a bit humiliated. I live in an empty room. There's nothing for me to do here. I'm temporary. I only came for you. I love you.

She's smiling. I can't decode her smile. Maybe she finds me pitiful. Maybe she's about to ask me to get back together. Maybe she wants to tell me we're finished, that there's nothing left to do. I don't know. I'm waiting.

But everything gradually becomes static, all images are frozen. Then, there's only one image; I see her smiling. I despair without her telling me anything. I despair deeply, almost definitely, absolutely. Because it's this feeling again. Your image is frozen and we are not together. Again. I wake up.

Think I've had enough of these dreams.
Think I need a new reality now.

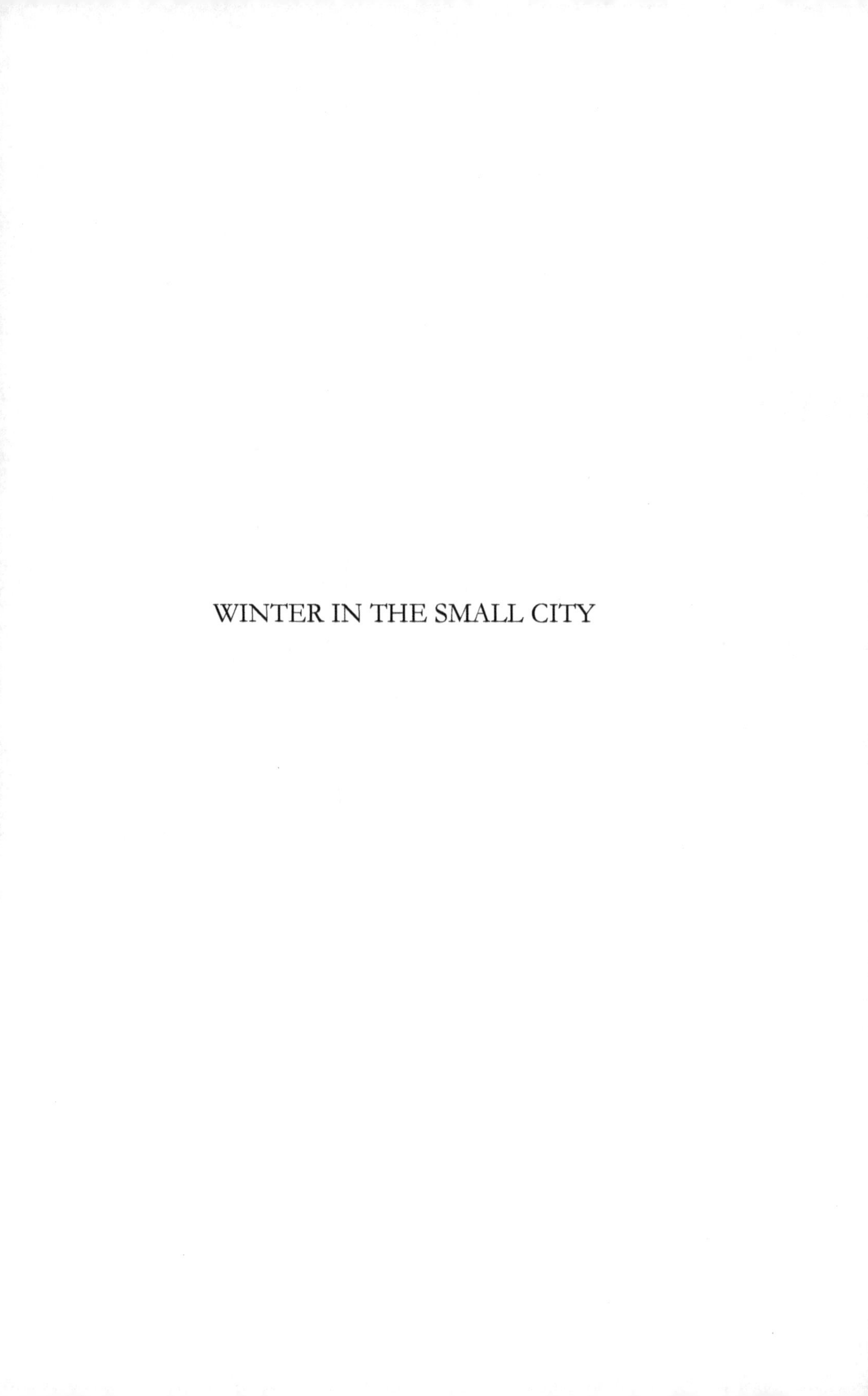

WINTER IN THE SMALL CITY

1. A walk by the fee

The best thing about the new city is the sea. It's always close, wherever you are. We take short walks by the sea every single morning during our first days there. I think it is a routine that helps both of us with adjusting.

Jazz doesn't eat the sand any more. But she's very fond of pebbles; she picks them up and throws them nearby or just hands them to me. I don't understand if she wants me to throw them in the sea (she calls it "fee"). She doesn't throw them near the water, she's not interested, she's happy with simply throwing them. The new thing she wants, though, is to dig a puddle. It's something I've always loved doing; a habit that was never abandoned. I did it last summer too, the few times we went to that ugly grey sea. She didn't pay any attention to it then, although I had dug it for her. Now she's watching me dig a small puddle; in the summer she didn't care so much, only once, when the puddle was so huge she could fit in it. Now she also grabs the sand in tiny handfuls and gives it to me and watches me toss it in the air. She likes this. She does it again and again. Then I throw pebbles in the sea but she doesn't pay attention. At least she's not afraid of water any more. It's winter and we can't go in, the waves are too high, but she goes near the foam and asks me to lift her up. I lift her up every time a wave comes so that her feet don't get wet. There's only one person in a hundred meter radius. I can't even make out what he looks like, but still, I find him annoying. I want us to be alone.

That's not true. I only do it for my own amusement. The fact that she likes it is only one more reason for me to repeat this absolutely infantile habit without shame. The truth is that I am the one who really likes digging puddles in the sand. When I start doing it I'm a bit ashamed, I check if there's anyone watching but soon it completely absorbs me, just like all illegal actions; just like all mischief. I forget myself while digging deeper and deeper.

I'm not interested in Jazz at all. I'm just looking for an excuse to dig the puddles.

I feel better now. At last, I spoke openly about the use of a baby in my life.

Also, it's the first time I discover there is some use in what I write. Yes, I feel better now.

It's weird but it seems as if she has grown a bit more after the journey. We're at home now, looking at magazines. She has started leafing through magazines as if they were storybooks and she points at specific things in the photos at every page, listening patiently to what I tell her, even though she cannot recognise some of the objects. When we're finished, she goes all the way back to the first page and starts all over again. Fairy-tales still irritate me. I often tell her they're a bunch of nonsense. I think I'm still allowed to say such things. Thankfully, none of the authors of the books I've read is watching me. I just can't get over the fact that the wolf gets assassinated because of that joke he played on Little Red Riding Hood's grandma – after all, he didn't eat her; in the last picture of the story, you always see her smiling, adoringly gazing at that bully, the lumberjack.

So, the wolf just goes away.

The same poor wolf goes away, after sloppily stitching up his belly, in the story with the seven young goats. A bit soaked perhaps, but still alive. I sympathise with the mother-goat but I don't see the point in loading Jazz's brain with one more murder. I don't think she particularly dislikes the wolf. I think he amuses her more than all the other characters.

The trilogy of the wolf's salvation concludes with the wolf chasing the three stupid little pigs, three pitiful compromised bourgeois, dying to put their heads under a roof at all costs. And the first two are complete idiots, that's all.

So the wolf actually falls in the cauldron. It's in all the pictures and also in the cartoon version she likes watching on YouTube. But from then on, I think I have every right to add that he simply got a bit of a scorched tail and then ran away. The little pigs are out of danger now, and all's well — so why not think of him roaming the woods, free and ready for new adventures? He's an amusing bohemian type and he's good at making funny impressions (OK, not perfect ones, but nobody's perfect anyway).

No wolf will die as long as I'm in charge. When she grows up, she'll be free to learn a different version. When she grows up, she will learn lots of nasty stuff; it's inevitable.

The only reason why we grow up is to learn the nasty stuff. Wolves die, people die and all the things we love will vanish one day. Also, the country is in recession.

What is exactly the reason why we grow up?

We are not used to the new house yet. I don't know how long we're staying here. It's a little ground floor house with a yard. Most houses in the old town are like this. The new part of the town is slightly pathetic. All those modern apartments. According to the people who live here, modern equals excessive, or, in my view, completely useless and unnecessary; large balconies, where nobody bothers to go out on, grandiose entrances for the cars to park, since there are no garages, vast useless spaces and a grand view to nothingness. Of course I know enough to keep my mouth shut — although talking with people doesn't happen too often to me.

Yet the sea is so close. Living here and seeing only the apartment across the street would be blasphemy. Anyway. We don't have a seaview either. The houses in the old town are usually enclosed all around. Nobody can tell what might be hiding inside them. They were built this way for protection during the Ottoman occupation, even by the Turks themselves. I guess people saw each other on the streets so often that they had no desire whatsoever to see each other when at home too. Of course, nowadays you don't see anything and you don't know anyone. We don't, at least. We have relatives here, of course, on my mother's side, but I haven't decided to pay them a visit yet. It won't be very pleasant. Anyway, the truth is that we were used to a larger space. Some of our habits have remained unchanged. We constantly think that we have more space to do stuff but we just wander in this large room which constitutes our entire house. It's a bit strange. But we'd better get used to it.

I wonder if there are any houses with some secret story around here. Medieval temples, Venetian villas, Arabic fountains, Turkish mosques; you come across all these everywhere. But most of all, I would like to learn the strange stories of the people who have inhabited those buildings. Yet again, you need people to tell you about all this.

I can't blame her, I especially, for not being very talkative, right? I don't feel like talking to anyone lately.

In the evening, her breathing sounds normal, but I'm always a bit worried. She wakes up early, around 8, and usually asks for beddy— bye. This means she wants to come to my bed. Unfortunately, she never falls asleep; she stays for a bit and then climbs down and starts gathering objects which she brings to me, while I'm still trying to have a bit of a lie-in.

I've noticed that I write in first person plural. Does this imply that I'm acknowledging more rights to Jazz in our life?

Last night we watched a movie for the first time, we watched about ten to fifteen minutes of *Ice Age 2*, dubbed. Of course, it's always the beginning I love the most, with Scrat. She managed to follow it for about ten minutes, although she surely doesn't understand a lot. Before this, I had played a DVD with a dubbed BBC documentary about lions for her. I stopped it when the lions started fighting but I was too late; one of them was already dead. I must find something more age-appropriate.

2. Penguins have someone to wait for them

Today we watched *The March of the Penguins*, that film about the life of the emperor penguins, dubbed of course. The penguins caught her attention at first but then she got bored. Every time I watch this I get annoyed with the narrators' corny quasi-romantic babble. It would be a marvellous film if it was silent.

I tried to trim her hair. I was a bit nervous, I had done it before of course, with ladies I used to date, but it's not easy to make this decision for a child. When I got a little more confident, the scissors slipped a bit and Jazz burst into her light crying; a sort of crying that can be prevented if you manage to distract her with something else. When it's classic crying, you just let it burst. Both types may last very little, though. Ferocious crying is the type you give up on and wait until it's finished.

Jazz let me cut her hair properly this time; last time I had only cut the ends a bit and she had found it amusing. This time I overdid it, though. She has short hair now. She's a pretty child, thankfully. Still a baby, I suppose.

I haven't made any progress with many matters. I'm still not quite sure how to put her diaper on properly every time I change her. It can't be that difficult. For some reason I get it wrong two out of three times at least. Perhaps I subconsciously see it as something degrading, and that's why I keep making this mistake. On the other hand, it might be mere chance. There's fifty per cent chance I'll get it right every time, since I find it impossible to understand immediately which one's the front side.

The truth is I was hesitant to speak about this matter up to now. Perhaps it's the same reserve I've always felt about this matter since I was a kid; it has been following me since then, preventing me to speak about anything related to this. Of course someone has created this issue of mine. But isn't it too late for me to look for the one to blame? At least I have overcome my difficulty to write about it.

What am I actually doing? Am I trying to get over my childhood traumas through my notes about Jazz? Is it possible that my whole attempt at raising a child is an attempt at growing up myself?

Tonight I got her to chuck the diaper in the bin herself, and she did it very easily. She keeps doing acrobatics though, and this is always dangerous. I'm not sure what I'll do with the punishment chair. I keep postponing it under various pretexts. After all, it was a piece of advice given to me at the previous nursery. Now we're going to a new one. This is also something we have been postponing for quite a while. I'm wavering between the rules that must be set and my own idleness.

There were 14 inches snow in New York today and the authorities have advised the citizens to avoid commuting unless it's for a good reason. While watching TV, we bumped into a soap opera. Two women dressed in black were having a conversation. Love troubles. One of them was older and plumper, her dress was more revealing but this didn't matter to me. All I wanted was to rub myself against the other one, the younger one, wearing a tight black sweater and tight trousers. I felt an unbearable urge to jump inside the TV screen somehow, to hug her from behind and stick my body against hers. Just this. Or just this for a start, I'm not sure.

It was the first time I felt something like this in a few months. Am I coming round from deep emotional lethargy? A bit like the penguins in the film, but with no mate waiting for me?

Then we changed the channel. We watched the European Swimming Championship for five minutes. I explained to her that this was a bit like the sea. The phea, she said. The phea.

I remembered the way my dad used to rub his face on my head or at the back of my neck, I'm not sure. But I remember this every time I carry her to the car in my arms. I've never managed to put her seatbelt on easily. It's hard, as hard as driving is for me in general. I often think that I might cause an accident or that something else, which wouldn't be my fault, might happen.

When she goes to bed in the evening, when I leave her in her little bed, it's the loneliest time of the day. I do long for this moment. Sometimes I even count the minutes to her bedtime. But the moment one is left alone with the television as their only quasi-company is actually too bitter and lonesome. You wonder if it will always be like this and you know it won't but also that you might start missing it one day. Nothing lasts forever. I thought that parents have their way of expressing their arrogance towards non-parents. When a non-parent asks them about something, they reply with such confidence, or at least they pretend they have complete mastery over a subject, usually having gone through a lot for each and every example they give. But they know nothing. It's impossible to know everything, to know how you would react, every single one of the millions of moments you will be required to react somehow, not to mention the countless possible ways you could react in the best (lots of quotation marks) way. No. Parents are lying, and that's that. They improvise. That's what they do. Now I know it.

You spend your life with a child improvising, because there is no other way. Not when it comes to basics; you must memorise some rules in this case. But when it comes to all the rest, you improvise every moment.

Tonight she woke up very early in the middle of the night. I went to her bed and showed her the shut window and said, it's still night, you have to sleep.

The fact that she actually calmed down was an incredible surprise, but it didn't last long. A five minute triumph of reason. Then she started sobbing, crying and eventually came to my bed for beddy-bye, in other words, about three hours of staying awake. We woke up late: it was nearly eleven but we couldn't help it.

We spend our days doing nothing special. We go for walks by the sea and we try to get used to the new house, the new city, a new world. I don't know if it's easier for her, but it's not easy for me at all. I keep postponing the visit to her grandma, or of taking her to a new nursery. I keep postponing the decision to start living a normal life. How can I live one though? I have no job and I have no idea how to get one. This is a small town, where everyone seems to know each other. I don't feel like meeting anyone new. On the street, I see women I would like to get to know better, of course, but the women I see around me increasingly resemble the women I see in my dreams; desirable yet unattainable…

If this is not our world, then which one is it? And where are we supposed to find it?

Obviously I suffer from some type of agoraphobia. I don't know how else to describe it. We go out all the time but we don't want to have any contact with people whatsoever.

What's this now? How is it reasonable to use plural in order to include a two-year-old child in my phobias? Perhaps because I am afraid of dealing with it on my own.

I suppose there must be a description of my state in some book; antisocial behaviour. It feels as if I've pressed the "pause" button on our lives. But why should Jazz pay for it? No matter what is wrong with me, I must do what's best for her at least. This city is not too bad. Well, it's not the city of my dreams but is there one of those anyway? One of Calvino's invisible cities perhaps.

Will she learn how to read? Will she enjoy reading? Will we ever discuss writers like Calvino? Will he already seem ancient to her by the time she grows up? And what difference does it make? All that matters is that she does whatever she enjoys most. But is a life in harmony with the world definitely going to provide her with more happiness? I don't know. All that matters is that she lives a better life than mine.

But I want to live a better life than me as well.

3. You must concentrate!

Jazz must start concentrating. These are the instructions I was given at the new nursery. She must be able to stay focused on something for at least a quarter of an hour. Perhaps for less at first. But she must do it; these are the instructions for the time being. I guess they have noticed a slight concentration issue. Does a child have to concentrate on anything at this age? And what could that be?

They didn't ask, so I didn't tell them anything about the few words she can say. They will figure out themselves. At least she won't have to go through the trouble of learning a second language, as she didn't quite get along with the first one anyway. Perhaps she was longing for this songlike idiom of the natives of this area. I wouldn't like her to speak exactly like this when she grows up, however.

On the way she was holding her new yellow toy-car, I knew she would like yellow although I never quite liked this colour. The first toy-car which I can remember was yellow, though. This consolation didn't last long. At school, she burst into tears and I didn't like watching her eyes shut tight as I walked away. Someday I will try to explain to her what the use of going to school is but now that I must, I can't do it.

Sometimes, when you look into her eyes it's like watching a movie trailer from the future. You try to imagine how it is, you think you can see it.

By now, she has also memorised cars and whenever she sees one in the magazine she points at it and says dada. But she also says mama and mimi, which probably stands for her name; Jasmine, Yassemi in Greek. They must have told her at the nursery. I call her different names. I should probably start getting serious about this too. I will only call her Jazz at home.
The highlight of the day, apart from her new shoes, is that she took the lens out of my glasses while we were fake-fighting. I still play this silly game with her. Therefore, it serves me right. It was hell finding the little screw that had gone loose and screwing it back in.

She gets genuinely devoted when she wants to read something, although she's not exactly reading. She usually grabs a magazine, she's been showing a preference to magazines lately. She opens it. She turns the pages hastily and then starts all over again. Nearly always, she stumbles upon the same pages and I don't know how she does this; it's probably chance. She always pauses on the same page though, and never reaches the end. The scene is this: Jazz opens the magazine and stops, say, on the second page. She points at something and tells me "mmm", I tell her "well, this is a car". She listens, seems to be thinking about what I said and moves on to the next page. She waits for me to say something again, she listens to what I say, *this is an orange car.* Sometimes, say, for a specific car, she adds something, *Daddy*, yes, I reply, it could have been daddy's but daddy has a red car. I have bought an old second hand Fiat. OK, she seems satisfied with the explanation and turns the page. She points at a little boat in a whisky advert and goes mmm again. I tell her, this is a little boat, which is in the phea and there's a bottle next to it. And that's how it goes. When the magazine is finished she puts it in front of me again and starts all over, usually from the same page. She could repeat this four or five times or maybe more if I don't stop her.

Some small random details from our life here:
Discovering things you thought were meaningless with her. For instance, during our boat journey; the lifeboat (the one she always got excited to see although it was the same one again in the same spot on the same boat) near

the handrail, when she had just learned how to walk but of course I wouldn't let her walk.

Children's leaflets only contain mothers. She reads those leaflets for hours, like the one they gave us when we bought the shoes. And another one that was handed to us in the shop where we bought our first glass. A plastic one of course. It's hard to believe yet she finds something familiar in everything; balls, swings, animals, dogs and cats basically.

Daddy cries sometimes — when he watches films. Maybe in his sleep too.

It's the first time she uses a glass properly. She finds it a bit hard but she likes it a lot and persists. She gets a bit wet but she persists.

We have acquired a new habit; we beat up cars. She goes near and gives a baby-slap to the bumper. Cars are parked everywhere in this city. I think they deserve a bit of a beating.

She erases the drawings on the little magic board immediately. I don't manage to draw anything for her and this irritates me. I need to show off a little.

We got a bit more soaked than I was expecting on the dripping wet slide. I was dumb, they warned us that the slide was soaking wet. It's been raining constantly for the past few days. There were two older children, a boy and girl, the boy was staring at it but he wouldn't climb. We just do whatever comes to our head, though. As soon as we had wiped the water from the slide well enough (with her clothes!), I saw them climb on it. We went to the swing too, where we saw a smiley mother. I smiled too and became much more talkative with Jazz, but nothing happened, she didn't pay any attention to us. She just left.

On our way back, in the stroller as usual, I told her the story about Anes. Anes are actually big birds. There were lots of them at the airport where we've been. It must have been a nest.

Anes fly really high; they take people with them and carry them around. They give birth to their little ones in springtime. You can see lots of little Anes in airports.

When should you learn that we eat all the chickens that go cluck and the cows that go moo and the sheep that go baa? My first girlfriend was very sensitive concerning animals. She was a vegetarian. She got really irritated when I was joking about seeing all animals as potential food. But I don't dare do anything like this with Jazz. I respect her more, or perhaps I'm more afraid of her.

Where could she be now? Who knows…

We must always think one beast ahead.

I had written this down somewhere and then forgot why. I kept it because I found it cute; perhaps I'll remember what it meant at some point.

We expect children to behave reasonably. We demand it. Because reason, which is our own invention after all, is convenient for us. We forget that the only reasonable thing a child can do is to behave unreasonably. Yesterday, she spent about twenty minutes lightly slapping one of the rotating animals hanging above her bed; a little tiger, I think. She gave it little slaps, very light ones though, a bit harder than caresses, and then she would laugh on her own again.

4. Daddy talks with the fridge

This is the first time she draws. Officially, I mean, at school. She made a drawing of No-White. Her teacher, a petite dark lady, is proudly showing me the drawing. Today we drew Snow-White, she tells me.

From her look, I get the impression that she's actually saying; *"the kid wasn't learning anything there, wherever that was"*. She might be right. Or maybe her look is saying; *"you're totally useless, and that's why your wife left you"*. But she has no right to say anything like this. These are all mere hypotheses. She's trying to guess. She might even be in love with me already. That's for sure.

I should probably stop imagining what people mean to say and ask them what they mean to say in reality.

Jazz herself isn't paying any attention to the drawing. She has this "It was all in a day's work" look, or something.

I can't keep up the same comedy of the couple here as well.

I'm all alone, madam. This child here, I am raising it on my own. And it's hard. And I'm very much alone, actually. Now you know who to turn to in case your husband has been neglecting you.

"Daddy talks to the fridge". That's what she would say if she could talk.

The fact that she doesn't talk is somewhat comforting. I will have to stop doing some things later on. But she can see me anyway. She might be thinking of it. Now she's just looking at me, waiting for her afternoon sweet. It's the good-girl-at-school bonus. Lately, she doesn't even bother to tell me "good mimi". She takes it for granted.

There's still a bit of water in the puddles on the limestone plates in the yard. With this water we write letters that will soon fade.

The look in her eyes has changed imperceptibly; I realise it when she climbs really high and sits on a box next to the painting canvas. It's dangerous, but I don't tell her anything. I let her enjoy it.

Lately, we've been carrying some plastic toys along with us to school. We walk a short distance every morning. When we arrive at school, she hands me back the toys calmly and I leave. When I leave, I feel really lonely.

Sometimes, we take another route, passing over a small bridge. When she gets her first notebook, I'll be waiting for this bridge, along with my own first notebook.

It was daddy's name day yesterday. Nobody was invited.

When she feels like walking, she gets off the stroller and we beat up the cars. I feel a vague dislike towards the other parents, especially the men who bring their children to the nursery.

The doctor here is bald as well. It seems like the previous doctor has followed us. He says the same things more or less anyway. Her negative attitude remains unchanged towards the new doctor too. She starts crying as soon as the medical examination begins. Don't be a pinchor, I tell her when we leave. I have no idea what it means, but it definitely isn't a good thing. Being a pinchor is not horrible either. It's a word of our own, though, and I believe she understands it.

Yesterday on TV, a little Egyptian girl, who couldn't have been much older than Jazz, was talking about the state of the country. She was saying that Mubarak throws stones and wood at people because they shout and they're hungry and they want a job. She was explaining why the people had gathered at Tahrir square. Then the reporter asked her what she thought would happen and she said, I don't know (it was before Mubarak left). Jazz doesn't know what Mubarak means or what Egypt or people with stones and sticks mean. How much can you expect from her, though?

Tonight, after putting her to bed, I watched *An Autumn Afternoon*. It's Ozu's last film. Once again, it's about the daughter who refuses to get married. There's a daughter like this in almost all his films; the daughter who doesn't want to abandon her father, without ever admitting it. I wonder why I am so touched by a theme that seems totally outdated. There's a scene where the father tells his son he should have a child soon because he shouldn't be fifty when his child goes to high-school, as this would be a problem. The son agrees. *This is precisely the problem I will have.*

The daughter gets married and leaves, though, and the father gets drunk already on the first night. What will become of him?

What will become of me when she grows up? *How many years do I still have with her before I become an oldster? Will she still want to see me? Will she forget about me or will she think of me as a necessary evil — as it usually happens? Will she feel pity for me when I get old, will she help me walk, or will she be living somewhere far away, never answering the phone? She will remember me when I'll be old and ill and she will come and find me but it will be too late by then. Will we only have time for a reconciliation scene, just like in American movies? Which mistakes will I ask forgiveness for and will she forgive me? Which things will she remember me for? Which days? Which ones will she be angry with? Which ones will she talk about to her close ones; I won't be her close one, will I? What do I have to do to be one? What do I have to do now, as long as there's still time?*

I have the same thoughts all the time. I think I should stop watching Japanese films. For a while at least.

I ought to find a job. We won't have money forever.

I'm not in the mood to write anything else.
    Winter must end.

5. As time goes by in the small city

The initial plan was to stay in the city until we got the house by the sea repaired. During the journey, this seemed easy and heroic. But when we arrived here and after seeing the state in which the house actually is, a house I hadn't seen in more than ten years, I realised that the initial plan should be abandoned. How are we going to live in a deserted house by the sea? The fact that it was still there was a miracle, but then again, this meant nothing at all. I'm not exactly the hero who decides to live a life of freedom in nature in Thoreau's *Walden*. And in spite of my lack of extreme sociability in the small city, I have no desire to become one. First of all, we would need a lot of money to repair the house. But even if we did this, with the money we got from selling our previous house, again, we would be completely cut off from the outside world. The closest village is 10 kilometres away. In the winter, the area is completely isolated. Of course, we would learn lots of things about squirrels and weasels, probably about rats too, but we would have a bit of a problem with the rest. Even if I wanted to, I wouldn't be able to make such a decision for the child. And I don't want this anyway.

We must face reality, as Mafalda says, holding a sledgehammer.

Jazz's world consists of the people we see on the street, the teachers at the nursery, the few relatives we met at the village (and the ones we will meet at some point in the city, I've already been talking to her about her grandma), the two or three acquaintances we've met here up to now. But the ones who pay the slightest attention to her are the ones who become her friends. The fact that she won't see them again doesn't bother her.

I remember a verse from one of the poems I used to like when I was a teenager: *When I see passers-by / I feel sad at the thought / that I won't see them again*

Fortunately, Jazz doesn't have such thoughts. And I don't want her to. I don't want her to become like me. Too much wasted time, too much wasted sadness. I managed to make some use of it, but I wouldn't like her to go through this. No way.

Food still remains a stable love and her greed has not changed at all. It might be a way of getting used to things, you know, feeling at home wherever you are. Jazz is a person who has habits. It's nice to see her feel good whenever she sees a bowl of food which is all hers. The fact that she eats everything is great. I'm a bit sad to notice that she clearly prefers meat, but I can take it. The new doctor also agrees (needless to say) that the child needs to eat enough meat. I haven't got the strength to argue with him, the way I did with the previous one. The teacher at the nursery always announces enthusiastically every time I pick her up in the afternoon that "She ate all her lunch! She asked for more! She wanted more meat!". Let it be, as long as she likes it.

She leafs through magazines and stops when she notices something she can recognise. She always finds something; a clock, a cake, a car, less than she used to, of course. Children attract her attention, as well as cats and dogs. She still notices airplanes; whenever she hears one, she starts looking for them in the sky and says: anes. She gets disappointed when she cannot find them. When a woman smiles at her on the street, sometimes she calls her mama or mamummy. At least she also calls me dadudddy. She insists on being very stingy with words. She even calls the pacifier her own way; she doesn't keep it in her mouth for as long as she used to, though, especially when she lies down, and yesterday I think she had a slip of the tongue and said wee- wee when I asked her if she needed a wee. The teachers insist that she understands more words and that she generally understands nearly everything, that's what they're saying. I doubt this. I've kept my promise and I haven't dropped any hints regarding my imaginary wife. If they ever ask me I will clearly tell them that our house is void of any mama. *No there's no mum.* I'll say, without any special pride about the fact that the child is growing up with me. And that will be the end of the conversation. Funnily enough, they've never asked me. Maybe what they say is true: in a small town everyone knows everything.

I got her a storybook with pop-out illustrations or something. She didn't tear them, not immediately at least, and they kept her interested, but she wants to go back to the same picture again and again and stares at it. She's not paying much attention to the story I'm narrating, a bunny called Carroty takes his spaceship (she calls this ane as well) and sets off to meet his space-friends. How on earth can you explain to her what outer space or space-ship or space-friends mean? They were colourful, though, and they gave carroty a carrot cake as a surprise-present. She recognised it, as well as the candles, and went phh, it was her birthday quite recently, yet she didn't know what to do with the candles then. She's clever, she's a dummy, or perhaps she's neither. I try to help her concentrate, although the most interesting thing we do is fake-fighting, which is not especially pedagogic, I suppose. I noticed that the name of the author of the storybook was nowhere to be found on the cover, and that wasn't very nice. However, she is amused when I pretend I'm hurt or when I lean sideways after a push or when I fall down after a pinch. I think she doesn't pretend much when she falls.

Jazz's mother and I were born in the same place, but none of us stayed there very long. We both went away, not together, when we were still young and then we went even further away. For a few years, I was trying to come to the island now and then, my parents spent the summers there, and then, when my father retired they tried to settle down there. I say they tried because even for people with no particular duties in the world, living in that isolated place was some sort of exile, for my mother at least. That's why they decided to split the distance between the homeland they had invented and the homeland they were trying to rediscover. They stayed in that house only in the summers. Crete is a beautiful place for vacation. And they kept fighting with each other over the house. So, after my father's death, my mother lost interest in the house. She just transferred it to me. Apparently, my father, in spite of the differences we always had, managed to transfer some kind of love for this house to me. But this proved to be only in theory. I don't feel like staying there at all anymore. Although I actually don't have any special preference for any place anymore. I am a person without a homeland. What I know for sure is that I wouldn't be able to stay there even if I wanted to.

I have to invent a new homeland for us. I must pretend I believe that this place here is our homeland. Even if it doesn't help me at all — I find it hard to convince myself — it will help Jazz. It's good for a child to have a homeland. That is, a place of her own. A place to belong to.

6. Mrs. Long-ago

We saw Mrs. Long-ago on the street, the lady with the shadows underneath her lilac eyes. She pretended she hadn't seen us before. We see her every day, though. The first time we saw her, we greeted her. Jazz waved with her plump little arm in her direction. I found this touching. So, I had to do something. Although I haven't adopted this habit (which is very common here, especially among the elderly) of greeting complete strangers on the street, I said "hello", in order to add some extra value to Jazz's gesture. The woman stopped doing whatever it was she was doing, planting something in a flower pot, or maybe simply caressing the flowers but that was all. She quickly lowered her eyes and kept making this incomprehensible movement. Maybe she was embarrassed to be seen in such a private moment. I felt somewhat insulted by her silence. Jazz's gesture had been wasted and this upset me. And I had also missed an opportunity to show off a little. We went our way. Then, when I brought her to my mind again, with these sometime-beautiful eyes, (they're still beautiful, even though they're surrounded by a dark wreath filled with years of abandonment and solitude), I decided that we should call her "Mrs. Long— ago". This was my revenge. Whenever we pass by that alley, we often meet her. She always seems to be occupied with something but we don't know what exactly. Maybe she stops suddenly when she sees passers-by. Maybe she doesn't want anyone to know what it is she's doing. But that's the point, I'm thinking maliciously. Nobody gives a damn about what you're doing anyway. Of course we never talk to her. Neither does she talk with us.

We simply co-exist in the same space for a while and then each one of us gets on with their life in their own world.

Jazz was dancing, bending her knees and moving her arms about as if she was conducting an orchestra, she must have learned this at the nursery. She doesn't throw the towels down when I change her diaper anymore. Furthermore, she has made some progress with words, water, milk, bag, she says them somehow, but not clearly and not every time; only when she feels like it. Of course she knows that hearing her talk pleases me but she doesn't grant me this favour often. The doctor we went to here said — her as well — that there is nothing to worry about. It's a matter of time. This is exactly what all the other doctors have said too. I noticed that the rest of the children at the playground, the ones her age, don't speak or they speak in a strange manner. However, there are some who speak constantly. Not perfectly, but it seems as if they're constantly practising a new musical instrument. Jazz is not crazy about learning how to speak. After visiting the park and walking on the streets and at the beach she has become very familiar with dogs. She's going through a phase of obsession with dogs. Something odd happened on the street. A little gypsy boy, who was wandering there, offered to clean up her clog, which was covered in mud. He just did it, before I had a chance to object, and then left. Jazz was staring at him with curiosity.

During her second visit to the doctor, she didn't cry, that is, she cried in the beginning, but then passed right in front of him in the stroller looking very aloof. Of course I told her to say goodbye but she didn't. The doctor himself noticed that progress had been made.

Lately she usually sits on the chair instead of the stroller, indoors and outdoors. She prefers it, just as she prefers eating with a spoon — or even a fork when she gets a chance. She tries to take control. However, she doesn't fall off the chair when you get her to sit there. She keeps uttering some little voices when she's in the stroller but she mainly sits silently. What could she be thinking of? She's not sad or anything, though. In the evening she was very cheerful, she pinched me black and blue, she likes pulling my hair and, after drinking her milk, while we were watching TV, she touched me with her hand, without any particular intention to pinch me. Also, she can imitate the woof woof much better now, as well as the gestures a girl at a café is making whilst telling something to her girlfriends. But she gets upset when people don't pay attention to her.

Slowly but steadily, she has started communicating on a different level. At first it was totally imperceptible, but when something is repeated several times, there is no doubt anymore. She always has a tendency — which has probably been nurtured by me — to make physical contact. She doesn't want to be cuddled or caressed, and she probably sees kisses almost as some kind of punishment. I mean, when I try to bring her close to me and kiss her, she reacts as if she was given a fake slap in the Pow! Game we like playing. She finds flying kicks much more entertaining; they're a variation of fake-fighting. That is, I grab her by the shoulders and lift her up with the edge of my foot. So while my foot is touching her, it looks like it is making her fly; that's the flying-kick (that's how I call it, of course). She also plays pillow-fight, that is, I throw pillows at her, she laughs, she's happy, she throws them back and here we go again. Something I find annoying is that when she needs help, in order to go up or down the stairs for instance, she asks for your hand. Then she pushes your hand away.

Just like she still pushes my hand away when I try to caress her because she knows this will piss me off and then the battle will begin. When she's in good spirits, she pinches me herself to wind me up, a bit clumsily, but it's still a pinch. She even does the sound: "pinch!" she says. Some afternoons we watch ball games, that is, football or basketball. She shows great interest, but it doesn't last longer than five to ten minutes. She always enjoys watching old black and white films and cartoons of course but I think she hates the news. And this is also a good thing.

If only I could also avoid watching the news. But the situation here is getting worse every month and that's a good excuse. Everyone says that the prime minister is an idiot. This is the most elegant word people use to refer to him. However, precisely because they take him for an idiot they don't make great demands of him. Generally speaking, talking politics in Greece is a slightly strange matter, and, especially in Crete, it always ends up in some sort of personal story. As I mentioned above, everyone thinks that the government is useless or bribed by the foreigners or both. Nevertheless, most of those people have voted for it and whoever admits this uses the fact that there's nothing else to vote for as an excuse. The others are even worse, they'll tell you. Moreover, everyone knows what the problem is as well as how it can be solved, but they are sure that it will never be solved. And then they end up narrating their life stories in order to convince you that they are perfectly able to survive without the help of any government. They're afraid you might think that they are somehow privileged by the government. This is not strange; the system here forces you to vote for one of the two leading parties in return for a job in the public sector. It doesn't matter what your job will be, as very few people work anyway, only doing what is absolutely necessary. They wouldn't be able to do otherwise, even if they wanted to, and this is again due to the system. The fact that they created or tolerated the system is something they don't like talking about. Usually conversations are interrupted or terminated with one more free shot of raki. I don't dare to confess to anyone that I find this drink awful. I just pretend I'm drinking, trying to swallow as little as possible. It's something like a medicine that cures the awkwardness of meeting new people. But it's ghastly. It's obvious that I don't have any real connection with this place. The natives drink raki since their birth, especially the men of course. There are no men who don't drink. You have two options: you either drink a lot or you drink an awful lot. Sometimes, I must admit, it didn't taste too bad. But it's usually terrible. Terrible.

And now I'm going to sit down and listen to that song by Fats Waller, "I'm gonna sit right down and write myself a letter." It's the music she was listening to when she still was inside her mother. I think it's the best way for the world to welcome a new child. And I also believe that it will help her see the world as this awesome pianist saw it. He died of pneumonia before he was even forty. He had three children.

7. An excursion to baby-land

It was as if someone had suddenly turned a switch off. Her behaviour changed. Since this morning, everything has become much harder, as if one more wall has been raised between us. It seems as if she has forgotten at least half of the words we have learned with so much effort. Regardless of the fact that most of them were entirely hers anyway, meaning that she had come up with them herself. It seems as if we have entered a darker room, where our contact has become even less. She cries more easily. She even started crying just because I told her we were going to school. And there, again, the usual scene; her refusing to go through the terrible door and holding on to me. I don't know what this is all about. It's like travelling back in time, an excursion to the past. An excursion to baby- land. A wall had already been standing between us anyway; a wall we had to gradually demolish with the help of words. But all of a sudden, this wall grew taller. It's a wall made of the stuff which is opposite to words; made of the missing words. The fewer the words she can say become, the taller the wall grows.

It's not just this though. Lately, her desire to leave the stroller has been gradually decreasing. Also, she has stopped making any effort to get to know the world better. Even television doesn't provoke her yells or her laughter, which somehow used to be her little comments on anything we have been watching till now. She just watches silently and solemnly, like some tired and disappointed old man. She doesn't even get enthusiastic with food anymore.

One more thing I find serious; she doesn't get upset and she doesn't object to anything. Not even school. She lets go of my hand and makes a few hesitant steps. You can sense that she doesn't like it; she expresses it with her entire being. But she doesn't turn around to see me with her sad eyes. She just keeps walking towards her inevitable future. Against her will, though. It seems like she has accepted the situation, but not in a good way.

Naturally, I have no idea what this is all about; or where I can seek the slightest help.

None of the books I've read mention anything in specific. There are a few scattered passages about behaviours returning to a previous age but nothing more. It's a possibility. It kind of resembles the behaviour of a child when a sibling is born (I had a peek at those chapters too, although I know I won't be needing them). This is when the child retrogresses in order to repossess the parents' lost (in the child's view) love. But this is a bit unfair. Jazz doesn't share my love with anyone whatsoever.

Are things that bad or am I simply overreacting? Am I projecting my own objections to our incorporation in a new world? Is she on my side, instinctively adopting my own profound desire? Or is it the exact opposite? Is this perhaps her revenge for all the changes I chose for her life? For her entire life up to now, the way I've shaped it with my choices?

I didn't ask her whether she wanted to leave, whether she wanted to change cities, environment or people, whether she wanted to change space, houses or habits. But what on earth could I have done? Could I have postponed all the changes in my life until she had been able to decide?

I could have done something. Surely, there must have been a way to understand what she wanted.

Yet, there will always be things that simply must be done a specific way. Wouldn't she rather learn this now instead of returning to baby-land?

It might be temporary. Just a bad day. I hope it doesn't last long. I'm not in the mood to deal with this as a problem, but as a passing cloud in the blue sky of her relationship with the world. Why is this happening, though? Is it related to the terrible twos? Have I done something wrong? Well, that's for sure anyway.

But have I done something terribly wrong? Was bringing her here a mistake, perhaps? And did I have an alternative? Yet I take for granted that we'll always do what I believe is best, so where is her own opinion, her own wishes?

I should pull myself together. Her wishes, the wishes of a two— year old are not to be taken seriously; unless they're about pacifiers or teddy bears. The rest is just something to write in the idiotic diary of my vanity in order to feel better. I don't have and I've never had the least desire to listen to what she wants. I'm just fighting depression and I want to feel like a proper father.

But Jazz insists. There's obviously something troubling her. I have the feeling that this sudden change of hers has made an impression even on Jazz herself. She realises something has changed, and that it's her own doing. Is this mode of thinking complicating things?

I think a lot on her behalf. But I have no idea what she's actually thinking of.

Last night was a nightmare; she was tossing and turning almost till dawn. Neither of us slept.

The slightest thing made her cry the following day as well. We didn't go to the nursery, of course. The only good thing was that she went closer to the sea by herself and dipped her feet in the water, each time she wanted to throw a pebble in. She even fell face down in the water once, she got upset, her eyes got red but she didn't cry; just a little bit. She probably came to terms with the fact that this is also part of the whole process. Nonetheless, she can tell whether something is her fault or not, especially when she has been naughty; she makes only very little noise then, just for the sake of it.

8. Walks in the park

Normally, even the stroller is an issue. Normally (what does normally mean, though?) we shouldn't be using it anymore. Despite her small build, she is too old to be carried in the stroller. I could ask perhaps, but taking a look around me is enough for me. Children over two don't go around in strollers. Still, I'm not sure; kids don't come with age-tags. After all, why should I ask? She wants the stroller. I want the stroller too. Therefore, pushing a stroller is our way of going against time. The idea of parting from it actually makes me sad. It's also for practical reasons. Her walk is not disciplined at all. And this is an occasion when discipline is vital, with the nightmare of the traffic, all those cars that never stop, the motorcycles that pop out from nowhere. Even bicycles, in the merely decorative bicycle lane of this city, speed quite unreasonably. Even I am in danger, as I keep forgetting about it. Also, I must admit that the stroller provides me with a sense of security, as well as a completely absurd feeling that she understands me better. I'm under the impression that what I tell her while she's nesting there, without any visual contact, has a better impact on her. Or — this is a bit more reasonable— I believe that it's more suitable for narrations of things I have the need to narrate to her. Doing this without a stroller would seem out of place.

Now she's crying again and I'm forced to stop. Is she perhaps crying on purpose just because I'm writing? Is what I write that bad?

Numb-a-thin

Numb-a-thins are tiny, they're teeny weeny, that's why they fit in oranges, large oranges with leaf verandas, but you often find numb-a-thins on the street weeping, just for fun. A numb-a-thin would never weep for real. Numb-a-thins live in groups and go to the sea all together, but they make sure there's not a lot of people around, otherwise they don't like diving, they just stay on the sand by the water and they slosh about. Numb-a-thins are so tiny that they can play football with a grain of sand and many of them know how to dance, carefully holding one grain of sand each; it's very impressive but only babies can see this when they feel like it. Numb-a-thins don't stay in cities for too long, apart from playgrounds, and they like the big lights by the pier when there's nobody around, or when there's someone who's so sad that he's convinced he doesn't exist. When someone is that sad, he can see the Numb-a-thins, but he doesn't notice them because he thinks they are tears. If that someone is so sad because he has no job and his baby is hungry all the time and he doesn't know what to do about this he may leave it at the Numb-a-thin village for a while, right on top of the weeds that grow untidily on the side of the highway. One can see lots of Numb-a-thins there, and some of them are so beautiful you wouldn't believe it; you mistake them for dream-flakes.

Of course I wasn't expecting everything to change with a fairy-tale. I liked the one I came up with but I actually know that it was terribly grown--up. I guess that the perfect fairy-tale would be written precisely in her language; in her own words if possible. The rest are for me to pass the time while pushing the stroller. So I had to resort to lonesome teddies, crazy bunnies and squirrels with enormous tails again. The worst part was that we watched even more TV as soon as we got back; more TV for a silent depressive family.

The following day Jazz is still shut up in herself, pensive, I might say, she whines a bit more than usual, but what's most terrifying is that she has lost her good spirit; she's sad. And that's too grown-up to bear. I've made a secret bet with myself, no kidding, for a while now. It is a very serious bet. I want her life to be happy for as long as possible. I want her joy to last as long as possible. And now I see her looking clinically depressed. What do I do with this? Just the thought of it paralyses me. I don't want to seek medical help. First of all, I wouldn't know how to explain it. Furthermore, I don't trust anyone. Moreover, it's my fault. Also, I want to find the solution myself. Perhaps because I feel it's my fault.

On the surface of the outside world, of my own world, this emerges through silence or through the fewest words possible. Of course, there's always the easy method of crying. But that's not what the problem is.

The problem is always this: which of all those rules she will learn should she actually learn? Which are the traps in which all of us are caught? Does she understand why I tell her off when I do so, I wonder. Can she tell the difference between teasing and irony? Does she get hurt by this? How much? For how long? Does she actually understand everything, no matter what she's told? Does she choose not to speak because she dislikes what she sees around her? And what could this mean? Have all the children who talk and communicate come to terms with what we have defined as "reality" for them? Is her refusal to speak a sign of her struggle against such a compromise?

I'm not in the mood for further theoretical pursuits. For our walks, we will keep using the stroller, which we have never abandoned. We will keep drinking with a baby bottle, which is simply the largest one (300 ml!) in the market. We will go on like this: I will be the one doing the talking, hoping that she understands me.

9. What if…

When will I stop keeping Jazz's diary? When Jazz becomes a part of this world. When she starts communicating properly.

What does properly mean, though? I guess I'll know when it happens. Is it possible that she'll be late? Is it possible that she will never manage to communicate properly? Who would bear this? No matter what you're saying, you just don't want your child to be slow, do you? The rest is just you trying to be a wise-guy. You want her to be like all the rest of the children. Is this the mistake everyone makes, perhaps?

Today she wanted to play with her favourite jigsaw puzzle — the one with the little bunnies and the hare that runs on his own — in the morning too. Fortunately, we managed to find the hare. However, when we are putting the pieces together, that is, when I'm putting them together, she just glances at it and then puts her feet on it and stops the hare.

Tomorrow I'll be 40.

Some old friends remembered me. I would like to see some of them again. But I don't know how Jazz would react to this. While watching an advert with Uma Thurman driving a car (are these her daughters?) she said "mama" again. No, I said in a steady voice, and after some thought. That's not mum.

The television stayed on during dinner too. We ate simultaneously and I saved my tortellini for later, after her bedtime. I don't know if I should read in front of the child. I got used to eating while reading, Mickey Mouse at first, then sports newspapers. My father would get furious. I still do it. However,

I won't get furious if I see her reading at the table. That might be some sort
of progress.

*Does she realize it when I try to deceive her? (I try not to lie to her but it's not always easy).
Why does she always say no? She only knows ten words, but does she know more perhaps?
Cat, mama, dada, nana, milkie, ya-a, ya-i is the pacifier, phea is the sea, woof is the dog,
bag, bob is the ball, bob is also the shoes and a few names. She can pronounce something
like water and clock and mmm instead of yes. Why is no so much easier than yes? For
children, perhaps learning how to say yes is an equivalent to accepting their defeat.*

*What if she refused to speak until the end? What if she remained in the same state?
Would she be able to be happy like this? Could this be the real, the only possible happiness?
Not talking and not communicating with others? My thoughts took a wrong turn again.*

I still go out for walks, always with little miss depression to keep me company. It
was raining a bit today but we had to go somewhere. I promised I would take her
to the swings, and, although she dipped her boots in the mud, we had to keep
going in order to reach the park where the toddler swings are. Of course she got
dirty when she decided to get off by herself. I hardly managed to put her back in
the stroller. At least it had stopped raining. The TV is some sort of consolation.
I swore we would never watch Little Lulu again. I never liked it, even less now.
It's boring and out-dated and totally American. I'm under the impression that she
only asks for it because it's easy for her to pronounce. Lulu! This way she doesn't
surrender; she still doesn't learn any new words.

This is the first attempt at communicating after several days: she gives me
a bit of her food and enjoys watching me pretend that I'm eating it. Can she
sense my hesitation, I wonder. But why am I hesitating?

It's normal for her to eat, they tell me at the nursery, at this age, but also for
a couple more years we don't restrict food as long as it's healthy, not a whole
piece of cake, some people don't give their children any sweets until they're
four, to prevent the system from getting used to them. Is she getting used to
them? Maybe not, but maybe she'll become a sweets maniac in the future. I
shouldn't let her become like me, I've always had a bit of extra weight.

She broke the ceramic doll at grandmas' house. The truth is I was convinced she wouldn't break it and that's why I gave it to her, but she broke it within a few minutes, in a way that it would be impossible to glue back together. She's not ready for anything like this. She doesn't mean to break things though, she's just reckless or, to be precise, she's not conscious of this danger.

She particularly likes an old Vogue issue with a little girl and a dog on the cover. I had never noticed this magazine amongst the chaos of the room. I don't know how long it's been here. Perhaps very long. She points at the little girl. She points at the dog and goes woof woof. She recognises dogs of any kind, as well as cats, she points at Kitty Cat and says, cat, cat. But further on in the same magazine, which must be a tribute to children, a children's issue, there's a photo of four or five children. One girl is making a grimace of laughter, possibly, it's an advert after all, but her face is tense and it makes Jazz cry. She cries and says that the girl has a mimi. This means that the girl is hurt and this makes her sad. But I have the feeling she gets sad over something more real. Or something more invisible perhaps? How on earth did this magazine end up here? I thought I had got rid of all this.

Later, we approach the sound system. She has learned how to ask for music but what actually intrigues her is the CD that goes in and out of the CD player. She has figured out that this happens when you press a button but she doesn't know which button in specific, so she experiments with many different ones. Of course I drag her away from there, so that we can listen to Dido. It's her first record, *No Angel*, which we have listened to several times already. I'm mad about the first song, although I'm not sure I can hear the lyrics clearly after the "here with me" bit. I think there's nothing more powerful for someone who is alone and at the same time absurdly "together" with someone else.

I think I weep every time I listen to it. Although I've learned how to hide it with time.

Jazz is swaying slightly, she's not crazy about this genre, but she likes it. Of course there are also CDs with children's songs. She likes some of them a lot, like the one with the war of vegetables that ends up with them turning into a salad. I have an issue with children's songs. Primarily because all the voices sound the same. Also because, like in many films and cartoon series, children behave like adults. This irritates me but I'm not always right. After all, I had also misjudged our good old friend SpongeBob.

She has invented a song of her own, called "yousida". She sings it very often, especially in the evenings. Of course I can't understand what it means. She still wanders around other people's tables the few times we eat out. She doesn't care that most of them don't pay attention to her. She has a tendency to do acrobatics, and this makes her funny. Fortunately she's been lucky tonight and she didn't hurt herself when she fell from the sofa.

The following morning on the street. Something happens and she trips. She doesn't fall, she doesn't get hurt but she bursts into tears. I kneel on the pavement so that we're face to face. That song pops in my head, I don't know why. Don't cry, I tell her. I sing to her intensely at first. Softly, really softly the second time. And once more. Whispering. That song, *Here With Me* is in my head. Again and again and a thousand times over. And this is when it happens again. She freezes. She's not crying. She's looking at me. She's not crying. Not her. She stretches out her little arm and I hear: "what is this?". Is this really happening? It's as if she spoke again for the first time. I hug you and I love you as if you were – and you are – the only person in the world. We start walking again. Here with me. Here with me.

10. While spring is approaching

She's feeding me for the first time. Of course she only gives me the bits she doesn't want anymore because she's full, but even like this, she gives me a slice of apple and she is amused to watch me chew it. In the afternoon she gives me a small piece of the almond I gave her — actually I shouldn't be giving her almonds — she could choke on them, they say, but I have absolute confidence in her abilities on this matter. I finally eat a small piece and of course she asks me to return the rest of it. The floor is covered in hundreds of building blocks brought to her by some friends, but she prefers to watch me build something, which she destroys; she tries to break them down to the smallest parts possible, but she doesn't bother to build anything at all. She likes throwing them all on the floor after I have collected them patiently. This happened a few times. I gathered them and put them somewhere she can't see or reach them.

Lonely walk at the playground, there's only a brunette with her blond son, who is nearly Jazz's age. They smile at us on their way out. We followed them with our gaze and then we went to see the woofs.

In the afternoon, we watched a dvd with Dora the Explorer. It was the first time for both of us. She likes the name Dora, the first time she saw her was on a balloon I had bought her during our trip and she keeps repeating it just like she used to do with Lulu. She watches the whole story attentively and when Dora is not on the screen she starts asking: Dora? Dora? She's worried she might have left. No, she won't leave, she's still there; I have to explain that she's just not in this scene, but this is something not even that wise little girl from Egypt would have been able to grasp. Dora usually pauses the action and asks the children questions. This didn't work with Jazz, but she's still too young, I guess. I imagine that when she's three she will be answering Dora's questions and when she's six she will be even brighter than Dora. Dora and her monkey, whose name I can't recall, are trying to cross a lake, to climb a wall and to reach the tree-house where there's a party. There are crocodiles in the lake. Blimey, are there any crocodiles in lakes? But that's not the point. Jazz knows nothing about crocodiles. She also doesn't know that there are wild animals that eat you. She doesn't know that there are also people who eat you. She doesn't know there are tame animals that we eat. She saw some little insects a while ago, she thought they were little birds, she called them papa, the fact that they're insects doesn't bother her, she's not scared, she's not disgusted, everything is papa, everything is colourful, everything is friendly.

There's nothing that can eat you, nothing to upset you. For the time being.

She doesn't like it when I take the pen away from her so that she stops scribbling on her hands or — even worse — on the sofa throw which I have no clue how to clean anyway. Or the big fork she insisted on using today. She liked my spaghetti though.

She knows nothing about bad things. Nothing. She will learn. Why is it necessary that she learns? If nobody learned about evil, would it still exist? Yes of course, since grown-ups would still exist. A world consisting exclusively of children should be created.

Amongst Dora's friends, there was an iguana called Isa. They fixed the wheel that was missing from her scooter. There was a wheel in Dora's backpack. I wondered what Isa would be like if she were a woman. Even though she was an iguana, she already had a blonde mane and she seemed independent and, you know, alternative, since she owned a scooter too. She slightly reminded me of an old friend of mine. Then I thought I'd better find a girlfriend because I'm already losing it. My other question was who paid the expenses for the party at the end of the episode.

I'm too old for fairy tales.

There's a light drizzle, which is not very helpful with the laundry, all I can be bothered to do is hang the clothes on the radiators. I mean I just can't face ironing, no matter how much I've tried; ironing and proper cleaning are tasks for the creepy woman who comes twice a month. Soon, we won't have any money left for her either.

Jazz is feeding me again, she gives me some omelette. Not because she doesn't like it. Maybe she just likes making me taste something, sometimes she even does it with her milk, she offers it to her dolls too, yesterday she was trying to feed it to the baby doll in the stroller, which she has rediscovered. Today she was saying poo-poo to the strawberry doll. She was even sniffing at her. So she gives me bites of food just like she used to offer me milk. I think she finds this business entertaining. Is there something like love to be found there perhaps? I don't know. When I hugged her good-morning today (or was it last night at bedtime?), it felt like she hugged me tighter. Yesterday she also did something new. While drinking her evening milk, she would turn and glance at me. The moment our eyes met, she found it funny and giggled a bit every single time it happened.

On the swing whoo whoo whoo whoop whoohoo whoo whoo whoo whoop whoohoo, I'm sitting like a wooden puppet, like a Pinocchio, immobile in the same place, and I'm waiting for her, I feel like a Pinocchio, this is what entertains her but not as much as I would like, behind us, on the wall exactly behind the swings at the end of the playground, there's a graffiti, *you ravaged our lives we'll ravage everything.*

11. Little stars, little flowers and everything falling back into place

Now she's absentmindedly staring at the little stars and the little flowers while I explain again and again how you put them in their place. I suspect that she's pretending she doesn't know how it's done on purpose, although she does. She slowly starts collecting a few things and puts them in their places, though. This is really important. The beginning of the great surrender to reality.

Jazz is out for a walk, at the chemist's, and the girl at the cash register asks her what her name is, she's a bit stunned, "nice name", she says, "she doesn't know it, though" I add. We buy a new feeding bottle. The most advanced one. There you go, one more step forward, amongst thousands of steps, visible or invisibles ones: the bottle doesn't have a teat, just a tiny hole, it's therefore similar to a glass, similar to what children do. She's not a baby — according to airline companies, in a week from today she will be charged more for an air ticket. We should go on a trip this week. But we're not going anywhere.

Today she took a little ball, the red one, to school with her.

The look in her eyes has started changing. Also, yesterday it was the first time she agreed that the building blocks can be placed in two rows. Until now, she would destroy them at once, when she saw me doing it. Now she allows it. But when I ask her to do it herself she won't cooperate.

She's been learning conjunctive adverbs but she doesn't get along with the ones indicating time. They're hard work. How do you teach time to a child?

More, down, good, nenia, she says when she watches *Hellenophrenia*. It's a satirical show about the situation in Greece. We don't understand every single thing but it's funny. We dance, moving our head and then our arms. Then we watch the news, with me, Jazz and the strawberry doll sitting on the couch.

However, a genuinely new thing happened this morning. She said the word scared for the first time. Lately, she's been waking up whispering. She whispers to herself. I usually tell her to go back to sleep, a bit of extra sleep is always good for her, especially on Saturdays. Today, she was asking if she would go to the nursery (how on earth do you explain that there's no nursery on weekends? She will just start remembering it at some point). After whispering, it's time for shouting, complaining, and if I don't go to her instantly she will also get started with the good old fake-crying. My theory about fake-crying is that it's not milder than real crying since it must also be caused by an unpleasant feeling she has. After taking the railing — it's still there — off her bed, hoping she will stay in bed a little longer — she never does it — she walks to the window with the view to the other end of the city and looks at the houses across the street — most of them are old and ruined. This is where some cats hang around and she watches them as if it was some kind of theatrical performance. There were no cats today, though; last night's downpour had created a small lake on the balcony where they usually chill out. That was when I heard her talk to someone or something. But there were no cats. I wondered if she was talking to herself. No, I started realising that she was addressing somebody called fy, fy. This fy creature was a fly that was flying around the upper left hand corner of the window, unable to go through the mosquito screen, which Jazz has dislocated as she bumps on it every single morning. I went near her, sat by her side and asked her what was wrong. Then she said the word scared, loud and clear. For the first time she said *scared* and she meant it exactly the same way as the actual meaning of the word. She was scared of the fly. We sent the fly away and I tried to explain to her that she shouldn't be scared neither of the fly nor of anything else in the world.

In the evening, Brownie the cat slept on the couch in the basement. Smooch wasn't bothered, he's very hospitable. In the morning, we go to the nursery. She likes it and looks forward to it. But she wants to take something with her. She takes the balloon. She wanted the plastic ball with the princesses, something girlie anyway, I don't know how it ended up here, I haven't bought this, but it was too big. She compromised with the slightly smaller orange balloon and we took it with us. On our way, I came up with the song of the balloon, which she kept in her arms all the way of course. She would turn and look at me now and then, something she doesn't do often. She liked it, she was looking at me with curiosity, perhaps with love, I dare say. The song wasn't amazing but it was tasteful. She recently discovered the baby doll in the stroller and she plays with this, then she played with the strawberry doll and in the morning she insisted on feeding it milk. I gave her some.

Just out of the blue, a young lady on the street told us: *you are the best dad in the world.* Why not?

She has got used to Dora and now she asks for more. But the DVD I bought her is scratched and it will only play the first episode. Jazz doesn't seem to care, today she said, there, for the first time, there, when Dora was again asking for our help with finding a tail or a lake, I can't remember, I make sure I respond to all the questions in order to set an example, and I have really come to like Dora and I wouldn't mind watching some more episodes. Today we had a morning incident, to put it this way, in the toilet, where I found everything covered in her poo. I don't particularly enjoy talking about this but I suppose I ought to talk about this too.

I'm thinking I wouldn't be able to imagine myself without her. Today she said "very" meaning to say what it actually means. Where does she learn all this? How many words does she learn because I repeat them to her and how many at the nursery? Does it matter that I constantly repeat to her what Dora says?

Dora's song has been stuck in my head all morning. I've been singing, dododododa Dora…

In the afternoon we played a new game with the paper tape. I stuck bits of it on various parts of our faces. She was quite amused. Then she started scribbling on the tape. Some lines that got tangled or something like circles, well mostly like smudges, but they look exquisite to me. Later, much later, I discovered one of those paper tape pieces still stuck on my foot. It was even scribbled on.

Dododododa Dora. Dododododa Dora Dora…

SPRING

1. Visits and Dreams

It's the first day of spring and it's raining. I had a hard time taking her to the nursery this morning. The rain wouldn't stop. On the way, I promised myself I would try to keep count of the nots and the don'ts I would tell her today. By the time we reached the nursery, I had already told her five of them. I gave up in the afternoon as soon as I got to 20. I bought her a 12-piece jigsaw puzzle, I couldn't get one with fewer pieces. I should have found one, but I didn't want to disappoint the salesgirl — she had a terribly sweet face.

She didn't pay much attention to it, probably realising that she's not capable of putting it together yet. Then we had some trouble with Lulu, the DVD I had bought was broken (why are they such cheats?) but she waited patiently for about twenty minutes, while I was trying to fix it and then we watched Dora. She remained absolutely focused but she talks whenever she likes, not answering Dora's questions. For the time being, I'm the one who answers; to set an example. Maybe I simply don't like the awkwardness which settles in during the void seconds when Dora is waiting for the kids to reply. I can't bear not replying to her.

It's called obsessive compulsive disorder, I'm aware of this.
And that's the good case scenario…

I keep trying to wake her up with some chit chat every morning. Yet in the afternoon she was crying as if it was her duty to do so. In the evening she was coughing. I went upstairs and turned the small light on, at times like this I love her very much, and I asked her if she had lost her pacifier, she said yes, but, almost immediately after I had turned the light on, she said, here it is and went back to sleep at once before the conductor's entrance.

To whom is all this important? To Jazz.

It's been raining constantly. Perhaps a visit to her grandparents might be a good idea. On our way to their house we see a baby in a stroller and she makes fun of the baby's pacifier. She's not able to tell us how much of that phase in her life she remembers. And when she will be able to tell us, she will have forgotten all about it.

Her grandparents are not very talkative. They only talk about formalities. I leave Jazz at their house and go. I hardly spend any time there. I think this is what we all want. I don't know how she spends her time there. Once, I saw a game with boxes that fit into each other. Then I saw it again. It must be their favourite game. I believe she must start doing more complicated stuff but I don't want to give them instructions. I also wonder how they manage to stop her from asking for food all the time. Yet she really wants to go there. It's almost inexplicable. They are elderly people, always solemn and probably without any other contact with children, apart from their other two grand-daughters. We don't communicate with Jazz's uncle and aunt very often either. They're not hostile but they probably feel a bit awkward, I guess. It's natural. Perhaps they're wondering what on earth I'm doing here. Moving to this city for the child is not a good excuse of course. I wouldn't say so either. Even I am not quite sure why I've come anyway.

I leave her there for a couple of hours, sometimes a bit longer, but never past her bedtime. Although she seems to be very glad to be there, she has never asked to stay longer. Is it possible that she only stays there for my sake? Who knows. She's not in a position to tell me how she spends her time yet. When I ask her she never responds. Her grandma gives her a formal farewell kiss sometimes or she welcomes me with a kiss when it's some kind of religious celebration I'm not aware of. Her grandpa has declared that kisses are not a proper way of saying goodbye and shows his disapproval to her somehow. A handshake is good enough for him. We never exchange anything more than formalities and we never talk about the past.

I feel their gaze is constantly interrogating me. I would also have lots of questions to ask them but I don't think I'll ever do it. The chapter of Jazz's mother ended abruptly for me when she left us. For her parents though, things are probably quite different. One would expect they would naturally want to talk about their daughter, excuse her, blame her or refer to trivial details about her life just like all parents do. They don't, though. And I wouldn't want them to. I suppose they sense this somehow. That's why there's always an unbridgeable void between us every time we meet up.

Tonight I saw my own mother. I was in a strange place, a sort of junction through which all the coaches passed in order to go to Europe. They would stop at the bus — stop but they would travel to virtually any place. I saw buses to London, Vienna and various other cities but I didn't leave. My mother arrived and found me in a hotel lobby. I felt restless. I had gathered some objects that belonged to her around me. I asked her if she was content with the objects I had kept.
Yes, she said, they're enough (the objects formed a circle around us). Yes, I'm fine with these, she reassured me again. She looked genuinely content. "I'll come back for them", she told me.

A weight was lifted off my chest, but a slight restlessness still remained. My mother would rarely say anything that could upset me. Perhaps I shouldn't have chucked so many of her things away after she died.

So is this our only way to communicate?

I always believed she would find a way to talk to me, to come close to me. To be honest, it's not even a matter of religious faith in spite of my mother having absolute faith in God and the saints, I was sure she would find a way to stay close to me. The fact that nothing like this exists, aside from dreams, is a cause of great disappointment for me. Perhaps I was expecting to find an answer to questions of this sort. Now I feel a bit lonelier. The world is an inhospitable place. It can't be possible that she didn't find a way to talk to me. If there was one she would find it, I say to myself. Totally like a child. Yet I am a child; her child, right? Why can't she find a way…?

2. Learning the rules

Today we started our day really pleasantly, we woke up relatively early, not too early because she dropped her pacifier and I had to wake up and give it back to her, she went back to sleep immediately, but I didn't, due to all those suffocating thoughts. Yet we followed our normal routine, milk and cookies as a bonus for her, coffee and cookies (there was nothing else left) for me. We gazed out of the window for a while, at the white cat with the drooping ears, in the deserted house across the street, we called at her and she lifted her head, awesome ears, and then I took Jazz to the nursery. It was really nice in the morning. The teacher said she has been hanging around with the other children, she wants to have things her own way yet she's more sociable than usual and she doesn't beat them up as I was afraid she would.

Are we actually holding a perfect creature in our hands only to gradually destroy it until we turn it into what we are? When does this start happening and why? Can't we do anything about it? No, we can't. Is the situation that terrible or am I exaggerating again as usual? And how could this perfect creature live alone in a world like this one? Along with other perfect creatures? What would life be like then? Could it ever be like this? Has life ever been like this, perhaps in ancient tribes, lost in time; has life ever been anything more than a game? And even if it has, what difference would this make?

I was slightly late to pick her up and that was a disastrous mistake. When she loses her rhythm, even only slightly, and she's not back home at the specific time, when I change her and put her to sleep, she loses her temper. She was crying incessantly, for no reason in particular. Any movement of mine would cause more crying, when I tried to undress her, when I tried to dress her. She kept crying until she saw her bed. That was when she lay on her tummy, pacifier already rapidly passing from palm into mouth, and she didn't bother me for quite a while, until the afternoon, when she woke up in tears again. You shouldn't pay attention to her, they say. You must pretend you can't hear it. But is this possible? She has the ability to start crying viciously from one moment to the next. Actually, there is no middle ground. She just bursts into ferocious crying all of a sudden. There is also light weeping, only when she has her eye on something and she asks for it. All the rest of the times, she cries heartbreakingly. That's how it is. Yet, when I accidentally tickled her tummy, while changing her clothes again, she suddenly broke into laughter. No, she's not a perfect creature at all.

She woke up too early in the afternoon. I was trying to write what I call "The diary of Jazz", as usual. It's always really hard. By the time I went upstairs, she had emptied an entire drawer. I remembered the rules. You have to put everything back in, I told her. I tried not to yell too much but also to be clear or at least to say it with the appropriate air one must have when addressing a child.

So, what is the appropriate air every time?

While she was putting the things back in, after I urged her a few times, she slipped and hit her face on the edge of the drawer. Wooden drawer. I couldn't believe that what I was seeing was blood. It stopped easily with a napkin. After a while she resumed tidying up. Of course she didn't put everything back in but at least she put some. I decided we should go out for a walk even though it was a bit chilly. Her little hands were frozen as we were passing by the sea. I gave her a small piece of chocolate rabbit. After a while, I asked her to give me a bit. She refused to give me any, and in the end I just took a little bit myself. I wish I were nicer, I told her. I wish.

I also wish I didn't seem so desperate when I looked at women. I wish I could describe them all, the ones I see down the street every day, almost every single moment I'm in the street. And not just describe them, of course. I wish I could touch them, get them into bed, *control them; that's the word I'm afraid of,* yes, control them.

I wonder if I'm the man who has walked the most kilometres with a stroller and a baby in this city. It must be tens of kilometres.

Some of them look easy, others less easy, none of them notices me. Maybe that's how the game is played but I never managed to learn it. Kostis was preparing his ceramics shop. He was arranging the objects of the new season. He's a strange kind of guy, perhaps that's why I prefer him to the rest around here. He knew the woman who died of cold in the park the other night. I knew her, he said, she had three dogs, I fed them cookies sometimes. She must have had a few, he added with his typical calmness.

We bought a magazine that came with a jigsaw puzzle of Dora. Guilt is costly. Today, she asked me for the first time. Where are we going? She said, auntie and uncle. I said, no, we're going to the sea. She said, swim, I said, no, it's cold. But it's nice to look at the sea at night, although it's still quite cold.

Jazz is coughing now, she has a cold all the time, but only a little bit. She likes playing with her nose, picking it. At some point she will learn that this is also a bad thing. What else is definitely a bad thing? Millions of things. She's greedy. Would she steal her neighbour's food if she was allowed to? Probably yes. Would she hit him if he reacted and tried to get it back? Probably not. Would she survive in the same conditions as Mowgli? I don't think there's any point in me thinking of this. I wouldn't like her to be a Mowgli, not for anything in the world. Even if she was brought up by monkeys with the utmost care. Now the only monkey she will be seeing for the next few years will be Boots, Dora's friend.

Of course she isn't a perfect creature. She is a sly, annoying, noisy creature that won't even let me write these lines. My lifestyle, seen from my perspective, compels me to have nothing other than Jazz to write about. I haven't got the slightest alternative. I can't write about adventures, bohemian lifestyles, late nights out, traveling to dreamlike places, alluring women who take everything away from you (if only they would), I can't write about criminals and poor neighbourhoods (although I've been getting dangerously close to what we call poverty), perhaps about unemployment, however, my case is too comical to derive any sort of drama from it.

I lost my job because I made a mistake. It's quite common. Now I live in a place where people lose their jobs all the time. And there's definitely no job for me. So, what can I do? I must come up with a job. Soon they'll be asking my daughter about what I do and she won't know what to say.

I made a stupid mistake with a stupid word. The only explanation that would satisfy me would be if I had done this subconsciously for Jazz's sake; if I had allowed myself to make this pathetic and absurd mistake just for the sake of losing my job because deep inside all I wanted was to take care of her. But I'm neither that nice nor that devoted nor that complicated. I simply made a mistake and lost my job, that's all.

I know that this tendency to fancy all women indicates that I don't actually desire any of them. To be precise, I desire them to desire me. But even if this were the case, I wouldn't know what to do.
In reality, I haven't made any steps forward since then… Yet I try not to think about it, inventing another self that doesn't resemble me.

3. Dreams for Jazz

She has started growing faster. Already the way she uses sentences is changing from day to day, even within the same day. It appears that there was already a word mechanism inside her little brain and she has just started putting the pieces together. That's not the case with Dora's jigsaw puzzle, though; she has no intention to take any advice, find the little flowers, match the little flowers, the monkey's hand etc. As a result, it's only been a week and we're already missing three out of the twelve pieces. She's terribly confident and when she makes up her mind you can't make her change it, she will try again and again. And yet she doesn't give up. She's been gradually abandoning some toys, such as the building blocks. I have hidden those away, because I got fed up with her scattering them all over the carpet, but she never asked for them again. So they're in the basement now. But I gave her a marker to draw on paper.

Her face glows every time I give her something new, whatever that is. We must buy some colors. Coloring pencils are not good enough for her, she wants something flashier. But who would dare to buy her markers? Naturally, she scribbled all over the small table and her arms with the pencils. I took them away at some point. By then she had doodled on several sheets, although it mostly looks like a signature. She draws a circle and then drops it. On other sheets — she uses newspapers — she persists even more. Her circles have improved a lot.

I placed a sheet of paper in the museum of memories. I wonder when the Conductor will go there too. I can't recall talking about the Conductor before, the blue penguin who plays music when you pull the string. This is what always happens when she's about to sleep, in the afternoon or evening. I'm not sure whether she needs it more than I do. I got to love this penguin terribly. She must have played his song more than 1000 times till now – a while ago she used to find pulling the string again and again very entertaining. I've promised him several times that I'll find a substitute for him so that he can take some days off but I never do it. I have a mild obsession with the Conductor. I suppose I don't want this era to end.

I dream of her living in Italy. That's what I told her on our way home this afternoon. I told her, this street is not pretty, but one day you will go to Italy, where there's lots of pretty streets. I love Italy, as well as Japan, although I have no clue what the latter is actually like. I'm working online and, in my browser, behind the window I'm looking at now, there's another open window; with a documentary film about the 100 years of Japanese cinema, directed by Nagisa Oshima. Will I manage to watch this with her one day? I'm not too old yet, but you never know. It occurred to me today, not at this specific moment, I just thought of it while I was going to the kitchen to grab an apple, so that I could watch the movie while eating, and this was when I wondered whether we will manage to watch them together (but I've thought of this before, about all the film noirs, the Japanese films, Ozu's films, the *Lost Weekend*, *Double Indemnity*, *The Maltese Falcon* and, above all, *The treasure of the Sierra Madre* – and all of Bogie's films. The journeys I never made, the films I've watched, the dreams I've had, the books I've read…

I've thought of all that a thousand times before, but then I thought for the first time that this might be the use of what I write. She can read them when I won't be around, near her, in case I won't be around. Yet I am determined to be around. Perhaps that's why I must write the entire truth, even though this doesn't exactly make me look like the perfect father I would like to be. However, it is a way for me to become better.

I was also thinking of those books that have a similar theme; someone is left alone with his child and he supposedly becomes very popular with women.

This is also the theme of one of my favourite books, *About a Boy*. In this book the main character pretends that the boy is his son, in order to win over a woman's heart. The funniest scene is when he goes to a parents' meeting, where of course he is the only man. I've brought this scene to mind several times. I've dreamt of living it myself.

But I haven't achieved anything in several months with this daughter of mine. Maybe I should take a note somewhere, that all these stories about me desiring all those women, all these probably degrading stories, are entirely fictional. But this might confuse her. Maybe I should set a rule that she should read it only after she becomes an adult – then she will understand. But no. I will be there to explain it to her. Yes, I will be there too.

There are moments when you feel like everything matches. Even the tray for the apple peel has some purpose in being where it is. Actually it's still there. It's been a few days.

And yet I enjoyed thinking about the children's version of the Adam and Eve parable. All children are like Adam and Eve. They live happily until they obtain knowledge. And yet, are we God or the serpent? We are a bit like gods to our babies. The serpent is the outside world, the already rotten world. That's what the serpent is. We do nothing to prevent it, the serpent shows the way to knowledge, that is, the apple tree etc., and children lose paradise. They are exiled out there in the cruel world, where they continue their lives in pain and torture. I must check if there's anything similar in Buddhism. Knowledge is the loss.

However, we just stupidly stared at the TV for at least one hour. We watched Rapunzel, the Disney version I think, and then a kids' programme with the good old pathetic children mimicking singers. Also a video clip of Bebé Lilly, ads for Barbie stuff and other instructions for little miss whore. It was the only way she would keep quiet until we walked to grandma's house at the other end of the city. Thankfully, we left quite soon. When we got back, I had to change her clothes for her nap. But while we were playing on our way up the stairs, I pinched her arm, perhaps it was a bit too hard, perhaps I underestimate the fact that she's still a baby. She shouted mama. I froze at the thought that I had behaved like a jerk once more. Fortunately, she forgot about it immediately and she even bit on my sleeve. I have started amusing her with a bit of tickle tickle on her tummy while changing her. Everything went fine and now she's still asleep.

Meanwhile, the state of the country is steadily getting worse. Greece is gradually falling into a crisis nobody is able to comprehend. To be precise, everyone is convinced that the orders Greece is given by "the foreigners" will lead to certain disaster. On the other hand, if Greece doesn't follow those orders, the country will be destroyed by bankruptcy. People react mostly in the big cities; in smaller cities, families act as a refuge from hunger while in Athens the homeless and hungry increase by the day. In demonstrations, however, one can only see the ones still standing. They shout, protest, curse the government and some of them even smash shop windows. Then the riot police arrive and people go back to their homes feeling lucky for not having ended up in the hospital. And there goes another typical day in Athens.

Today I went to get her in the rain, which later turned into hail. They never forget to tell me the news of the day every afternoon – during the last hour she was upset, probably because she had arrived early and had stayed longer. Something nasty happened on our way back, though. Perhaps because I got distracted by the waterproof stroller hood, I forgot to tie Jazz properly, therefore, on our way down the stairs, she fell out of the stroller, along with the protective cover. She was wearing her jacket and wasn't hurt at all but this mistake of mine was completely unacceptable. I apologised to her a million times, I called myself an idiot another million times, and then I thought that reckless mistakes are better than the ones I make due to my personal weaknesses. I promised I wouldn't shout at her for an entire month. I hope I'll keep my promise. I also promised her sweets in the afternoon. But she started screaming for sweets as soon as we arrived home. I gave her a piece of chocolate. Then I realised it was too big, so I took half of it back and ate it. She complained and I told her she would eat chocolate in the afternoon too. Life with Jazz is an endless sequence of compromises.

This afternoon, we watched the film of her first year onwards. We already have a tape (I use a really outdated camera, while everyone films with their phones) of her first year. From then on, we've been filming on another tape which will last until she's three. She watched her grandma, her godparents and Smooch eating his birthday cat-food, her first steps. Up until last summer, she couldn't recognise herself, she was saying, *the baby* and was quite amused. After the summer, she started recognising herself. She says, Mimi. She always likes herself. Yesterday, she opened a small window, just to look at her reflection on it. Today, more or less on the same spot, she made a different face, I told her "you climb" (on a pillow) and she said, "I climb". Downstairs, while I was changing her, she said, *I like this*, referring to a cardigan. She uses imperative a lot, go being one of her favorites, as well as the future tense, especially when it comes to food. *We'll eat.* She also pretended she was feeding the baby doll in her cradle. She has done this before. But now she's weeping softly, pretending it's the baby, and when I told her she should stroke it and tell it to stop whining, she said: No! And she threw the baby out of the cradle.

The great book of animals, which dates back to the era when I still had a job, is one of her new interests. No more clockwork hare that runs all around the large jigsaw puzzle with the little frogs, no more furry fairy tales, no more book of animal sounds that I had got for her at the airport, hoping it would be of some help on the plane as well. We look at the animals and she demands of me to tell her which one is which. The not so nice part is that there are lots of insects, which I can't recognise and I also see no reason in describing. Sometimes I suspect she does it on purpose. She should be able to recognise bear cubs in any form, for instance. The house is full of them; Teddynormous, Radioteddio, Teddycat, Teddykeychain. And more of them, god knows where. And yet she insists on asking every time she sees any kind of bear. She's still afraid of flies. She discovered the worm herself; *gorm.* That was her sole success. Besides cats and dogs, woofs, birdies, ducklings in general, I am supposed to tell her what all the rest is. She doesn't show any inclination to memorising. However, she enjoys this process, leafing through the book always backwards.

Yesterday we watched the Tom and Jerry movie, I thought it was really bad, but we only watched a few minutes, I fast forwarded it as I wanted to watch the news. Then I yelled at her because she wouldn't get away from the TV. Of course she can recognise Yorgakis, the idiot prime minister (or the prime minister who pretends he's an idiot) and she laughs whenever she sees him. But I'm not sure if that's a good thing. I yelled at her, though, and she seemed numb, and then I told her calmly that she must listen to me and that she should do as I tell her sometimes. Nah, she'll be doing the same tomorrow. Why are they doing this? I mean, why are they destroying something so beautiful? The Pink Panther used to be a fantastic show. I can't wait to watch it with her. I started watching it when I was ten, but Jazz is more intelligent. All children are more intelligent nowadays. However, the sequel of the Pink Panther – or the second series, or something — sucks. Totally silly. It's neither suitable for children nor for adults. I don't understand why they're doing this. They did the same with Tom and Jerry. A movie that bore no resemblance whatsoever to the old cartoons. Not to mention Mickey, Duffy, Bugs Bunny. An industry of pseudo-modern silliness. Mickey's club is endurable. It's a bit Dora style. But Jazz remains loyal to the original.

My father always used to say: let's go build this or that but he always built it himself. I must do better than this. Yesterday, we went shopping at a department store together, she was really patient at the queue, where, among other things, the machine broke down, that is, the memory was deleted, so we had to wait for quite a long time and she took off her boots and socks in the meantime. I promised her an ice-cream and we ate it together. I was surprised to see that she immediately tried to bite the bottom of the cone, just like I-still-love doing.

Diapers are still hard work for me, after all this time I still find it hard to find the right side where the little animals are supposed to match. It's a neutral activity; neither repulsive nor pleasant. The people at the nursery told me I should get a different type of diaper again, something that looks more like underwear. We'll see. We don't like sudden changes. I'd rather if she showed some willingness to learn how to do the job herself. I hope she will this summer.

5. The biggest moon in the world

She came to sleep in my bed. How pretty she looks in the morning light. It's the first time, it also happened last summer but only because she was very tired. In the past two or three days she has acquired the habit of waking up early and wanting to sleep by my side. She doesn't sleep of course; it's just a new game. She usually doesn't stay long. Today she did, though.

Her grammar and syntax change on almost a daily basis. Of course they didn't exist at all until now. To be precise, they are not actually improving. It seems as if this process consists of thousands of little pieces that are slowly falling into place. Of course she imitates what she hears, but the fact that she doesn't make mistakes is impressive. She can recognise the prime minister, she calls him: the ath-hole. She copied this from me of course, even though I've only said it very few times in her presence. I'm trying to establish "dumb" instead. She keeps asking questions. Where are we going? What are you doing? (she asks this all the time, it really amuses her). 'Im? 'Im? Everyone is 'im'. What is 'im', less often; only when we go through the animal encyclopaedia. And another variation is: *daddy, daddy, 'im?*

Today I got her her first Mickey Mouse comic book. She liked it a lot. While we were leafing through it, I told her the names of all the other characters one by one, as she only knows one, Mickey. Black Pete made an impression on her. It's been thirty years since I read my first Mickey Mouse. My elder brother had brought it home. I don't see him anymore; he lives really far away, from every aspect. We saw a couple with triplets on the street. She looked at them with great curiosity but I didn't let her examine them closely.

I dream of being able to ask her if she's happy and she replying, yes. For as long as this can last.

There are a million ways of making mistakes. For example, something entirely stupid, putting her shoe on while she's standing. It's so easy for her to fall backwards. It seems elementary to us but it's not elementary for a baby.

I dreamt of my mother again last night. I was some kind of prisoner in a house and she was trying to help me.

I'm watching all these disasters in Japan. I would like to go there. I'm thinking of Haruki Murakami, he's the first Japanese person to pop in my head. I only know Japan through films and books. Coincidentally, today I received his first book by post — translated in English of course. When I opened the parcel, I noticed that the wrapping came from a bookshop called Kinokuniya. He mentions those bookshops quite often. He definitely mentions one in *Norwegian Wood*, there's a girl that brings the main character back to her place, and I think her parents own a Kinokuniya. This makes his stories feel more real. I kept the wrap. I haven't grown up much, after all.

Another book of his that I like is *South of the Border, West of the Sun*, in which he talks a lot about only-children. He believes they are entirely different to other children. In this book, all the characters are only-children.

Could the world end? Not when I look into her eyes. I find it impossible to accept that my walnut-eyed girl might ever stop existing.

Then I thought that lots of parents must have said the same and perhaps they — and their children too — were lost in the earthquake.

On our way to school this morning she kept repeating "malakas", which means something like "asshole". It's the most common Greek swear word. The Greeks use it in more than thirty different ways in their ever-day conversations. Let's hope she'll forget all about it. I was wondering if she saw any posters of the prime minister on the street. I can't afford another Dora DVD. I decided to download some episodes and watch them on the computer. What can I do?

I think she looks a lot like Dora. I've often wondered what Dora would be like. She resembles her, for sure. I really enjoy watching her focus on putting the Dora jigsaw puzzle together. She tries to match the shapes of the pieces but that's the only instruction of mine that she follows. She doesn't look at the little image, she doesn't listen to me saying that Tico and Dora and the monkey should appear upright, she never makes sure she starts from the letters on the upper left hand corner, she doesn't get anything. Does this indicate that she's a bit of a dummy? Or just stubborn? No idea. Yet I like watching her; her slightly rosy plump cheek forms a perfect semicircle as she leans over, her cute little eyes also leaning over the table where we have also glued Dora's stickers, and her whole little head leaning over her task attentively. That's how hard she concentrates on whatever she does.

I try to eliminate the morning crying, it's probably impossible to do the same in the afternoon. She can't bear not crying, it's absolutely absurd. In the evening she had another fit about one or half an hour before she went to sleep. It seems as if she rushes into the final battle and messes everything up. And, of course, when you ask her to put everything back she just freezes and pretends to be stupid. But the latter behavior doesn't indicate stupidity at all. While I was carrying her to the bathroom in my arms, her gaze paused on the fridge. All her photos since she was only a few months old are there. One of them is really pretty. She says, "babez asleep". The babez is you, I tell her. And you're not asleep. You're just having a lie- in; precisely what you don't like doing now. Yet she's not able or willing to realise that it's her in those photos.

I wonder how much longer I will have to go through this torture of the morning awakening. I should also mention that we saw miss Desert again this morning. Miss Desert has stunning eyes of some rare colour which makes you try to find a way to describe it. But I never get a chance, as I only see her now and then, and she's always in a hurry. Her body is not equal to those strange eyes but who cares? Most local girls also have a bit or a lot of extra weight. This doesn't reduce their charm; it actually makes them match their surroundings better. Yet we don't exist for her. Not even a smile to the little one, which is something that nearly everyone spares. Naturally, I named her Miss Desert. I think I named her like this because she seems so distant. Where does she go in such haste? Nobody is in a hurry around here. They only get furious when you block their way somehow. Even though there's nothing urgent for them to do. I sometimes wonder if they have anything to do in general. But I shouldn't judge people according to my own problems.

Tonight, they're saying we will see the largest moon, because the last time it came this close to earth was in 1982. Jazz is not particularly interested in the moon. She can recognise it but she doesn't pay much attention to it. This afternoon I lifted her up to see it over the wall, and she just mumbled something.

The evident progress she has made is pronouncing more and more letters; she can pronounce V much more clearly, for instance. In the morning we watched cartoons for too long and we got a bit of fuzzy brain. I shouldn't do this again. She watches a whole load of video-clips and ads for CDs and fairy tales and Barbie equipment and perfect Ken who can talk and answers our questions. He says, *I love Barbie*. I hope she stays away from all this bullshit for as long as possible. Yet, it is a solution on Saturday mornings.

6. Freedom on the sand

We went for a walk by the sea, this is her favorite. I promised fifteen minutes of absolute freedom on the sand and I almost managed not to tell her any don'ts or shouldn'ts or stop-its and all that. In the afternoon we watched Dora playing football. The golden explorers were playing against the dinosaurs and naturally they won. She still has this habit (she might be poking fun at me though) when Dora is not in the shot she will definitely ask: Dora? Dora? I try to explain it to her. It also took too long for me to explain that she should only have her milk and no more than one cookie, that afternoon she had eaten loads, she only stopped when there was nothing left — and a bit of ice-cream (she commented: nice), and I also warned her that she will get fat if she eats that much and she will swell like a balloon and she won't be able to walk any more. Oddly enough, she seemed to understand. Then I gave her the one and only cookie we had left. She didn't like it very much, she gave me a couple of pieces back, and she only does this when she doesn't like something. When she likes something, there's no way to take it away from her. She mentioned the babez who is asleep again. I tried to explain that the babez is her.

I tried to take a photo of her on the floral mattress, lying down, radiant, with her hair spread out, it reminded me of something from the 60s but I don't remember what exactly. But when she's in front of the camera, she freezes. It's OK.

Her relationship with the cat has improved. I still don't trust her of course, I still need more time, but I've noticed the cat has been approaching her increasingly often and he stays close to her. Of course, saying gooood gooood can easily turn into pulling his tail or fur but she seems calmer, Jazz I mean, Smooch is always calm. She has started calling him by his name.

On a rainy Sunday while I'm trimming the trees. Jazz wants me to always be there for her; she's looking at me, asking 'what are you doing' every five seconds. Am I too obsessed with Jazz? Will I turn out to be like the people I used to make fun of? I'm waiting for her to grow up so that I can travel to the islands again with her. Relying too much on a child is not right. I could leave her somewhere and go on a holiday. Not now; some time. Of course, I'm not considering it now. Later? What will happen later?

She woke up early again this morning. It's raining. The light comes in through the windows, now that we've trimmed the trees. She's crying, having a little conversation with herself. Yet, crying is much more usual. Stop it, I shout, everyone's still asleep. This surprises her. She asks me if everyone is asleep. Yes, I reply, "everyone is asleep". She pauses for a while. Then she starts asking names. Is auntie Voula asleep? Yes. Mrs Nony? Yes. Anna? All the names she knows from the nursery. She goes on with unknown names. Teetys? Babis? We come to Dora at some point too. Yes, Dora is asleep too. I'm the only one who's not asleep. I must do something about this.

This Saturday, the children from the nursery will gather at the main square with their bicycles. We're going too. We don't own a bicycle yet, but we're going on foot.

I think she has grown up. It began yesterday but it's still happening today. Yesterday, we started having a nearly proper conversation since she woke up. How did you sleep? Fine. This is one of the questions I ask without ever expecting any response. It might have been a reflex, though. Maybe she has just learned that she must respond 'fine' to this question or to all questions in general.

Then, in the afternoon, I asked her what she wanted to eat. She said grandma's cookies. OK, I said, but I've cooked some runner beans, would you like to try? She said yes. And it seemed as though she had agreed mostly to be nice to me. She had had runner beans before at the nursery. I put some runner beans in her plastic dish after cutting them in half. She said, nice, before even trying them. She didn't eat much, though. So we went back to grandma's cookies. She knows very well which box it is. She ate one, then she wanted more. I explained that they were running out, mostly in order to avoid the consequences of their absence the following days. So we moved to fruit. She ate very little, naturally. Then I told her we would watch Dora, and I asked her where she wanted to watch it (I've also brought a DVD); whether she wanted me to bring it upstairs or if she preferred to go downstairs. She chose downstairs and we went to the basement, she climbed on a chair and waited. We watched Dora again, the episode where her assignment is to reach an enormous horizontal bar.

Something even more impressive happened today. She suddenly woke up early in the afternoon, she hadn't actually slept properly, her cough is still bothering her. She woke up and started crying. I took my time with going to her, hoping she would calm down. Eventually I went upstairs. She was crying loudly. She hardly ever goes back to sleep once she has lifted her arms. She lifts her arms in order for me to take her out of bed. I gave her the pacifiers she had dropped on the floor (probably due to frustration) but this didn't calm her down at all. Then I told her, slowly and steadily, Jazz, darling, you get some more sleep. Please, I want you to try, it's still too early, it's still noon and I don't know what to do with you and I'm tired. I'm very tired and I want to take a nap. There's nothing for us to do now but I promise I'll do anything you want when you wake up in the afternoon. Please try to sleep a bit more. The initial success was the fact that she didn't interrupt me with her crying at all. But the most incredible thing was that she replied, yes, when I asked her: will you try to sleep? And then again, yes, when I asked her, do you understand me, do you understand what I'm saying? Again, yes. And she didn't make a sound for the following hour and a half. It was marvellous and incredible. She's growing up. This is making me a bit sad but it's still marvellous.

The bicycle fiesta at the square was not for Jazz's age. She doesn't ride a bicycle and she doesn't show great interest in doing so when she's at grandma's. Only when you push her. But we met the young teacher and a little girl Jazz called Anna, if that was her name. She didn't utter a word. She came over to the bench where we were sitting and showed us a really small balloon, not inflated yet. Jazz took it and handed it to me. I looked at the little girl. You couldn't tell from her expression. I tried to inflate the balloon but it was impossible. I gave it back to her. She was with two women; one of them was quite graceful. She came back with another balloon, an orange one, a bit bigger. I could inflate that one, I gave it back to her and she gave it back to us, I gave her Jazz's ball and she gave us a party whistle. She had one more whistle. She didn't reply to anything I asked her. Meanwhile, a little boy approached us and asked Jazz how she was. He was quite older and I was surprised to see him paying attention to Jazz. Then another little boy passed by on his bicycle. He called out at her too. They seemed like wolves approaching their prey to me, although I know I'm overreacting. And that it will take me a long time to get used to the fact that Jazz will hang out with boys, perhaps she will even bring them back home. The silent little girl's mother asked her from a distance to return the ball to us; she must have been quite nice as far as I could see. She didn't seem keen on getting to know us better.

We're drawing a new era. That was a song by the Specials. I couldn't remember it was by them of course; I googled it. Who remembers the Specials?

A walk by the sea. It's not a very good day today. She's constantly asking for something. I've given in about ten times, giving her a cookie, a bun, half a cheese roll, and another half, and another half. As soon as she eats them up she wants more. I decided that she had stared at the TV long enough and that we would go to the seashore. The truth is she could also walk instead of going in the stroller, but I won't risk it. It's a beautiful spring morning, an early spring Sunday. The clocks changed and Jazz resembles a computer where the time changes automatically, she's hungry according to the new time, even though the clocks went one hour forward.

I dream of holidays in the islands and of a grandchild while I'll still be thriving — at seventy — but this morning I woke up with a nightmare again. I've been gaining weight and I'm afraid I'll die; I see suffocation scenes or something like images from hell. I don't want to. I don't want to die or to go to hell. I should just eat less. But the beach is unbelievably dirty. She grabs some sand with her hands and tosses it further away or she happily brings it to me to toss it. I had noticed again last time that she doesn't care what I'll do with it. She doesn't even notice. She is already busy with the next handful of sand. She also discovers a piece of a broken beer bottle, she says glass, right, but we'd better get out of here. It was pure chance that she hadn't collected broken glass the previous day at the playground, when she was doing exactly the same. At the square we did this absolutely absurd thing: we put soil or a little rocking-horse on the swing seat and I would catapult them really far shouting dodododododooo

A dog is approaching. He's small, white and cute. He's running towards us. I look at his mistress. She has a beautiful, sweet, white, clear face and slightly wavy hair. Her figure indicates an older woman but it might also be the distance. I would really like us to approach her but the dog doesn't grant us the favour to come closer to us. He slows down and returns to her. She might be very beautiful. I think her gaze might be somewhat melancholic yet it might just be my imagination. We go back. Jazz is hungry, according to the new time. As soon as I take her shoe off, the floor gets covered in sand.

She sleeps enough in the mornings. She wakes up with her cry-mumble but she's soon ready to answer my questions, to have a chat with me. This morning she made a drawing on her small magic board, we also have a bigger one. Dad, daddy, she said triumphantly. I took a look at it. The other day I was trying to explain that when we draw a face we must not only make a circle, which she can draw quite well by now, but also a nose and a mouth. So now she has drawn a circle containing another smaller one, a bit like an oval. Good, I say, now draw Mimi. She takes it back and again draws a circle with a little curved line inside. She generally avoids doing things that demand a lot of effort but she is capable of remaining focused on something for a few minutes. Yesterday she was searching something under the living room chest of drawers for quite a while. She rediscovered the yellow toy car we had lost some time ago. She was happy but such things don't interest her any more. On the contrary, the ball is of constant value. Whenever she finds one of the balls we've got, she kicks it and says goal. She only uses her right leg and she has learned how to take a few steps backwards and then to run forward and shoot. One of those balls, a plastic one with Mickey, ended up in the recycling bin yesterday. Most useless toys must be chucked away. They fill up the little space we've got. Naturally, she doesn't want to part from any of them. But I don't tell her, of course. I just have to replace them with new ones as much as I can. Jigsaw puzzles were not a good idea after all. Even twelve pieces are too many. Besides, even I wrote down numbers on them in order to remember how to put them back together. There should be jigsaw puzzles of four to maximum six pieces.

The children's conspiracy. Is there some kind of link that connects all children? Are all children somehow held captive by parents? Perhaps it's not as dramatic, but I believe that every child goes through this phase somehow. I like thinking that I've made an agreement with my "grown-up" self; to stay on the children's side. However, the children's conspiracy means that they know what's up and they express this solidarity with each other, in spite of the fact that they fight with each other sometimes. Perhaps they understand that what connects them is bigger than age. Perhaps I used to feel this too, I don't remember.

I hope I'll be her hero for a few years.

On our way, I smiled at a little girl and I asked her mother how old she was. She seemed a bit younger than Jazz. The mother didn't respond. Maybe she didn't hear me. Someone gave me a suspicious look. Perhaps he thought I was just looking for an excuse to get to know her. That's also correct. Yet, a simple response would suffice.

We're sitting on the sidewalk, watching the sky. It's nearly dusk. It's a beautiful spring sky that refuses to part from the clouds. A bird is flying above the roof of the house opposite us and disappears in the faraway clouds, beyond the antennas. I wonder if she remembers that game we used to play a few months ago. When does a child start remembering? Isn't it a shame that all these present moments will vanish? My memories begin from when I was about three. Yet I'm never sure whether I remember something through my own experience or through my parents' narrations.

In this case, we have to start all over again. It's a bird, can you see it? Duckling? No, a birdie, not a duckling. Duckling! She confuses me a lot, maybe on purpose, by not accepting that the birdie is a birdie and not a duckling.

The truth is that she usually calls Tweety a duckling when we watch it on the computer. I ask her, what do you want to watch and she says: duckling, She means Tweety — with Sylvester of course (there's also a modern version of this, with the granny as the main character — for heaven's sake, I could strangle all those people who came up with all this). It's not the first time she calls birdies ducklings. And what's the bloody difference anyway? Could I be even more of an idiot? What matters is playing. Besides, when she's in a good mood she shows some understanding when I try to convey all this knowledge to her, she calls them birdies. Like now. There goes another one. Look, look. Another one. She likes this one. I want more.I don't know if another one will pass by. Maybe. And it does indeed.

The truth is I'm teasing her, as there are always birds passing from that spot. Now she's having fun. I want more. I want more. She feels as if she's the master of the sky and wants one more bird to pass by the horizon. They keep passing by, one, two, three, birds are passing by from every direction. We must get going too. I lift her off the mantel.

One more film by Yashujiro Ozu for the evening. It is *Akibiyori* — something like late autumn. Once again, it's about the child that doesn't want to abandon the parent, in this case it's a daughter who refuses to get married so that she doesn't leave her widowed mother. My beloved Setsuko Hara is playing the mother here. Up to now, she used to play the part of the daughter or at least the old maid who doesn't get married in order not to leave her father alone. I don't aspire to such fate. I wouldn't desire it either, I would prefer, contrary to the mother in the film, to remarry and let my child go her own way. I would happily get married to someone like Setsuko Hara.

I searched for her in Imdb to see what has become of her. This wonderful woman is still alive! She's nearly ninety. This is Ozu's penultimate film, and one of her last ones. She stopped acting shortly after his death, when she was forty-three. She also lived like Ozu, without ever getting married or having children. She has lived in solitude for over fifty years.

If only I had known this fifty years ago, I would have gone straight to Japan to find her. And we would have lived happily ever after. I think she would have been a wonderful mother to Jazz.

I suppose I'm going insane.

I should take care; fewer cigarettes, less food, less gluttony, more discipline, more jogging. All the above don't guarantee anything of course, but at least I'll know I tried. I was short of breath and this upset me a bit more, perhaps I had eaten a bit more, perhaps I had smoked a bit more, even one extra cigarette would be enough to cause this. Why do I do it then? Also, why should all those morning erections get wasted? Isn't it a pity? I think I'd better get used to the idea that the good old days are long gone. But I'm still sad over the fact that women never cared for me, they never took advantage of me. I thought of buying a porn magazine from the kiosk but I was ashamed, so I bought the Thelonius Monk CD collection. OK, I like Thelonius Monk. Yet, I'm not quite sure whether I actually needed this collection. I've already got lots of his CDs. And that documentary about his life. It's nothing special but it's the only one ever done. At some point, his son is talking, saying that there were times when his father (who had serious mental health issues) was in such a state that he wouldn't recognise him. That's probably not the best thing for your child to remember but at least Thelonius was a genius. What am I?

I was ashamed because there was a woman in the kiosk. When she asked me what I wanted, I asked for the Monk collection. She gave me her number in case I wanted anything else from this series. A strictly commercial move, let's not make more of it, besides she was quite old. Not too old actually, just a bit older than me. Isn't this some sort of ageism? But I get a taste of my own medicine by all the girls who never look at me twice. At some point I have to order Monk's biography online. Perhaps some porn too.

I found this phrase in that book by Yoko Ogawa that I've been reading: *he believed children suffer from troubles, which are much more serious than the ones adults suffer from.*

She wasn't exceptionally pretty. She had some wrinkles around her mouth, her skin was slightly dark and worn — out, but when she smiled she changed a lot, her face would lighten up. She had a son, not particularly good-looking either, and rather pale. Probably like most boys around the age of four, he was quite abrupt. Jazz was watching him with great interest, as she always does with children. We had come back to the swings, after the slide, the merr-go-round, which she calls ring-a-rose from the song, and the seesaw, at which we had to take a closer look in order to ensure that it was broken. Then she kept asking this as a joke: the seesawz? To which I was supposed to reply, 'he's broken'. The woman stood behind the swing and pushed the boy. She overheard our seesaw conversation and smiled. On the pine tree there was a canary that kept chirping monotonously. I tried to show it to her but it was too high. It must have been scared to death. Maybe it had flown away, probably unintentionally, a few hours before. It was getting dark. It got quiet at some point. We left. At home, she didn't demonstrate any tiredness after all this running around in the park. We came back on foot, she asked for this herself. She walked slowly, she had tripped twice in the park. I was trying to write something now, but she's making such a terrible racket upstairs, that it's quite impossible for me to do so.
If all these notes ever get published into a book, I should — after a few years (after I will have become famous) — write the true story as well. I must confess I'm a despicable guy. But I guess any cautious reader must have realised this already.

There's something like a children's party in the afternoon, at a fairy tale book launch. She doesn't understand and she's quite right. Fortunately they're giving away sweets on the way out. In the evening, she's drawing on the magic board. She has found her own way — nothing to do with my instructions

— of drawing everything. A circle, almost perfect, some dots and then some lines here and there. Is this hair? I ask her. No response. Only the names change. Ane. She'll draw an ane. She's drawing it the same way. Then grandma. The same way. But then she's drawing the teddy-bah. She drew, accidentally maybe, two circles inside each other and this actually resembles the teddy-bear we've got on the couch. Teddy-bah is one of the difficult names she avoids saying; she has only said it once before. I think we shouldn't erase this, I tell her, but she doesn't care, she just erases it with a single gesture. So we go to sleep. I think she returned one of the guilt-caresses I gave her.

I was there just before dusk. Perhaps half an hour earlier. He didn't show up. I pushed the swing mechanically. I was a bit disappointed. I don't know what I was expecting. I kept looking towards the far end of the road by the playground. I know nothing about him. The child might not even be his. That's not bad, it might be better that way. Here I go again, getting carried away, daydreaming. The boy is looking at me pensively. It's dark. A tiny moon has already appeared in the sky between a few clouds. I just wanted to see him.

I like imagining that she would have these thoughts. We didn't manage to go. Time is not always ours. The following day we were there. On our own. I just wanted to see her.

Later on, some little girls come along, some are foreigners, quite dark, two of them are sitting on the swings. They also have a baby with them; a few months younger than Jazz, a little girl probably, although I can't be sure. They speak an unknown language. Jazz gets close to the baby-girl. She smiles at her and tells her incomprehensible words, she examines her and gives her a handful of soil. The baby looks at her with curiosity, and just opens up her fist in order to take the soil, but she doesn't make any other attempt at communicating. I think she doesn't belong with them anymore. I have the strange feeling that she has abandoned this tribe. I think the baby understands that Jazz is on the way to something else. She's not one of them anymore.

At some point another group of dark children came along. The eldest one must have been around 12. They crawled on the swings and the merry-go-round. They weren't aggressive but they also wouldn't move away from there. There were hardly any swings available. The seesaw had been repaired, but she's not crazy about it. I guess she also wants me to climb on it, but that's not possible. So we stayed in the swing. I saw one of the boys rolling a cigarette and then handing it to the girl who was sitting on the swing, talking on her mobile. I wish it was just tobacco, but it wasn't. I didn't look suspicious to them, though, or they simply couldn't be bothered. I suppose that the task of each generation is to shock the previous one. We would have shocked our parents if we had been smoking cigarettes at this age. Later on, we tried marijuana and most of the people I know from University used to smoke and still do. If our children smoked tobacco, we wouldn't be especially shocked.

We left fairly soon. Thankfully, she didn't complain.

9. A smile for Jazz

She has started becoming obese. And I'm beginning to get really worried. Is she what they call bulimic? I have no intention to ask the doctor, I didn't even manage to find him and ask him about the cough that has been bothering her again in the evenings. I improvised a bit with some local herbs, then I asked the chemist and I bought a syrup, that's what they do in this city. Nobody bothers to find a doctor. I drank a bit of the syrup, trying to show her that it tastes nice. But when it comes to this, children have been the same throughout history. They are never convinced when you try to advertise something to them. By the end of the evening, I had drunk more syrup than Jazz had.

My money is enough until September. I don't know what we'll do then. Maybe we'll sell the house by the sea. I could refurbish it and turn it into rooms for rent for the tourists. Everyone here earns money from the tourists. I could do it, if I were prepared to spend all my money down to the last nickel. I don't think taking that risk is a good idea but waiting till all the money runs out is not a good idea either. Why am I so calm? I have no idea. Maybe I have started resembling the locals so much that I've come to believe in an inexplicable happy ending. Maybe it's just that I have watched too many movies with a happy ending.

We went to the playground in the afternoon. I get this sense of loathing for all the other parents that do the same things as I do, as well as this certainty that Jazz is the prettiest child in the world. I'm looking at her. She is something special. A special child. I know what they say. All parents believe their children are special. A woman leans to hug a child, it's not her child, his parents are further away. She's wearing sunglasses and a black t-shirt that gets a bit pulled as she bends, so that I can see a bit of her cleavage, but not much more than this. I'm thinking that I joyously do what other parents do as a routine. It's a bit like a happy marriage. But this only lasts for as long as I'm chasing her from one end of the double-slide to the other, jumping like a hare to catch her.

Back home, she asks for a second cookie again, she eats her own cookie really fast, she tries to grab mine and then she runs towards the place where she believes the cookie-fountain is. I get angry of course and I shout at her. Obviously, she bursts into tears and there goes all the pride I take in enjoying fatherhood.

She has definitely made progress with words. They also confirm it at "school". You realise this from details, from adverbs and exclamations. *Ah, this! Let's go now!* or similar stuff I can't quite remember now. She's having a bit of trouble pronouncing 'th'. Yet, today she counted up to five. After listening to me count before her. Then I asked her to repeat it but she only went up to three and then went back to two. She might be making fun of me, though.

I can't keep up with her words anymore. She repeats all the verbs she hears, she can count up to six, she says short or longer words, having trouble only with 'th'. She shows interest in whatever I do, she wants to do the same stuff or she wants me to do what she does, she keeps asking me what I'm doing, and she wants to do new things all the time. Sometimes it seems as if she's just looking for an excuse to start crying. If you give her something too soon, she will want something else. If she gets devoted to something, she will ignore anything you tell her about anything else. Perhaps this is what Despina means when she says that this age is the first adolescence. She has a son herself, a boy who loved and still loves food, but is extremely tall at least. I don't care at all.

Life with her is a never-ending negotiation. Let go of this if you want that. No more cookies, you'll have some later. Let's stay on the swing a bit longer, but no seesaw. Drink your milk standing on the table, but at least drink it. I try to teach her the everyday basics, what we do in the morning, the afternoon, the evening, at night. I mean us two.

We wake up in the morning, she usually wakes me up, we drink our milk, we go to school, we come back home, we sleep, we wake up, we watch Dora, we eat fruit, we play or go for a walk, then we take a bath, we drink milk and then sleep. That's what we usually do. Of course, there's also a big part of my day she's not aware of and she's probably not able to understand at all. It hasn't been going too well lately. I have no job or any prospect of finding one, the only thing I'm busy with is Jazz and the only thing I write is her diary. And the money is gradually running out. But I even have a hard time writing the diary these days.

I think I have a smile only for her. When I look at her in the morning with the pacifiers and the milk and the clock she always puts somewhere else, looking at the cat with the drooping ears that hardly ever comes and the beads of the already old abacus, which I bought two years ago because I had come to like the little second-hand shop with the books and the toys owned by two lovely girls. I used to have money for things like that back then. The most important thing that has been coming to light — as they all do — these days is the fact that she tries to call everyone she knows by their name, even Smooch. She still makes small sentences. She must have been happy at the beach. On our way, she kept singing songs which sounded familiar and other, unknown ones in her own language. There was also a swing there. Everything was abandoned. Nobody; only one person about five hundred metres away.

She's greedy. Could this mean that she's missing something and she's trying to substitute for it? The answer to what is missing is always love. Is my love not enough for her? She gets more than she needs. Or not? What does loving a child mean?

At night she uttered a little scream. I thought she was having a nightmare. I wondered if I should wake her up. I don't want her to suffer, not even in her sleep. Sleep is not insignificant at all. As far as I'm concerned, as a rule I have nightmares when I'm going through a good phase. And when everything goes wrong I find consolation in nice dreams. It's like my dreams are trying to compensate me; sometimes more, sometimes less. Sometimes the sensation is so intimate that I'm convinced, for a few hours at least, that they are all somewhere around here; all those beloved, smiley faces, the women who accompany me and are always in love with me, even though we rarely make love, I never come in my dreams, all the rest is enough. Yet there are consolation dreams to satisfy all tastes. A few years ago I was invited to play with the national football team. It was a great joy. I still remember the atmosphere in the locker room. I wasn't the odd one out; there were more people I knew around. The German coach, a strange and stern man, was waiting for me. He especially wanted me to play. And yet again, I went to the pitch but for some reason I couldn't get dressed on time. I never saw me play. But I still remember the joy I felt when I was invited.

When I was a kid, I wanted to be a football player. Then I had to wear glasses and then my father forbade it. I had to study. Football was a waste of time. Later, as a teenager, I wanted to be a writer. I was probably looking for a way to be loved, I was a reserved child. My father's mocking voice when he found out, is still echoing in my ears. And now, as always, whenever I write something I still wonder what the point is. A waste of time.

Most of the time, I really think that Jazz is the only lifeboat I've got in life. The rest of the time I just don't think of it.

10. When will I stop?

When will I stop writing about Jazz? When she utters the first complete sentence that would mean she will have signed her first contract with the life of grown-ups. How long could this take? No idea.

We had various problems at the house by the sea during the Easter holiday. I was definitely expecting it would be different. I was dreaming she would have all the sand to herself, the beach is enormous, and that she would be free to do as she pleased, free at last. Yet, I don't know what doing as you please could imply when the only things available around are sand and sea, in which you can't swim – the water is still cold, and of course she doesn't know how to swim. The first day she learned the meaning anemos, the Greek word *wind*. It was very windy indeed and although she took it bravely at first, then she started saying, my eyes, every time some sand got in them. We stayed less than half an hour. The second day was better. In the morning she ate some chocolate bunny, which she didn't particularly like, neither did I. The house is still cold from the winter. I lit the wood stove as soon as she fell asleep, although I would have liked to share this joy with her. It would be too great a temptation for her to simply watch. So, the house got a bit warmer.

In the yard, there is dirt and stones from unfinished repairs. Jazz settled down there with her little bucket and then started carrying stones in a big tin cask. She wasn't sure if she wanted us to go to the beach, she could remember the previous day's hassle. We went, though. It was a bit better. We stayed for about an hour. She gave me stones and I tossed them. When she couldn't drag them out of the sand, she would ask for my help. Then I tossed the stones and I prompted her to watch me but she didn't. She was busy digging the sand or looking for new stones. The result doesn't matter to her. It also looks like rewards don't matter to her either. Yet, she kept sending me to the sea for water, as there was also a watering can amongst her equipment. That night, I had a long dream, in which my dad was the main character, which is reasonable, as he was the one who built this house — which I'm still trying to finish. The question is whether I should use my last remaining money in order to fix it. And what then? Would we stay here? Probably impossible. Perhaps not entirely. Would we get some tenants for it to earn our expenses in the city? I've already started thinking of our future in plural.

The third day, it was even better. Meanwhile, we saw a shepherd with his sheep and dogs, two beautiful small hunting dogs. The shepherd was impressed with how remarkably at ease Jazz seemed near the dogs. He said he had never seen a child her age without the slightest fear of dogs. Other than this, he's disappointed in the situation, if it goes on like this, he will give up his flock of sheep after thirty years of work. He's very lucky he doesn't owe any money, or just a very small amount. He would burn down the Parliament if he could. Many people here share the same fantasy. There's actually lots of people in Athens who try to make it happen in reality every day. But at the end of the day, all that remains is more casualties due to the riots with the police.

In the evening of the second day she was terribly disobedient and upset. I nearly despaired. She was constantly asking for something and when I gave it to her, she would ask for something else. When I didn't give it to her, she would burst into tears. The following morning we stayed at the beach for quite a while. It wasn't windy anymore. But she suddenly stood up without a word and started running towards the little stream, about half a kilometre away. I had seen her run before, but I didn't expect her to manage to go all the way to there. She did though, and by the time I started heading towards her it was already too late and she walked into the stream, what's worse, she sat down there. I lifted her up. Of course, I had to walk into the stream too. It wasn't more than twenty centimetres deep, as it was really close to the sea at this point, but we both got back home in a mess. She asked for a hug, she was exhausted by then. So was I of course. She slept a little and now she's coughing louder. It was stupid of me to let her go to the stream. This evening, though, she said the word tree while I was changing her. A bed-sheet with a tree painted on it that is hanging in front of the window instead of a curtain. In the car she was singing and she would ask 'what is this'. I couldn't know and I couldn't turn my head all the time, so I decided to explain and describe to her all the things we could see in the night. How do you explain to a two and a half year old what a village is and what people do there?

She's learning *gelio*, the Greek word for *laugh*. I'm imitating her laughter. She's laughing mechanically too. It's not the first time. She has a type of laughter that I call her laughter of courtesy. There's also the type of laughter that diminishes; when she likes something and she laughs at it and when it repeats and it's not as impressive anymore but she still laughs. I'm saying the word laugh, laughter and she's listening and she's repeating. The following day something else happens.

She woke up in the worst mood I've ever seen her. Maybe it's the sun and the sea. The truth is, one of those days it was a little cloudy and not hot at all, a nice spring day, and this weather was kind of misleading. She woke up in a really bad mood. She wouldn't stop crying, she wouldn't calm down by any means or speak properly, not even when she was asking for something. Then an old joke of us came to my mind, perhaps our first one. It must have been last year or the year before but no, she had already started laughing, so it must have been last year. I pretended I was the flying fly-beater. I stand up and clap my hands, I jump in the air a little, a bit like a clown, and when I reach up I clap my hands. The first time I did this there were actually some flies around the light-bulb, it was noon, she was in her bouncer, I'm not sure, and she burst into laughter. And now she seems a bit better and she's laughing. That was very nice. Later in the afternoon after the swings she wouldn't part from, I thought again how few things she's able to understand. She saw something on a balcony and said, I want it. She might have been referring to the balcony. They say that children understand much more than we think. In a way, I also believe this. However, I'm quite astonished at the fact that she understands lots of things which are absurd or difficult for a child her age to grasp.

Another excursion to the sea on Labour Day. This time, again, she's clearly having fun; she's singing during most of the trip, improvising on songs over two lines long. Every now and then she remembers the ane and she wants to know when we'll be going. To reply, I use words like days weeks, in a little while. I wonder how much of this she understands. The surprise is that she counted up to ten out of the blue. She's constantly asking 'what is this' and I explain to her again about the trees and mountains the villages the houses the animals. She gets really excited with sheep. She snatches the dog's bread and then gives him a smack. She is terribly enthusiastic about new shoes, it's almost an addiction, while tops and trousers don't interest her as much. She doesn't like skirts, as it's probably not easy to play with dirt in them. I tell her various things about flowers but she's not interested in them either since she has stopped eating them. The walk back home tired her. She slept for more than 12 hours. At the nursery they told me she played the dead duck.

11. She talks with her toys

She talks with the little white teddy and with Eeyore the donkey. Also, with strawberry the doll. She doesn't play with her baby or the stroller anymore but she likes feeding the animals. Not only does she talk to them, but she also dresses them, she even puts a nasal stick up their noses, just like I do some (tormenting for both of us) times. We even had to buy an inhaler mask and some drops and syrup but at least she finally came to terms with the doctor after getting a yellow balloon in return. I think she even promises her toys to take them for a walk if they behave, but I'm not sure.

How much does she miss an extra presence? She hasn't asked in a long time, yet I wonder. Will she always be missing something? Am I enough? How many problems could this absence cause her? I don't know. The last few days she's in a jolly mood, though. Her eyes are shining in the sun. She is my beautiful walnut-eyed girl.

I yelled at her again because she wouldn't speak on the phone. She rushes to pick up the receiver but the game ends there, she almost always keeps silent as it always happens when she hears a voice at the other end of the line. Tonight she didn't want me to take her upstairs. And yet, we had had a nice day. When I lifted her in my arms, she started imitating the exaggerated moaning sounds I make, supposedly because she's too heavy, every time I lift her, a bit of an inside joke, and of course I like this a lot.

Then we went to the playground. This time I am beginning to notice that only foreigners go there, or at least mostly them. While she was climbing on the slide, a little boy her age came close to her, he must have known her from the nursery I suppose, and as soon as he saw her his face lightened up. I've seen this scene too many times already to mistake it for something else. The boys her age fancy her. I'm not sure if I like this, I guess not. I watched her doing a new trick on the slide; she goes to the spot where she needs to let herself go in order to slide down and then turns around and falls on her tummy. She's really proud of this. I don't know how she came up with it. She had a bit of a nasty fall once, but this didn't discourage her. Every time, I get a bit anxious that she will not want to go but in the end she always obeys after getting a few extensions. Danger was lurking at the crossroads, though. The car had stopped, a woman was already crossing, a tourist perhaps. We started crossing as well, when suddenly the car started moving. I halted the stroller abruptly, but the guy had already pulled the brakes, he pointed at the sun, it had blinded him and he hadn't seen us, I made some gestures to show him that there were no hard feelings but it had all been a matter of seconds and metres. Jazz didn't seem upset at all, but she started shouting, nearly crying, outside of the bakery across the street, because she knows very well that there's food she likes in there, she has done this once more while we were passing by a souvlaki place where we had only been once; once was enough for her selective memory. She persistently refuses to call the cow by its name; she calls it moo or wolf, on purpose of course, just to get on my nerves. Meanwhile, just before we reached home, a neighbour invited her in her house — where her beautiful daughter was lying down. She accepted the invitation at first, I had no objection of course, but she soon changed her mind.

She still chases Smooch, rather violently actually. Probably out of jealousy or perhaps just habit. I told her that if I had to choose between my two children, I would keep Smooch. Not very pedagogical, I thought later.

It was a difficult evening, at least at first. I had to go to the house by the sea, we might be able to let it for the summer, we must find some money somehow. I left her in the company of that girl in case she woke up early. I would prefer it if we didn't need a baby-sitter, but I couldn't take her with me again, besides she was still a bit ill with coughing. In the afternoon, I found her awake, she was getting along very well with the girl, she even agreed to tidy up everything without any complaints, and she also took her medicine in good spirits. Because she saw me drink the syrup, her gluttony prevailed at last, besides I've also been coughing, she asked for it herself. It's not as easy with the inhaler mask, although I also put it on; I put the mask on without pressing the button that releases the gas she's supposed to inhale. She must be suspecting the fraud, however, although counting for me when I wear the mask entertains her, you must count up to seven, and I don't miss an opportunity to make her count, she must be suspecting my little fraud and she complains when she inhales.

The girl left at nine and left us alone. She stayed awake for a bit longer than usual, until I had prepared everything, but as soon as she went upstairs she started coughing. I felt so much pity for her, I felt incapable of doing anything, until eventually, when I was already about to go to bed, I decided to take her downstairs for one more milk with honey and chamomile. We went downstairs, she was in the mood to play with the building blocks and this time she let me build a double wall. We played for a while and then listened to Radioteddio — a teddy bear with a radio inside. He's still working quite alright. She picked him up and put the mask on his face. Then we started the sleep procedure once again. She paused a bit to take a look at the photos from her first months, still on the fridge. I hadn't taken all of them. Mimi, she said. That's how she still calls herself. *'Mimi eats rock'.* This was a line from her first summer when she was tasting the sand and especially the small pebbles at the beach. She did this once then and once this year in the beginning of spring. Yes, I explained, you were a baby then, and I talked to her about each of the photos. She likes listening to stories. Then we went upstairs. While I was putting her down on her bed she looked above us and asked 'what is this'. I told her, our shadows, mine is this one, it's a bit larger. I thought it was touching. But she was referring to the Mickey Mouse sticker I have placed on the wooden wall above her bed.

12. The night and the rain

Yesterday I also showed her the night. This is not something we can do often. Only because she woke up in the middle of the night, coughing. I pulled the shutters up, I opened the window and in spite of the bright street light, I tried to explain that this is the night and this is why there isn't much to do, it's dark, that's why we sleep. I mentioned all the people who sleep at this hour, grandpa grandma uncle aunt voula (one of the nursery ladies) mama godfather godmother. She likes listening.

We listened to that song again, *rain rain go away, come again another day*. The rain in Dora's land is a plump little cloud, a bit ugly. They kept sending it away and this made me feel a bit sad.

The moon wasn't there at first. I could see it high above the window but she couldn't. I lifted her as high as I could but she didn't pay a lot of attention, she was playing with the jasmine flowers that blossom this time of the year. Then the moon rose even higher. We went out in the yard to see it. I didn't have to lift her much, just a regular hug. It's like a ball she said. Yes, it's true, my love, it's like a ball, I said. She leaned her cheek on mine and we gazed at it. The moon, I told her, visits us for a few days and it sees us and then it leaves again. It will definitely be here again tomorrow, it has come to our city to see us and it will go away and it will come back again, that's what the moon does. Then we went upstairs to see the new lullaby crib toy, the one that rotates, today I put some batteries in it at last. She had been taking it for lost all this time, and perceived it as something new, she herself had told me to buy it. It is a rotating musical crib toy. In the morning we read the book where Dora goes to school three times. She likes it a lot. We learn some of the colours on her pyjamas. Blue, orange, red, green…

What will she remember of all this? Will everything be erased from her memory, as if nothing ever existed? Will she look at me curiously and then condescendingly and even later will she be bored to death with listening to what her first songs were like, her first animals, her first mischiefs? Will there be any point in me telling her all about it?

One morning a few days ago, I sang the most famous of all the songs I used to sing to her, *Mr little mr sweet he was always very tender, he was always very tender mr sweet mr little mr sweet mr little…* that's how it went again and again, swapping and playing around with the words tender, little, sweet, I referred to her in the masculine gender back then, it probably suited the songs more, but it also sounded cuter, perhaps because we had learned more about mr teddy rather than mrs teddy. She stared at me without any special reaction. She reminded me of those films in which someone is trying to restore an amnesiac's memory.

What do I remember? I definitely remember my father taking me out in his arms after an earthquake, but I must have been three then, perhaps even older. I can calculate this according to the cities, my father was in the army and he had to move to a new city every two years, so that was my life until I turned eighteen, when I entered University, from which I never graduated though. In a way, I'm still a student. Perhaps I only grew up now, after Jazz's birth. Yet, I remember that small town where I was born, I have one single memory like a photo (two dogs, a white one and a black one on a balcony across the street) from then, and I also remember the following one, we had moved to the capital then, I only remember an oblong room, the table is set and the food is orzo, which I never liked. There's also a cousin of mine in the image, he must have been about twelve back then and he seemed really old to me. But are these memories real? It's hard to be certain. The one with the dogs is too distant to be real. But the table with the orzo might be, yet why this scene in specific? There's nothing special about it. Maybe something had happened that day, who knows. Maybe that was the day my memory started working.

I heard that they have discovered the depression gene. This is one of the silliest things I've ever heard, but I also think that thanks to Jazz I have escaped a lot of stuff that used to torment me. There's no time for such luxury now.

On our way to the sand, I'm thinking that the distance between us is vast. We are still two different worlds. She will understand me and she will love me only if she agrees to learn the world according to my own terms, that is, if I teach her the way she can understand and love me. Of course, she also receives stimuli from other directions. She has started saying the 'm' word every time she hears me honk at someone or even when I overtake another car. She surely hears stuff at the nursery and formulates some views, thoughts, sentences. The young teacher showed me some photos on her mobile, and she was very excited; it was Jazz wearing large sunglasses. I didn't make any comments. I don't even find this funny or cute. I guess she realised, she put her mobile away and hurried away.

When we go to the house by the sea, I remember my father. He wasn't especially affectionate and sometimes he would become irritating, just like I do now. I remembered something he used to do. He used to stick his nose on top of my head and tell me that I smelt like a goat. I have no idea how goats smell, I didn't then and I still don't. But I wonder if there was some truth in it — my father had grown up in a rural area — or if it was just a joke. It was nice when he made jokes. When he didn't, it was a problem.

When I carry her in my arms I sometimes have the feeling that she is caressing me. We went to the stream again – we are at the house by the sea again — but the setting didn't excite her as much this time. On our way back, she demanded me to take her in my arms. This has become quite hard. Then we went to the beach, but she got scared of the wind there. The poor child's eyes were in tears and she was rubbing them. I felt pity for her. She said, no sand, then she said, yes, when I asked her if she wanted us to go to the sea, she probably meant to say, *I want to go but I don't like the wind.* In the end I shouted at her and she got so startled she fell down on the sand. She had probably stumbled. A bit more guilt for my collection.

13. Episode in the park

The first thing I noticed was the strap that had slipped down her right shoulder while she was jogging. She was quite slow, but not as slow as the ones you immediately realise that it's the first (and probably the last) time they're attempting to run. She was in her fifties, perhaps a bit younger. She wasn't pretty. To be precise, she was one of those people that never make you wonder whether they're beautiful or ugly. It just doesn't matter. She was quite nicely built, with a bit of flab slightly spoiling the image but to local women this is some kind of symmetry… I paused for a bit and waited for her to catch up until she slowed down and eventually started walking. Her breathing was normal when I talked to her, therefore she runs regularly. We walked together till the end of the park and then we arrived at her house. It was very easy, almost as if we had organised it. I wasn't sure if I should do it, but her house was nearby and I still had a few hours of freedom thanks to baby--sitting. However, I felt like I was about to betray someone, myself or Jazz, I'm not sure. Her house, a little ground floor house with a slightly unkempt garden, was charming, there was something friendly and lonesome about it, along with a musty smell. You felt it was missing some company. We talked a bit about literature and, almost without me requesting it, she read out some poems she had written. In her regular life she was a teacher. I couldn't tell whether I liked her poems, I didn't like her either. But I felt an uncontrollable urge to hug her, so I said I did like them and I hugged her at the same time and we made out on the sofa of the little room that served as a living room and kitchen. Then I felt a bit disgusted with myself, after we were finished with what we did. She was still holding me tight. Now the urge I was feeling was getting out of there as soon as possible. I waited for her to finish talking and I told her I had a child and that I should go back. "Oh", she said, slightly untightening her clasp. I don't know why I didn't even mention I was single, with a child, yet single. I waited in silence for a while and then I left her there and went out. It was too fast and too silly, I thought. But I had managed to be done with everything half an hour before the baby sitter was supposed to leave.

Out of the past

His voice at the other end of the receiver sounded pretty strange. I hesitated to speak for a few seconds. I could just hang up, I thought. I didn't, though.

— Who is it?, I asked.

— What's up you jerk?, the producer yelled. Already forgotten all about us? Having a ball in that hole where you've been hiding? Come on, vacation is over. Pack your things and get your ass over here. We've got some business to do.

It was just like that movie with Robert Mitcham; my guilty past had tracked me down. And now I had no choice. I had to go back to all that shit.

— I thought I was through. Isn't this the way it usually works?

— It wasn't easy, to be honest, after the way you fucked up. But we managed to convince them. We need you, boy. Don't worry. You'll stay out of the limelight. You won't even come to the shooting. But there's lots of work for you back there in the office. No need to thank me. We love you, you jerk.

— Listen, I have issues here. I have the child. Someone needs to take care of her. I'm on my own now.

It took him a few seconds to take it in.

— Look, we start preparing in a couple of weeks. We need you here. Bring the child along. She can't grow up in that shithole you took her, right? Come here and we'll take care of everything. Just buy the tickets now and production will cover the cost.

— Right, thanks, but it's a big decision. I think I've left all this behind.

— Come on, cut the crap. What's your problem? Take the child and come. We'll find a hot babe to look after her, one you can fuck too. Couldn't ask for more, right? Get on with it, coz there's lots of paperwork involved, we should have already started. Give me a call as soon as you get the tickets.

— Yes, I will, I said.

There was a bit of silence. I was waiting for him to hang up.

— Look, we fought real hard to bring you back here. Some assholes were pretty mad at you. This is your chance to get back in. Give me a call tomorrow to let me know you took care of the tickets.

— I will. Have a good evening.

So I now had a chance to sneak back in the game; to get my job back, to finally earn some money somehow. Isn't this in Jazz's best interest? Having a father with a job and not a ridiculous, depressive guy taking her to the park; isn't this what everyone wants for their children? A secure future regardless of me being buried under piles of paperwork, picking questions, doing all the dirty work no other person with some TV experience would stoop to do. In reality, this was what the producer's proposition involved. To be in charge of what we call the "depot" of a TV-show; that's a job for a freshman. But the work would be better done by an experienced guy who would accept the same money just because he fucked up and therefore has no other choice.

14. Exactly two and a half

She's now two and half; time flies. We are in the midst of the terrible twos. I try to make her understand that she shouldn't be asking for things all the time. She wants a cookie and when it's finished she wants a fiffy (a chocolate fish) and when she eats it she wants to watch Dora, and when she watches Dora, a birdie and lately a pavvot, because I showed her the intro from the film *Rio* where parrots sing and dance.

Yesterday she brought the white teddy to the couch in order to give him some nasal spray. I didn't understand what she wanted initially, but then she went to the bathroom and brought one, that is, a small phial that actually looked like a nasal spray and she stuck it in teddy's eye. I explained to her and I helped her put it in his nose and we actually did this, in both nostrils, and then she put some more on his cheeks and tummy. She really enjoys taking this role.

She woke up coughing during the night again. I used some towels to lift her mattress up. We both cough all the time, I'm on antibiotics now, I couldn't take it anymore. Fortunately it was easy for her to fall asleep. But she wanted the lullaby crib toy, which kept playing for ages. I turned it off in the end. I had pleasant dreams, which means I am sad.

We all have a deep pain, says someone who plays God in *Final Frontier*, the fifth *Star Trek* movie.

At the nursery they told me that I shouldn't be having any trouble communicating with her by now. Yes, I said, I have accepted her terms though. *It will always be according to her terms*, they said.

I still can't describe to her all the things we see when we go for a walk. I like thinking that whatever interests me interests her too. It feels less futile since she has started forming sentences. It's like fishing. You have a good time for a long time and at some point something happens. Yet, I hate fishing. My father took me fishing once. Only once. I must have been about twelve. It was easy. They cast a long fishing line from the boat and the poor fish came out of the sea in fives or even more. It disgusted me, also because it was easy. They threw some of them back in the sea. I said nothing but I must have looked so frustrated that my father never proposed it again. I tell her stories too. I also tell her things that will happen later on although I know that she can't grasp the concept of time. I have also started counting the days using her little fingers.

We discovered an abandoned playground. It looks a bit like Greece. They started building it but it will never be finished. There were only slides there. And some posts and ropes. She examined the slide and soon discovered that it had two exits, so she could have me chase her forever without ever catching her. At some point we finally left. I tried to explain that soon we would have to bid the stroller farewell. It has gone through a lot already on these streets that have no pavements. She keeps saying 'more'. We see a dog and she asks, more? I'm not sure but she probably means that she wants us to see more of those. The same happened with the cars, the taxis and a bird that tweets constantly in the neighbourhood. I dreamt that a somewhat elderly woman was taking care of me.

Now she also likes the roadrunner and the coyote. She likes the beep, she's crazy about it, although I think she's overdoing it. She actually wants to have some things she can love. I told her that the coyote is a wolf. She realises that he is suffering, she says, *he fell*, when he falls in the canyon or when he falls from the airship he has built. He fell? She asks. Yes, he fell. I like the coyote, I was always on his side, but I thought that there were two roadrunners, perhaps there were in a specific episode. As a means to improving her behavior, I threatened her with the wolf of darkness that eats feet but I wasn't very convincing and it's also a bit too late for such threats. She didn't take me seriously. Her clothes are a complicated matter. Every outing of ours, every move to another place requires hours of studying and planning. Luckily, the weather is getting warmer and clothes are getting less. A kid is endless hours of boredom, her aunt said, and I couldn't disagree. But appearances can be deceptive. When I reprimand her for playing with the rabbit-wheels on the wall, I'm thinking that the restrictions are so many and that most of them must appear completely unfair and inexplicable to her. The third time she disobeyed I shouted at her and she burst into tears, of course.

Our first demonstration. I was a bit nervous. She was cool. Of course I had made sure I had various little pieces of cookies and bread and cheese with me to feed her. Then we went to Goody's, she deserved some fast food, and then we got back home. Is anything going to come out of this? Who knows… yet, one day she'll be able to say that we went to her first demonstration when she was still two and a half. There was an even younger baby there. Sure, but we could understand what was going on. People protesting for a better life; I think we're both aware of the fact that this is nothing more than a fairy tale. The demonstration at the small city is much more harmless and boring than the one in the big city. There is very little action here, most people know each other, they shout mild rallying cries about bread and freedom and kicking the bad guys out of the country. Then we all go back home. Even Jazz can realize that the bad guys will stay around just like they always have. She came out in the veranda. She helped with sweeping the leaves. But she overdid it again. Because then she started plucking the petals of a geranium so that we could get to sweep more leaves. In the veranda, she also wanted the stroller with her baby as well as Teddynormous. But I didn't let her. In the evening, the usual threat, you either drink your milk or we go upstairs. Upstairs? Yes, upstairs. So, she got up and went upstairs by herself.
I went there just to lift her up and place her on the mattress. The Conductor, then the crickets from the lullaby toy, the pacifier which she grabs precisely the moment she lands on the mattress. She always knows where it is, no matter how dark it is.

My evening cough kept me awake and I arrived late at the village. The handyman was gone but he came back. I emptied the space. We will soon start refurbishing. Let's see if we'll manage to make some money out of this, renting it to tourists. We live in a country that might go bankrupt any minute. But I'm bankrupt already. Still, I simply can't picture myself as the jolly hotelier who welcomes tourists and shows them around the house. Yet this is what I must do. Jazz needs to be fed and the money is running out. Unless we find Hansel and Gretel's gingerbread house.

There was a ladybird on the wall when we went out in the veranda. Look, I said, this is a ladybird. The ladybird is a beautiful insect. She's very beautiful. She's red with dots. This is a small ladybird, she's not very red yet, she's quite yellow. They say they bring luck. This ladybird came to us. Jazz climbed on the bench to look at her closely. Then she wanted to climb at the top of the bench but of course I got her down. I wasn't quite sure about her intentions. After a while I saw her holding the broom but I took it away from her. "Look Jazz," I told her, "this ladybird is too small, too weak. You shouldn't catch her because you will harm her. She might die. She will definitely die. And then she won't exist anymore. Which means…" I felt we were touching upon a really huge subject which there was no reason to get into. It will hurt a lot at some point, though.

We enter the house. I'm wearing short trousers. Jazz always showed interest in my legs. What is this? This is a leg. We have two legs, human beings have two legs. In the old days people used to have four legs. But now all people have two. You have two legs as well. She thought of it for a bit. "I have two" she mumbled, not very enthusiastically. Then she craved the strawberries I was eating just because she can't stand not trying something someone else is eating.

In every life, the same song returns again and again. Somehow at some point you will be sad to realise that you will not exist forever. Is there an appropriate time to learn this? I don't think so. It's probably the only thing I would like to avoid explaining to her. Perhaps because

Yesterday at the square — another protest — her manners were impeccable. There were more people than last time. No huge crowds, it's just a small town. We sat down and listened to the first speakers; a girl who said that we should buy local products, another one who said she was very happy to be here, a Spanish guy who spoke in English, an elderly man who said we should burn all politicians (lots of people applauded), another guy in his fifties who apologised on behalf of his generation. These things happen everywhere around Europe these days. It's nothing magic but it is something. Jazz was quite attentive, she seemed to be enjoying it, she did something like a dance for as long as there was music, then she started crying for some mysterious reason, so we left.

It was a heroic and absolutely idiotic decision. It was perhaps idiotic of me to believe that we live better here, that we live better this way. But this is how I feel.

— I can't do it, I said to him. Thanks but I can't come back there.
— I understand, but you're making a stupid mistake, replied the producer, after giving it a bit of thought.
He made one more effort.
— Think of the child, he said.
— That's who I'm thinking of, I replied.
— I don't know how you're getting on there, but if you need a job this is your only chance, your last chance.
— I know.
— We'll miss you.
— You'll manage.
I hang up on him as well as on an entirely different kind of life for Jazz and myself. I didn't know if it was the right thing to do. You never know till the end of the movie…

SUMMER

1. Getting used to water

There has been a significant shift in her relationship with water. Now she gets close to the sea, which she insists on calling *fee*, and splashes about up to the point where the water can reach her. Of course I stay nearby, digging puddles that fill up with sea water. She enters those fearlessly. What she enjoys the most is tossing pebbles and then bending down to lick the water, giving me conspiratory looks. No objections to entering the sea either, where it's still shallow though, or to doing a swimming dance, while I keep hold of her arms.

By now she warns me when it's 'potty' time, yet she can't tell the difference between 'poo-poo' and 'wee-wee'. She says it though. What she refuses to say is 'yes' or anything affirmative. It's not that she feels any sort of shame; on the contrary, I think she's probably proud of it. Besides, I promised her a sticker with Dora or the rest of her friends for every time she tells me. I found them in the Dora magazine we got at the kiosk.

Her clothes in the morning are still a source of anxiety for me, even after such a long time. Officially it is summer already, although we got some thunderstorms a few days ago, and the clouds are never gone for more than half or one day max. We need fewer clothes in the summer, I say to myself in order to lessen my anxiety. Yet it gets me. I'm afraid I won't manage. It's the remains of that massive panic of the initial months. I pick her clothes the previous night. The garments are divided into categories. Undershirts, t-shirts, trousers, skirts, track-suits, dresses, thin socks and that's all. The truth is they're a bit mixed up, as I can't actually tell the winter ones from the summer ones. I'm always anxious — I still can't get over the fact that I made her wear socks that weren't matching. I did the same with her shoes once too, luckily I realised it as soon as we walked out the door. I'm always afraid someone might notice that her clothes are not matching or that they're not suitable for the time of year. But the weather isn't very helpful. Even now that summer's here, the temperature varies a lot.

Dressing her up is not such a difficult task. I do all the housework apart from ironing, which I've also had a go at. I don't know, perhaps I'm resisting internally. Furthermore, I don't tie her hair in pigtails. I do it sometimes but I don't want her to look ridiculous at the nursery. I still remember the times I stood out for some reason when I was a child. Yet the children at this nursery seem quite harmless. Also, in contrast to me, my daughter appears to belong with the teasers' side — I hope not extremely — rather than on the side of the ones who will get teased.

I decided to create a website. I started doing it today already. I must do something before it's too late. It will be about people like me. Not about men raising babies; this sounds nice but it would be too cinema-like. Life is a bit different. It will be a webpage about literature.

Yet, before I even had a chance to get started with it, they called me up. There was something wrong. Jazz was asking for me. I went of course, almost instantly, interrupting a skype conference with a technician regarding various technical issues I can't quite grasp. She didn't seem bad. She must have been hurting, they said, because she started crying for no apparent reason and didn't play at all, something which is not like her. She never gets isolated. You must be flattered she asked for you, they told me. I was wondering whether the sole witnesses of my existence were the people at the nursery. The slim blonde teacher told Jazz that she would take her out to dinner at some point. Not a bad prospect at all, I thought to myself. Then I picked her up and we left. Her mood didn't seem foul at all; she wanted to go to the swings and I granted her wish after stopping by the post office. Then, while I was preparing a salad, I let her play in the yard by herself for a while, with the broom that has no broomstick— the internal thread is messed up — and the dustpan, trying to sweep all the leaves that had fallen off the ryncospermum (what kind of a name is this for a plant anyway? Yet it's such a beautiful plant). Jazz had already had lunch, but she also likes the stuffed vegetables as well as the legume recipes I cook. I try not to feed her meat too often, although she likes it. She identified the red colour of a car in the street. She kept asking me about the other colours.

She likes listening, but not to the long fairy tale I offered to read to her. Is she going to like it later on perhaps? I can't get the ideal American family images, as they're manifested in movies, out of my head. Kids listening to the fairy tale their dad is reading to them, then they ask something smart and a bit surreal, and then the dad says, it's bedtime. He carries the child to bed in his arms. He says a couple of things, perhaps the beginning of a short story, and the child falls asleep instantly. The father glances at the child tenderly and pulls the covers. He always pulls the covers. This is also the case with lovers, but whenever there's a child involved this always happens. Then he goes to the living room, where his beloved is waiting for him. They have the entire night at their disposal. They can order pizzas and talk about all sorts of irrelevant stuff. Later on they might make passionate but also tender love. I wish I could at least get to do the pulling-the-covers bit. But she will be sleeping without any covers for some time. That's how it's supposed to be, everyone says so. Yet I've never seen a child sleeping without covers in any film.

Up till now, I used to be anxious about my own life, now I'm also anxious about hers and I can't get rid of this feeling. I try not to think about it, I avoid thinking anything related to it, but I can't entirely get it out of my head.

My financial state, perhaps my life in general, is going downhill but I am compelled to put up an optimistic front for Jazz's sake.

In the meantime, as I can see on TV, the people have started persecuting politicians quite openly. Booing, throwing yoghurt and stones at them, chasing them up to the protection shields of the special security forces, well, they don't dare to walk about without them anymore. Of course they are such cynical crooks, that they actually claim that all those people, old men and women, kids, youths, middle-aged people, the people next door, are all agitators executing some obscure plan, they're fascists, communists, anarchists, anything but what they actually are. Indignant people, watching their lives fall apart simply because politicians and their customers' gangs have been incredibly greedy thieves for the past decades.

I'm still on antibiotics, a solution against asthmatic bronchitis, which is either to be taken orally or inhaled through a device activated with breathing. That's what the doctor said. I hadn't been ill in ages, since my father's death, when I had caught pneumonia.

There's a German storybook I've bought because I like the sketch of a dog it has on the cover. Although I had taken German lessons for a few months as a child, my system keeps refusing to learn this language. So I hardly understand any of it, but the sketches look really pretty. It's a family of dogs, behaving exactly like humans. It's a very loving family. A few days ago I took it out of the bookcase, as I usually do with books I believe Jazz is ready to look at. Her stash of books will last until she turns ten at least. She liked it indeed. Today we were looking at it again, she asked for it. There are two things that make a deep impression on her. One of them is the fact that there are two children in this family — puppies. They share a double bed, a bunk bed. I show it to her but she never repeats it. She probably doesn't like the idea of many siblings living in the same house. There's also another issue, though. I explain to her that this is mummy-dog, next to daddy-dog. Daddy is feeding one of the puppies and she is reading a book to the other one, just like we do. The dogs' book also contains a rabbit. Of course our book also contains one, since it is the book containing the dogs reading a book containing a rabbit. Jazz says, *she's her grandma.* Grandma is reading the book to her. She never calls the female dog next to daddy any other name. Grandma, grandma, grandma.

Professor Edo's book about children is quite small, comprising of no more than thirty to forty short texts. Some pages only have one or two phrases or even just a few words. This book contains lots of stuff about children which is worth learning. There's hardly any information about professor Edo himself, regarding where or when he lived and most importantly for the curious reader, whether he had children himself. Perhaps it doesn't matter, though. It's so small but also so dense that reading it is a never-ending process.

There is only one single word on the first page:

Patience

2. The child is always right

By now she knows we go to the open market on Saturday mornings. She requests a walk to the open market by herself, not necessarily on Saturdays only. This time she nearly stood up in the stroller and snatched an enormous onion — we didn't need any onions. We got peppers, cucumbers and tomatoes for the salad. She grabbed a pepper and started nibbling on it. I took it away. Today we got very few things, we shouldn't spend too much; a bit of cheese and some fruit, fruit are really expensive, even the ones in season. We bought pears and apples, she wanted bananas but we didn't find any, so she grabbed a pear and started biting the peel. I'm not sure if that's right. So I showed her how the bunny eats. It gnaws the pear peel off with its little teeth and only eats the rest. She only left the stalk and some of the seeds, which she handed to me. As soon as we had left she wanted us to go back.

It's a bit out of place, I know, still going about in a stroller. She's old enough now. But I'm not in the mood for changes. And that would be a big change.

I guess this whole business will end as soon as we let go of the stroller. Was my mother taking me out for walks in a stroller? It's impossible to remember. I can't match my father's image with a stroller, though. I don't think he would have taken me. When we put the stroller aside, it will be a new area.

She can identify Saturday by now, not in relation to the rest of the days, but mostly as a name that stands for something different. Cartoons on TV in the morning — SpongeBob of course — and then we're off to the open market. It was really hot today, though. She had a temperature when she woke up this afternoon. I realised because her skin felt really warm. I waited for it to pass, but she felt hot in the evening as well. Her mood hasn't changed, she was just a bit more affectionate in the evening; she wanted to stay a bit longer in my bed after taking some children's paracetamol, so I let her. Now she's sleeping with her strawberry doll.

My asthmatic bronchitis is still full on. I'm worried it will never actually go away. Those awakenings in the middle of the night or at dawn would always bring forth my existential issues, and this has been going on for more than twenty days now. I'll go back to the doctor. I wonder if this sort of virus Jazz caught will be tormenting me next.

Meanwhile, more than half a million people gathered in Syntagma, the central square of the capital on Sunday. We went to the square of our little town but only for a short while, we met some acquaintances, but we ended up going back by ourselves. The prettiest girls of the movement gather at 'Melo' café, before and after. They're rarely on their own, escorted by enthusiastic boys wearing their hair long, like in the 60's, but also by more mature, politically aware intellectuals; late in the evening they all turn into one big company and yet again this doesn't matter much. I feel too old to enter their conversations.

In the meantime, Smooch has been roaming the streets for the past week. A cat on a hot tin roof, as the expression goes, and that's where he probably has been, since there are quite a few such roofs in this town. It's unbelievable for a cat who will be twelve in August and who could hardly climb on the armchair to lie down till last year. It must be the sea air. Jazz waves at him when she sees him. I see it as an omen of the teenage-girl who will be soon leaving the house, coming back whenever she pleases without taking the slightest notice of me. It's a nightmare. You can't do anything about it, you can only hope for the best.

Hope for what exactly? That she will keep coming back.
For how long? This is something you don't want to think of.

She still breaks my heart every time she wakes up in the afternoon and refuses to go back to sleep. She says, no, no. I talk to her softly, slowly, quietly, I tell her how many things we'll do when she wakes up and about the cookie we'll eat and about the Dora episode we'll watch and perhaps the walk we'll go for (I don't want to lie to her about anything) and I tell her she should go to sleep because everyone else is asleep, I'm asleep too along with all the rest of the children. And yet, although I convince her to go back to sleep nine out of ten times or at least to stay in bed without crying, I feel unhappy. I put myself in her shoes and I feel horribly claustrophobic inside this tiny bed, not because I'm big, no, it's not this, it's because I have no way of defending myself, no way out of there.

Who could tell how desperate she is because she can't get out of there? And who can be so certain that it's that important for her to sleep every single afternoon? Is it because everyone does so? Because it's convenient? Because it's good for her health?

Yes, but when she feels desperate, when nothing can help her escape from these tormenting hours of captivity in the bed, how the fuck is this any good for her health?

And who could tell the size of her sorrow? Why should our own sorrows and stupid troubles be more important?

Smooch is back. A bit mussy, with his tail a bit plucked, covered in dry leaves and more, with some scratches above his eye and ear, but he's back at last.

The repairs at the house by the sea are in progress. This is where most of the money we got from selling my mother's house is going. We use the rest of it to get by for now. Perhaps it will be possible to host some people there next year (although I still find the idea of being a hotelier quite repulsive), perhaps we'll live there at some point. Who knows if Jazz actually needs to go to school and all that? We could go and live there and I could be teaching her everything she needs. At least I thought about it. Yet I haven't got the guts to do it.

I dreamt I was in love. She was a sweet brunette. She must have been pretty young, around 25 but I shouldn't have been much older either. Ten years ago perhaps but this doesn't matter in dreams. And I was saying and feeling and thinking, I'm in love, I'm in love. And I had this feeling, you know, that only happens then. I didn't think of it afterwards, I could actually feel it the moment I was dreaming. I was also saying, I remember this, I was saying to her, it's marvellous, no matter how long it will last. I said it looking in her eyes and waiting for her to say exactly what I felt she was saying, I heard her in a dreamlike sort of way: It will last forever. I woke up early, I tried hard to reconstruct her figure out of the leftovers of the dream. And yet she exists somewhere, I just know it, I am absolutely certain.

Jazz keeps asking: what is he saying? *What are they saying?* On TV, in newspaper photos, when I let her use earphones to listen to the radio. *What are they saying?* It's just stories. They're talking about their own stuff. She looks at me in disappointment. She demands to know what they're talking about while she's not making any effort to learn how to talk… Her progress with the book of animals has been insignificant. She has memorised a few more names, but only when she's in the mood, mispronouncing terribly, gonkey instead of donkey, sorhe instead of horse, phelepant instead of elephant, grof instead of frog and so on. There's always the possibility of her making fun of me. At least she can finally say cow, turtle and seal. But not squirrel, for which I have fought really hard.

Another thing. She's really amused when I hold the remote control and she tells me 'neither' and I change the channels. Something she really likes must be on for her to stop saying 'neither' — sometimes she says 'other,' 'other'. It's been a long time since she used to throw it on my head.

Without me noticing, she fell off the swing in the park. The truth is I kept telling her to be careful, the belt was rather loose, but apparently I wasn't watching so I suddenly saw her fall on the ground. She looked like that picture we have taken of her lying on the children's carpet with the little flowers, like a little hippy, the only difference now was that she was crying instead of singing. After making sure she hadn't hurt herself, I mostly got concerned with not becoming a spectacle at the playground, there were unusually many dads around, which I didn't like much since it made me feel less special.

On the second page of Professor Edo's book there's only one small phrase:
You are wrong!

I get the impression he is saying it in a rather strict voice

And then, on the third page one can read this:
The child comes from a world which doesn't belong to you anymore but which you must always respect. The child is always right.
The mistake is yours. Just try and find it.

3. How does a child grow up?

How does a child cross from one side over to the other? Is there a sudden click that makes the child abandon the baby world forever, just like another age will be abandoned later on and another one, just like the multiple "deaths", which occur throughout our lives according to Heraclitus? I should re-read his maxims.

Do children suddenly one night or one morning, stop being babies, do they stop doing all those things we call nonsense and start playing according to the rules? Is this when they start remembering? Is this when they start dreaming? Is this perhaps when they stop living in a dream and they come into reality? And if this happens gradually, if it's a day to day process, why is it that I don't realise it? Is it possible that one day she'll wake up and say, dad I'm not going to throw stones all over the place anymore, because they're stones that you've arranged in our garden in some kind of order and it's not right for me to throw them? Will she stop opening cupboards, grabbing knives that I've left at the edge of the sink, where she can only barely reach on her toes, showing them to me with a smile you might even call sarcastic? Will she come to me one morning and say that she doesn't want to be naughty anymore or something? Will she stop being silly while I'm trying to dress her, kicking or jerking her legs around, snatching the towels from the hanger beside her and pulling them down? Will she stop taking her shoes off when she's waiting for me to take her out or throwing her socks out of her bed when she doesn't fancy sleeping anymore, crying when I don't give her a cookie or chocolate and screaming when I take the enormous piece of bread she has snatched when she found it forgotten on the table? Playing with the remote and the cell-phone? In other words, will she grow up?

And then what? Will I have to share a home with some person behaving like a work colleague? Someone giving me the usual consolation talk whenever I'm in despair, mechanically asking me how my day was? I know it's simpler and I know that all children grow up somehow. Yet I can't understand how it will happen. Time will tell.

I try to identify the differences to last summer. She goes all the way to the sea on foot. She asks about everything, although I know the answers disappoint her and fill her with new questions which she simply doesn't know how to formulate. So she starts all over again. *What is 'im? What's she saying? What are 'ey saying,* she asked me at the beach. They speak a different language, I told her in order to console her, that's why you don't understand. They speak German. I wasn't entirely sure but the discipline, the seriousness, and the coldness they showed to each other drove me to this stereotypical conclusion. Also, and this is important, it was the first time she showed some interest in participating in digging my puddle. I enjoy digging puddles, it gives me an almost sick satisfaction. I should include them in the reasons why I wanted to have a child: So that the puddles I dig in the sand would become justified. They are now. She played for quite a while putting sand in and taking it out of the puddle. However, it was impossible to convince her, through a variety of arguments, that she shouldn't lick the big rocks and then say *nice!* I despair over my inability to explain all the evil reasons why she's not allowed to do it.

Evil is still absent in her world. The cat chasing Tweety just wants to play. The fox stealing things in Dora is probably a bit of an idiot. The driver who nearly crashed on us is of course an asshole, but even an asshole is nothing more than a character trait mostly belonging to the prime minister. She still calls him this wherever she sees him. Also, she still recites poems her own way. I can barely identify the poem but I acknowledge that she is actually following the rhythm. The words are dreadfully deformed, though. This morning she was really entertained by a little variation of the song "Little Bunny Foo Foo", of which I made an arrangement with her as the main character.

Later, while we were eating fries and omelette and my own version of Greek salad with cabbage, lettuce, arugula, carrot, sundried tomatoes, capers, avocado and some oregano and myzithra (a type of local soft cheese we really like), she asked me if I liked it. Of course I like it, I said, I prepared it. In the past few months I have learned how to prepare exquisite salads as well as some very tasty simple dishes. If I were a Meryl Streep movie I would already be rich.

In the afternoon I had another nightmare about the house by the sea. The first one was the day before yesterday. I saw people assembled at the front yard and having a feast — not with my own food but with food they had brought in my own yard. Just outside of the yard, the situation was even worse. They had formed a circle and they were dancing, making sure they didn't stand too far from the fence, so that the cars driving down to the beach wouldn't run over them. The second one was much nastier. I got back home and I realised that all the taps at the ground floor had been left running. In reality, the house only has one tap outside in the yard, and we have cut the water supply even to this one, due to the ongoing repairs, but in the house I saw there were even some small fountains; jets of water darting really high and then falling back on the ground for no purpose whatsoever. I realised the plumber had come again, the previous one, not the one working there at the moment, another one, a distant relative. He had come, he had turned all the taps on and, from what I gathered, he had made himself comfortable downstairs watching TV without even bothering to let me know. In reality he was a weird guy indeed. But it wasn't actually him (later I thought that this nightmare must have been the sequel of another one, in which the plumber breaks in my house – because the images felt familiar, I knew what was going on). While approaching the TV though, I didn't see the plumber but a company of guys looking like crook-politicians fighting for independence. I started shouting and eventually — although they had brought lots of gaming chips — they left slowly and contemptuously. One of them mentioned something about my father but I didn't quite get whether it was meant for or against him. In both cases it would be against me, though. They finally left at some point.

The webpage is going quite well. It's nothing much yet but it has a few tens of visitors already. I find some things quite difficult, I struggle for hours with things that would have been very simple if I could have some help. I find myself literally alone within the tempestuous virtual seas. But of course I prefer it this way. And it's not only because of the money. I've been uploading some of my texts. I hope I won't have to keep doing all the writing myself for too long, it exhausts me. Besides, the plan was to build something which would be open to everyone. I don't know how easy this is, I'd rather not resort to tricks you can use once you've paid in order to get more visitors. I don't want a lot of people. I want people like me. Not entirely; that would be boring. And it wouldn't get many visits. I also have no idea how I could make money out of this. This is also supposed to be one of my aims. Yet I don't want to take advantage of anyone. And, especially in Greece, it's really hard to make money once you set such obstacles to yourself. But I'll go on. It's good for me.

What would happen if she grew up right at this moment?

There, if she just grew up instantly. Would we start chatting or would the generation gap come between us? How will I keep her close to me? Isn't this very egoistic? Of all the things I do which ones would she criticise if she grew up this instant? Would she ask for more TV? Would she find the house suffocating? Would she leave home at that very instant?

4. Does the sea go to sleep? Where do birds go?

We don't go anywhere without our fitchy-fitchy; that's what we call the sunscreen lotion. If she gets more of it on one arm, she asks for more on the other one too. If she gets more on her nose, I have to put some on her ears too. If there is enough of it on her skin, I have to put some on mine too. The fitchy-fitchy ritual had a rough start but has now become an excuse to go outside. Each day begins with endless demands. I wonder if she composes a list of all the things she will want the following day, during the night, while I think that she's sleeping. She obviously finds the sea quite impressive; even though it hasn't won her over yet. She talks about it again and again.

Yesterday afternoon we stayed on the veranda to watch the birds. I promised myself that I would resist television at least until the pathetic eight o' clock news start, and that I'd stay with her outside, waiting for the birds to pass over our heads. This is one more habit we picked up this summer. It's getting dark, it's also a full moon tonight, as well as a red moon eclipse, but all these don't matter to Jazz. However, the birds, which — I explain to her — have their own home, their food, their toys, their mom and dad perhaps and their grandma (she has a little think and asks, "don't they have a mom?" I let it pass) and now, not now, now yet (the sense of time that has been bothering me my entire life is tormenting me all over again) now, at this hour still, they fly towards their jobs and their toys and dinners so they will pass by here and they can see us and we can wave at them, they can definitely see us.

Hello bird, hello birdie, there's a big one, she gets crazy with excitement when she sees more than two, *hello bird, this one's small, no it's not small,* I tell her *it only appears small to us because we are far away* and they won't stop passing by. And the sun, as they change direction, shines on their reddish and golden bellies and on their wings too. Just before eight o' clock, since it's obvious the birds have already started going to sleep, I heard her ask: Does the sea go to sleep?

Right, the sea, well that's a good question, the sea doesn't sleep, not like us. The sea is water, you know. Water. That's why it doesn't sleep. You know, it's not like us or the animals or the birds. It's water. But sometimes it moves slower and other times it moves faster. This is when waves are created, remember? (*Remember?* She repeated it two three times when we were going through the path leading down to the river). Remember? It was actually worth carrying her all the way down there on my shoulders in order to see the little river.

Now we're playing a game. It's dusk. We're on the small balcony. We don't come out here often. All you can see is other houses and roads. But also roofs, balconies, antennas. And a detached house with a tiled roof, empty, deserted. Sometimes we see cats in there. Now we're watching the birds. We'll call the birds now, I tell her. I know that birds fly around at this hour, perhaps looking for a hotel room for tonight. I therefore know that every now and then a bird will appear, crossing the part of the sky that we're watching. Some of them land on the tiles of the old house, others on the antennas, some bolder ones on the ever-shut-down balconies. "Call the birds and they'll come," I tell Jazz. She produces a small cry. Jazz believes she has summoned it herself and this makes her really excited, she gets crazy with the sense that she can actually summon the birds. We play this game again and again and again. Isn't it magic? It is for me, for as long as it lasts. And when a bird appears a bit late, I get anxious. But there are birds flying constantly. And Jazz is happy. Again and again and again. Until it gets dark. She wants more. We'll call them again tomorrow, I tell her; they must go to bed now. She doesn't object to this — I adore her.

Today is one of the longest days of the year. One more week for the days to keep getting longer. I can hear music from somewhere. Music? She says to herself. It sounds astounding when she says it.

I wonder if she understands every time I tell her that everything is OK when I hand her the pacifier she has dropped. Everything is all right. Everything will be fine. I would like her to believe it; I would like at least her to believe it. .

I always feel remorse on Saturday mornings when before or after the open market I let her watch TV. A tornado of commercial temptations, which she doesn't know how to handle yet, but it definitely leaves some traces. During the commercial break, Bebé Lily, Bob the Builder, Rapunzel and some miserable stories with mummies. It's time for stupefaction and compulsory consumerist education, which I don't like at all. At the open market, the old man we bought rusks from, managed to confess his desire to have all 300 members of parliament burnt at the stake. Just to make sure even their seed will vanish, he added distinctly.

Meanwhile, we must learn thousands of self-evident things. Why can't they learn all these automatically? This is probably what all the people who haven't gone through this process must believe. But it's nothing like this. Two years ago I would have believed the same. Which letters can you still remember? O, a, e, i, none of those. She can't remember anything at all. I would dare say it is absolutely despairing if I wasn't suspecting that she's actually playing a trick on me. Somewhere deep inside her brain she knows them, it can't be, she knew o last year, it's a ball, she can't have forgotten this as well. I suppose she's is no mood to learn the letters. She's in no mood to learn anything at all. She only learns the songs from the nursery and she even sings those her own way. As well as the prime minister, whom she calls an asshole with enormous pleasure. I was hoping the government would collapse and at least we would get rid of this, but that impossible guy got away with it for the time being, by giving away part of the power to his worst intraparty rival.

Yet today she was terribly cheerful, while we were leaving the nursery. I let the beautiful lady know that we were going on vacation, hoping for a drop of sorrow on her part in vain. On the contrary, she actually seemed happy to get rid of Jazz. You'll have a great time, she said. I, on the other hand, wasn't that optimistic. It won't be easy, I told her. She won't listen to you, she assumed pensively, and a red line was drawn between us. I wonder how much stricter I should become in order to compel Jazz to listen.

Suddenly, while she was watching Dora, she sprang up from the chair, came over to the sofa where I'd been trying to read Franzen's *Freedom*. It's so addictive I'm getting quite sad to watch the remaining pages shrink, and yet I want to read all the time — could an author hear a more ideal comment? She sprang up and hid behind me, just like a cartoon. My relatively large back was protecting her from the object of her fear. She gradually got over it, I suppose she got scared by the mountain transforming into a giant red hen, a really enormous one, compared to Dora and Boots, who could fit comfortably in a little corner of the hen's head. Her reaction astonished me, though. She has become really experienced with Dora by now, there's no reason for her to get scared by anything, she has repeatedly watched the episodes at least 150 times — according to my calculations this means 75 hours of freedom for me. As compensation, I melted a bit of vanilla ice cream, got some crisps, and took her with me to the yard to water the plants, but she insisted on watering the tiles instead of the plants, which she finally started watering after the fifth time I shouted at her. When we went upstairs we got to see the last birds going to sleep. There's no moon anymore, and tomorrow we're going on vacation.

Mr Kitten is a true hero. He's not a cartoon character. He's an incredible man who feeds the cats in our neighbourhood. And not only in our neighbourhood. His love for cats spreads over a vast area, which must be more than one kilometre wide. He sets out every afternoon at 5 sharp, from a house nearby. The end of his route is the city park where he leaves rissoles and replaces the water in the little cans he has placed there. This saint of cats feeds hundreds of souls and every afternoon at 5 o'clock sharp you see all the cats from all places gathering at the agreed meeting spots and waiting. Of course, he knows all of them by their name. We also give names to cats but they don't always suit them. Sometimes we have a chat with him. He is, of course, a really gloomy man, very disappointed at humans. He talks bitterly about their behaviour. He knows when a cat is hurt, when a cat is ill and even which ones are missing. When a cat doesn't turn up at the common meal Mr Pussycat gets even gloomier.

What's this? This is the sky. It's blue and it's above our heads. Yes, it's very high. We can't reach it.

5. A journey

While we're in the cab, I'm looking at her nose with admiration. It's one of those moments she looks perfect to me. A perfect creature who knows everything, in her own world, the ideal world. I always wonder about her landing in life, though.

In every cab we get at the big city, she asks, *who is he?* She wonders if he's our friend. How can you help her understand that *he* is doing a job and his job is to drive people to places and I do another job (I have no job at all at the moment but there's still some money left for trips), and I need *him* in order to go from one place to the other, so we get in the cab and we go from one place to the other, and we get another cab to go back and at the end of each ride I give the driver a colourful piece of paper. Who is he? Is he one of the people I'm supposed to know about? Why doesn't he look happy to see me like all the rest of the people but he just stares at the road holding the wheel?

She says "red?". And then, *more?* Yes, this is red. We'll see more of them. This is also red, and this. There, look, this is red. That is green.

She's not interested in learning the colours. What she's interested in at the moment is red. I remember I was one year older more or less, when I asked my father, who was holding me by the hand. How red is blood? My father seemed impressed and mentioned it to the man walking by his side. He was also wearing a suit and a tie. He wants to find out how red blood is. I was impressed to see he was impressed so I still remember it.

The question "do you remember?" contains enormous power. It means that she has inwardly understood this entire mechanism, to be, to exist, to have existed, to bring something back, to share it again with the person I had shared it with.

I require her to prove to me that she has grown up. I am a type of traitor but what can I do? I am such a cheap character that I prefer the easy way out.

A strange dream about my own existential issues, which are passed on to her as well. I'm trying to be on time for a family celebration or a party or something. Jazz is already there and she somehow explains to me what's going on. In the party, there are some unusual toys, looking a bit like balls, perhaps with the enormous balloons we saw last night, and loads of sweets. Yet I'm sad, especially the moment we leave on a weird open-top bus, because I won't live forever. But I'm thinking this is also the case with Jazz.

She shows a special interest in music, not exactly music, songs. All sorts of songs. As soon as one begins, she wants to make sure that more will follow. This afternoon we watched music videos. She quite enjoyed the one with Bruno Mars, *Grenade*, in which he is dragging a piano in the street. I asked her again and again what she liked about it. *This, this.* Walking down the street with a piano? *Yes, yes.* Perhaps it reminds her of our broken stroller. The music video is slightly melancholic, because after walking the whole way and arriving at his beloved's house, he sees her with someone else, so then he has to go all the way back, dragging the piano with a rope.

Yesterday, in the street, she said, "song." We could hear something but as soon as we got closer we realised it wasn't a song. Some old man was screaming in a loudspeaker in order to save the world from its impending disaster. Of course, some people were laughing at him. I thought something similar must have happened to Jesus.

In a way, the journey to the big city is a journey in time. We do nothing much, just some necessary jobs and some necessary visits. Taking a glance at what we've left behind. I think she feels — although she is unable to say so — that living in the small city was a wise choice. I don't know how our life there will be in the next few years but it will definitely be better than what it would have been here. We're both in a hurry to leave this place.

I can't think of a movie scene that is sweeter than the one where Gru (in *Despicable me*) the misanthrope, is forced to accommodate three orphan girls at his house and he must also read them a bedtime story. I don't know how much of it she understood, we'll watch it again sometime but to me it was magical. I still have the right to watch cartoons, right? Do I still have the right to weep? I guess it's too much for my age, yet I can't help it. It's not my fault. It's Gru's fault. Because he resembles me so much. It's also the three girls' fault; especially the youngest one's. Because she definitely resembles Jazz a lot.

Athens is a sad and sorrowful city. It looks like an aging theatre company that keeps performing even though nobody gives a damn anymore. The visitor--spectator feels this kind of pity and finally a sort of fondness. There are cities that look indifferent or hostile towards visitors, but Athens is not one of them. It is hostile only towards its own people, something that looks like a just revenge for their behavior, or at least for their fathers' behavior towards the city. In some places the ugliness is horrifying. In other places, it hides clumsily behind the remains of the past, since some of those can't possibly lose their beauty. People go out in the streets and protest quite often. Nothing changes of course, but I have the feeling I should do this too, at least once.

I arrive at Syntagma Square at around one o'clock. Jazz is safe, miles away, at her auntie's house. I spent very little time there. These contacts are always awkward for me, but Jazz was excited to play with her elder cousins. I leave her there and go to the demonstration.

I arrive exactly before the rough part begins but I not aware of this yet. I observe the crowds arriving. Most of the people are organized in groups according to their political party or workers' syndicate. I'm walking just next to the pharmacists, I recognize their banner. As usual, I feel guilty about not belonging anywhere. But that's the way it is. Further back, there are more groups, some of them are more imaginative, with colorful flags and balloons while others are wilder, wearing their distinct black attire. This time, the demonstration is enormous. Thousands of protesters start heading towards

Syntagma square. I hear some explosions and the chase begins. Smoke emerges from various sides and people are running in panic. I can see the riot police behind them, with their shields and truncheons. Of course, I've already started running too, there's no time for too much thinking. Later I will find out that what triggered the riot were Molotovs thrown at the Parliament building, which stands at the upper side of the square, protected, of course, by thousands of cops. The smoke is getting thicker. People are screaming with terror or anger, some are picking up stones and are throwing them, while the police respond in the way they know best. Although my mood is perfectly fine, tears start running down my cheeks. A kind of fog is spreading, a fog of tear gas. The demonstration is over. All I want is to get out of there. I have no idea where I'm heading. To a place where I won't burst into tears over nothing.

There's nothing else for us to do here. I don't know if we belong to the small city or anywhere else. We belong to each other.

6. Man pushing stroller

Today she tore a book with horses that I brought her. She might have been looking for more images. But I guess I'm just making up excuses. Then she tossed the last spoonful of her food, ostentatiously, because she was full already but that was still not a good excuse. In the morning she tripped and fell while she was running, her little face is a bit swollen, therefore I treat her a bit like an asylum seeker. I stopped the crying with a piece of melted chocolate (the only one I could find) and of course her clothes ended up in a mess. It's generally been a tough day. How is it possible that I still can't bear the "poopoo" very easily? Is it possible that I haven't placed the diaper properly? We're going to the swings on foot. We miss our stroller. When it broke I thought we should try and see if we can live without it. But I'd better fix it.

The thing is she keeps going backwards. As if she's trying to suspend it as much as possible. She has a date with growing up, which she keeps postponing. She's staring at the tiled mantel. "The wa-er!", she yells. She's referring to that game I used to play, watering the tiles in the yard, and then watching it dry up. "Remember?", she asks me.
This word sounds absolutely enchanting, since she has started pronouncing it. Re-mem-ber? As with many other words, it's like I'm hearing it for the first time; to be more accurate, as if I understand it for the first time.

"I remember", I tell her and then I water the tile again so that we can repeat it. It's also part of her mania for water, which might be a common thing. She's touching the tile, playing with the water and then licking it. I let her do it.

The cab-driver who drove us to the station — our car too has broken down — recommended I should take her to swimming lessons this year. He had taken both his children apparently. Now they're about 15 or 16. He wasn't much older than me.

Another sudden change. She didn't want a stroller anymore, she said "feet". Is this the end of the road? But it wasn't just this. When I told her we should take it along just in case, she insisted on pushing it herself. It was a bit funny to watch, yet a deeply serious matter. She didn't let go of it at all until we arrived at the swings; only when she was forced to, in order to cross the main avenue that separates us from the park, and then we couldn't help it.

I frankly don't know which one of the two of us is most afraid of the great change…

At the playground everything went as usual, except from her launching like a rocket at the first slide, falling on the ground and hurting her head slightly. She didn't cry much; when she realises she's kind of responsible (well, she must have done something wrong, probably pushing harder on her way down the slide) she doesn't overdo it. Yet she approached a little boy with a swollen cheek in order to ask him — what are you doing? The little boy, I see this quite often, was speechless and probably stunned. There is a terribly sociable part in her, which I have no idea where she got. Not from me, that's for sure.

The construction site has acquired a name. "Will we see the bulldozer?", she asked, "in the afternoon?". I explained to her that bulldozers go to sleep in the afternoon so there's no fear in passing by that place. She probably enjoys a bit of danger. I've noticed that the amount of words she uses in each sentence has increased. But when I ask her why she was told off in the park, she only says an incomprehensible, "thyer", pointing at the bread; the loaf of bread that she snatched, cut into pieces, put in a plate and rushed outside to eat it, breaking almost all the related rules. I understand that as soon as she starts speaking properly, having conversations, we will have gone on to that notorious next phase. I don't know how much I want this, but I'm definitely pursuing it through punishments. Can I do otherwise?

For the first time, she doesn't want to watch any more of Dora. She watches about five minutes, and then starts asking for the duckling, that is, Tweety and Sylvester.

This morning I am ill, lying on the couch. I'm trying to gather up some strength and take her to the nursery. She comes over to me, it's easier now, since she has gained some height and our noses are on the same level, so we can play all sorts of games, rubbing our noses, touching our eyes, our hair, searching for each other's face.

She still has a bit of a fear of the sea. She never lets herself go, she stays tense in my arms so when it gets a bit more surging she ends up gulping much more water than normal. But she adores the sand and her feeling that everything is ours gets out of control. I can't understand if there's a better way to explain it, than constantly telling her that all these are not ours, they belong to other children, other people, they're not ours. At the deckchair next to us there are two couples, two women with enormous breasts, similar to the local baby-watermelons, and two rather beefy men. And two little boys. Further away, there was another woman, thin lips, beautiful eyes —I managed to take a glimpse at them during the split second she took her enormous sunglasses off — and an aloof look which came in contrast with the generous exposure of her body as well as the cheapness of her yellow bikini. Jazz went straight to the towel the two boys had spread out and started playing with their toys, tossing sand over their plastic swimming pool. One of them threw sand at her face. Just a bit of sand. I thought that was a cruel learning method concerning these joint ownership ideas of hers — which is actually more of a tendency to regard everything as hers. She took a few steps away and then undauntedly got on with her playing. The two boys went in the sea at some point so she was free to do as she pleased, until I carried her away. Yesterday at the birthday party at the nursery she got shocked by the number of people. I realised she can't bear being among groups of more than ten. As a woman, who introduced herself as a philologist, explained, children's tolerance to groups is restricted and increases as they grow up. She asked me what I did for a living and, by the time I managed to explain what I had been doing before and to find something worthwhile I intend to do in the future, the conversation was interrupted by someone who asked to have a word with her.

Evening stroll at the playground. We were practically on our own. She enjoyed swinging as much as she could and a bit of the slide. A Barbie doll was abandoned there. I showed it to her and told her that if the child didn't show up we could take it, then I wondered if this went against the rule I have set for some years now, no more thefts, so I changed my mind. I left it there, lying under the slide. Luckily, she forgot about it quite soon. Then the whistling lady came along to shut the playground and told us we should leave.

I think we both suffered due to the lack of a stroller. Because of this we had to change quite a few things. Jazz could also tell somehow that we were entering a new era. We were no longer the dad pushing the stroller, whispering stories to his baby. Now, we are a man and a child holding his hand, walking down the street together. Down the street, where we heard the bulldozer roar from a distance. Jazz asked what that was and I told her it was a bulldozer. It wasn't exactly a bulldozer, it was an enormous vehicle with a drill opening holes in the ground but of course I don't know what you call this. Once we got very close, the noise became too loud. Jazz was quite scared and I took her in my arms, running away from the noise, a bit like one of those images we see on TV, of distraught parents running away with their children in their arms in order to escape from some catastrophe.

He uses clay to make some terrifying puppies, which he paints himself. It took some time for me to realise that he made them so ugly and scary on purpose. They looked totally out of place in a space where all the items are happy (and nearly all Chinese) and somebody making something ugly, especially if it's on purpose, is almost an insult. He's an outsider though, like me. He picked this city because he liked it. I, on the other hand, had no choice and I can't really tell whether I like it or not.

We also see people in an entirely different way. While we were chatting, he told me he didn't want to enter into close personal contact with anyone. He might belong to a cult or something, who knows, I didn't dare to ask him. I, on the other hand, would hang around with almost anyone. Yet the result is the same. We are both lonesome guys.

We don't have much to talk about whenever I go there; we might not even feel like it. We sit amongst the ugly puppies and share a beautiful silence. Funnily enough, Jazz also keeps rather quiet, compared to her standards, in Mr Kostis' workshop. Of course she broke a puppy that he had made the mistake of giving her. Since then she has been quite sensible. She'd better be. It takes him about three hours of work to make each puppy. This guy is genuinely placid. I would have strangled her, I guess.

I mended the stroller. It wasn't hard work but I couldn't help boasting a bit. "Your daddy fixed the stroller," I told her twice just to make sure she understood. "Think nothing of it," she said and I have no idea why the hell she picked precisely this phrase. Once more, I feel like we're in familiar waters, though. I don't know for how long, it's definitely a little trick we have played on time. We both know, OK, I know for certain, that reality will beat us in the end. But it's easier to use our stroller as we used to. I believe we're both feeling better now.

Along with the stroller we keep moving a bit forward – both of us – that appointment we have with time.

7. From now on we will live happily ever after

I think my cooking has been constantly improving. I know I will never become an amazing cook, but I don't mind. I don't intend to become the type of guy who gets all the women of the company (which women and which company, are an entirely different matter) thanks to his awesome recipes. To be precise, I will always be a conservative guy — I have come to terms with this by now — with artistic tendencies. And intense nostalgia. Those are my main ingredients. Speaking of nostalgia, what I intend to achieve through food is to hold onto my mother's memory. This might be a clever way of preserving memories. My aim is to learn how to cook ten, maximum fifteen, dishes as well as possible, no more. Most of these dishes will be an echo of my mother's cuisine. I want to retain that aroma. My mother never showed me how to cook anything, she didn't consider it necessary; on the contrary she would have been afraid of losing something if she had allowed me to cook as long as she was still alive. Between my fifth and twelfth year though, at least, I spent countless hours next to her in the kitchen, watching her cook. So I gradually discovered that I remember lots of things, even though I never tried cooking systematically. These things are always around. When I'm finished with a dish, it took me some time to realise this, I compare it (as an image first, then in terms of its smell and finally in terms of taste) with all those dishes that still exist in the depths of my brain. And that's a bit magical; when something goes slightly wrong I already know what I should do the following time.

My favourite art is the art of the salad. My mother's recipes are not a
great help in this matter, as she wasn't very interested in salads, that's my own
thing. I feel very lucky I can find plenty of local products in the small city.
There are vegetables, greens, legumes and herbs I had never seen in my life.
Now they're all at my disposal. So, after picking the ingredients, each time I
begin the game of colours. Colours are the souls of vegetables. A cabbage is
heavy and somewhat idle. It's a slightly boring friend who is always there to
fill the gaps, though. Also, tomatoes are always there when you want to add
a bit of certainty. They only stay out when the green colour and its shades
refuse to mix with other colours. The lettuce is slender, a bit more bohemian
perhaps. The rocket is a bit like a girl in a folk costume. The avocado is the
strange guy who will add a bit of extra colour to the company. You always
risk some people's displeasure once you invite the onion. It gets along with
tomatoes and peppers but the lettuce and the rocket are not on good terms
with it. The art of the salad is a combination of painting and party invitation
technique. My salads are nearly always the same yet always different. Just like
a party that happens with the same guests each time but there are also some
new people invited, just to break the monotony. My daughter is, at least for
the time being, much more conservative than I am. She always prefers to take
a few pieces of tomato and cucumber in her plate, ignoring the rest. I don't
lose heart, though. Improving is the only thing that matters.

*Playing the father is perhaps a role. A role which anyone can — just like all actors
can, apart from the ones who don't want to become actors — learn with time. Does this
mean that all fathers are acting the same part? No. It means there is an archetypal role
which can be learned and is then adjusted to the needs of the theatrical play each person
performs in — that is, his life — and to his personality. After long rehearsals, during
which he repeats the same basic scenes, the play starts flowing effortlessly. Does this mean
there's no room for improvement? On the contrary, you may improve through sticking with
the same general script, yet refining the small pieces of this jigsaw puzzle.*

She is a merry woman. You wouldn't say she's beautiful. Not ugly either.
But not exactly common either. There is something special about her. Yet
it's probably tightly sealed beneath this impeccable, cheerful — of course

— professional attitude of hers. I haven't come here to get to know her though. I came here because the people at the nursery suggested I should see a psychologist. Naturally, it's a bit awkward — first of all, explaining my relationship with the child. It's something special. A father on his own. I don't feel the usual pride I have acquired after all these months of single parenting. Yet, I've made it, right? Let's say I've made it. The reason we are here is Jazz's frequent crying. Apparently she cries much more at the nursery rather than at home, and yet she never objects to going there, some mornings she even rushes out of the door as soon as I open it.

She doesn't make any comments when I describe to her exactly how Jazz is being brought up. She's just listening, that's her job, I guess. She also doesn't say anything when I explain that this visit was not my idea, but her teacher's suggestion. She only asks me whether I believe that the child is being brought up normally, if I can see any problems. That's a difficult question. Is a child brought up normally, as long as the mother is missing? If we set this aside, then, no, I can't say I can see any particular problems. She cries of course. But isn't this what all children do?

"Why does she usually cry?"

"She cries when she doesn't have things her own way. Most of the times."

"Does she also cry for no reason?"

"She does sometimes, yes," I admit.

Jazz has been watching the conversation all this time. She's feeling a bit awkward, I can tell. But I feel equally awkward. The psychologist has given her a jigsaw puzzle to keep her busy, but Jazz only glanced at it condescendingly, started putting it together and put it aside after a couple of minutes. She has played with much more difficult ones. Perhaps she thinks it's too easy for her.

Then she decides we've done enough talking. She's trying to attract my attention in various ways. I don't want to seem too strict but I must stop her. "All right," I tell her many times. "All right. Don't be noisy. We have to talk."

She leaves us in peace for about three minutes. She's pretending she's busy with a toy. Then she gets stuck on me, as if she's ill. She uses her vocabulary as best she can. I get no chance to talk about the words and whether she should have been talking more and about the terrible twos. For some reason

I just feel an urge to get out of there as soon as possible. I would happily have this talk with her over a romantic dinner. If I were entirely sure that Jazz would be safe with someone else. Yet nobody inspires such confidence. The truth is I didn't look for anyone.

If this were a movie, I would fall in love with the psychologist, who would be a bit troubled until she realized that she is also madly in love with me. I would leave Jazz with a seventeen-year old baby sitter. She would also be in love with me already, secretly though. She would make an aggressive pass at me on a rainy night, after getting high on something. But I would manage to help her pull herself together. I would explain to her that she has her life ahead of her and give her a paternal cuddle. Perhaps I would kiss her a bit too. Well, it wouldn't be entirely paternal — I'm no saint. The following morning she would leave a post — it on my laptop and I'd never see her again. I would get married to the psychologist and Jazz would be a jolly bridesmaid at the wedding. End of story. From then on we would live happily ever after.

Nothing came out of our visit to the psychologist. A child cries because children cry. A child doesn't say many words because some children don't say many words. That's all.

End of story. Besides, if one of us two needed this woman's help, that one would be me.

From now on we will live happily ever after.

Jazz and I.

8. Where do you live, Mr Moon?

She asks more and more questions as the summer goes by. Soon I might not have the right answers anymore. Maybe I've never had them. But I love her and I think there will always be something for me to tell her.

It's the great August full moon, when she asks me where Mr Moon lives.
— He lives in a house far away and he sleeps all day and goes out at night.

She keeps asking questions beginning with 'remember':
Remember though we went to the sand?
Remember though we went on the boat?
Remember though we went to the parade?
Remember we went to the music?

Her little arm is stretched towards me as if she really has the need to feel I'm there.

A dream in three doses, that's a first, I would wake up wanting to see her again but each time she was even further away. A young woman who desired me, her cell phone was like a tree full of branches spreading out to unknown worlds, to which I'll never gain access. Who is that woman? She must exist somewhere. She knew about the child yet she didn't mind. She was tender clever funny sexy wonderful. Where is she? How can I find her?

Jazz knows very few things about the world she lives in. Nine out of ten times the world demands her not to do things. Usually, what she wants to do is annoying and the best case scenario is we simply tolerate it if we let her do it. Other times, we grant her what she wants as a favour and we ask for something is return. Yet, what are her options, regarding the world of grownups? Even the process of learning the basics, to her especially, must be exceptionally irritating. So she keeps stumbling upon denials. She knows food is something she likes. But she shouldn't eat whenever she likes, she shouldn't eat whatever she likes, she shouldn't eat most of the food grownups eat, and even when she does eat, again, there is a restriction in the amount she'll eat or when she refuses to eat, again, she is either forced or she makes an effort. Therefore, even when it comes to food, which belongs to the things that are familiar to her, she is facing a pile of problems. How easy is it living in such a world, whose beginning or end you are not aware of, whose logic, whatever that is, you can't comprehend, and at the same time having to obey all those rules you cannot understand?

And you go through this when you're still at an age when you have only just realised that you are something and others are something else. One must keep all this in mind before getting angry or abrupt with a child; one should get this elementary picture of how unequal a relationship between a child and our world is.

Things that are important in her world:

A leaf of ivy that gets plucked and is tossed in the air. A little jump from the lowest step with feet together. A dog suddenly growling aggressively. These are the important things in her world. Not the news. Not the salary that doesn't exist anymore. Not a coffee with someone you are in love with. Not a little bacchanal you've paid for with the good old guys from work. Not the country's bankruptcy. Not the government's stupidity. Not the fault in an air-conditioner or a TV. Not the no to a wedding proposal. A little leaf you pluck from the ivy and toss it in the air. That's what's important now.

The turning stroller wheel, covered in mud. Touching this mud and rolling it around in your fingers. That's what's important. After all, how reasonable is a pair of pink shorts that cost a fortune because of their designer's label. A leather handbag? A fur coat? An enormous amount of money in bonds that equal the bankruptcy of a country as well as endless misery for a few millions of people who are not to blame? A bottle of tequila you managed to gulp down in order to feel like a real man and then crashed on the lamp post? How reasonable are all these? Why are they more reasonable than plucking a little ivy leaf?

How easy is it to understand her world?

Another passage from Edo's book:
Try to think like the child. Try again and again. Don't try to become a child. You are not a child. If you were a child you wouldn't need to try to understand.

9. I will make mistakes, but why?

I often despair of myself. In any case, I never trusted myself much since I was a kid. I mean, I loved myself but I didn't believe in myself very much. Not as much as it would take to feel good, if you know what I mean. I believe that the worst part of my childhood was between 8 and 12, what I call the charmless years, perhaps this is the case with all the precocious creatures at this age, and this was definitely the case with me. This was the worst period because it was the peak of my parents' relationship crisis, my father almost openly cheating on my mother, while she was putting up with it to some extent. Then, when she realised she had lost all control of the situation, perhaps apart from her crying and the hysterical scenes she would barely try to hide from me, she moved on to more aggressive gestures. She started following him closely, perhaps with the assistance of well-wishers from within or outside of the family, friends, my father's colleagues, who knows, in order to catch him red-handed, something she nearly achieved with me as an unwilling witness, after forcing me to spy on him on previous occasions, and informing her of all his moves, sending me with him under some ridiculous pretext. My father was aware of this, of course, so his hostility was taken out on me as well. So, during the revelation scene, when she finally caught him having coffee with his girlfriend, I was also there against my will. Later they sent me back to the car but the damage had been done. I remember I used to get fits of hysteria when I was ten. I grew up to be placid on the surface but rather irritable and sometimes, especially between 20 and 30, I always ended up getting in quarrels with the slightest cause, usually crappy drivers who did something stupid while I was riding my motorcycle. I had nothing to do with cars till I turned forty. This tension that overwhelms me and bursts out in uncontrollable ways is still quite typical of me. Therefore, even when it comes to the child, even though I try to be as calm as possible, many times I can't help shouting at her and grabbing her fiercely, lifting her up, something that usually doesn't frighten her, and trying to terrify her in order to make her behave. But how does a two year old become a good child? Usually when she leaves you in peace. This is the moment when her good manners align with your best interests.

Yet, what could a child full of energy, like Jazz, do, shut in a rather small house for hours? Of course, causing small damages is her attempt to pass the time, to look for objects, but also to impress me. It makes sense for her to cause some damage in order to attract my attention. What is also at play is her opposition to the rules of peace and quiet, which look totally irrational to her. She has therefore developed a range of reactions for every time I tell her to do something. She either stays silent, looking at me as if she can't understand, when we both know she does, or she keeps doing the damage she was doing or she does the exact opposite to what I tell her. Fear is the ally of rules, an essential requirement in order to achieve something with a terribly weaker creature such as a child. How honest is that? How easily could it cause her the same problems that I used to — and still —have? Is it perhaps a never-ending vicious circle? How can I resist this and how can I still set some rules, as the child should know that, say, she shouldn't cross the road by herself, that she shouldn't touch dog-poo, that she shouldn't take an object she sees at a store and another million such things, justified and unjustified.

Where do the real rules for her safety begin and where do my own phobias and obsessions end? And who can define that it's bad, say, if she drops an ashtray at the café, if she snatches the bread from the table next to ours, if she smacks the neighbour's kitten? We are surrounded but nothing other than rules in a hostile world. How much is it the rules' fault that the world has become like this? And how can we ignore them since we are compelled to live in this world? I should try to be calmer, calmer, calmer, just this, and to love her as much and as firmly as I can. When she laughs after her crying, it's much more beautiful than the sun appearing from behind the clouds. It's a new hope that I haven't completely messed up everything.

One more, a rather strange one, passage from professor Edo's book:

The child is wise.
Your job is to make the child stupid.
Careful not to overdo it.

I'm not sure I understand it.

10. Let's go find the summer

There is an absolute logic within the child, all mine, all free, all to all. Jazz is not the most free creature in the world, compared to a baby at least, but due to her stubbornness, (one could also call it love for life) she is still in a state where she is unaware of all the basic human restrictions. Who could help envying her for this? And who wouldn't rather stay in this state for as long as possible? Of course, she's aware of a few restrictions, very specific ones, though: don't touch the ground, don't chuck the garbage, don't pee on the floor. She knows there are rules, and she has already discovered some ways of fighting them, it is impossible to escape even the smallest basic rule (what would happen then? Would it really be a nightmare as we're afraid it would?), but she hasn't grasped The Rule; the general rule that will contain and organise the rest of them. Let's say: We don't disturb others. With a million specific sub— rules. We don't disturb daddy. With thousands of applications. We don't say whatever comes to our head. All right, this one will come later, they also call it logic. But when this comes, something will be lost forever.

You watch her run everywhere, amongst the people, around the deckchairs, by the sea, you're scared, because she might ask for anything she likes from anyone and "expose" you. Because that's what you're scared of. She may take whatever she likes, play with whatever she likes, greet anyone she likes, while we're scared, ashamed, awkward, neurotic, full of phobias. At some point, of course, Jazz will learn how to respect other people's property above all, and this will be the end of the story.

I watched a film. The main character is a writer. He invents the perfect woman and sees her in his dream and then starts writing about her. And one morning she appears in his house. And she is perfect. Then he realises that he can form her exactly the way he likes, since she is his own invention. He forgets about it at first and simply enjoys their love affair. Then the outside world gets closer and trouble begins. He gets tempted to keep writing about her. First he wants her to be with him all the time, then to become a bit more independent, then to live on her own, then to get stuck on him again. And there's a problem with everything. At some point she manages to leave in spite of the obstacles he sets. He meets her again in the end. They might start afresh yet I doubt it.

I got a bicycle.

The girl I was chatting with online turned out to be a guy. Not gay, he said. Just a man who enjoyed talking. I can't say I wasn't disappointed. I had been making some plans.

A few days later, it just seems funny.

One of those stories you like narrating.

Later.

I miss Tania — that was his name.

He could have been the ideal woman.

In another story perhaps.

The image of the nursery festival, parents with their iPads, sweets and presents, the children's play in which they don't actually want to perform, the beautiful mother attracting all the looks, my thought wandering off. I'm worried by an image of her holding a ball and looking for children or asking them to play with her and being ignored.

According to Tao, love is analagous to that spontaneous and implicit goodness which only small and innocent children give away spontaneously to anyone who treats them kindly.

Usually at the end of the story the hero has learned stuff, he has changed his life, he has compromised with the situation, he has even found some company. In some beautiful stories he's even about to get married. This way the reader can finish the book peacefully. Have any of these things happened in my case? I'm afraid not. I'm afraid I haven't learned anything, at best I managed to forget a few things — not even the basic ones of my troubles. Let's not even talk about finding company. Also, I haven't got used to this place at all yet. I like the town, I liked it in the first place. But the people… This will always be an issue. Have I changed at all, I wonder. I'm scared of looking the reader straight in the eye.

Yet, Jazz has changed. That's for sure.

But she would have changed anyway.

Let's go find the summer, she told me this morning.

A nice, long, complete sentence.

I think something is coming to an end at this point.

Yes, that's a good idea.

Let's go find the summer.

Perhaps I wrote all this, thinking it would be a way to bring her back.

The only thing I brought was a few pages on Microsoft Word.

Mommy is not coming back.

But if we are good…

Could another mom come?

Better not.

I'm not quite sure.

But we must be good.

Have I been a good kid to you?

Normally a woman should appear at this point of the story. It's precisely that moment before the happy ending. At this point comes a wonderful woman who loves me and Jazz, she is very intelligent, she laughs a lot, she plays with us and in the end the three of us walk towards the sunset holding hands. I would be prepared to do anything for her. She would wear her hair long, maybe not too long, her eyes would be tender and (at least at first) we would spend hours in bed in the weekends (Jazz would be away on a trip, it would do her good). We would spend hours talking about various things, I would tell her all about my past until she wouldn't bear to listen anymore and she would tell me about her past too. Then we would watch a silly rom com about a couple ending up together in spite of all the obstacles and we would fall asleep in each other's arms. I think she would be an artist of some sort so that I could have her at home more. I would do the cooking but not all the time. After all, she would be a better cook. I have started liking this woman so much, I'd better stop this at once.

This is just a diary, nothing more than a diary. And it's time for it to end.

EPILOGUE

— So where's mom? She will ask me one day.

We'll probably be sitting in front of the TV watching MTV or something, without looking at each other. It won't be too long till this happens. Maybe in a few years. Just before her fifth birthday perhaps.

Anyway, I'll be pretending to be completely absorbed by some music video, buying a bit of time to think about her question. But after not too long, I'll respond:

— Listen, don't take me wrong, it's not that I don't want to talk about this, but I really think I'd better tell you a story instead. You're still a kid after all.

— OK, she'll reply. Tell me then.

— Well, let's say that once upon a time there were two squirrels living in a big tree in the forest. This is where they lived, having a good time, as far as we know, and they had loads of nut — the squirrels adore nuts — and their life was easy. The boy squirrel was called Pappie and the girl squirrel was called Mappie. They spent their entire day climbing on trees and playing games and chasing each other, you know, just for fun. Then they somehow built or they made, if you like, a nest. I'm not quite sure but I think it was inside the big tree. And one day a little girl squirrel was born, and they named her Zappie.

— Seriously?

— Yes, why not? Zappie is a rather common squirrel name.

— No, that's not what I'm asking. That baby squirrel simply appeared out of thin air inside the nest?

— Sure, this is more or less how things happen. When there's a boy and a girl of whatever kind and they build a nest, if they're lucky enough, a baby squirrel or whatever kind, will come.

— OK. And were they happy after this?

— Sure, why not? They really wanted this little baby and, I must say, it was the prettiest baby squirrel ever born. Well, they were really happy with all this. But there was a small issue. Someone had to take care of the baby all the time, because the forest was a dangerous place to live, with loads of enemies around. So now they had this really pretty baby but life wasn't as much fun as it used to be. Fair enough. That's how it is. But then something strange happened. Mappie, the lady-squirrel, suddenly discovered that she wasn't a squirrel after all…

— What was she?

— Good question. She felt she was something else. Something with wings. A bird, for example. Which bird do you like?

— The parrot!

— The parrot, eh? I didn't know you liked parrots. OK, then. Mappie was a parrot. And, to make things worse, she remembered she had left a nest behind somewhere. And someone was waiting for her there.

— I don't like this fairy-tale.

— Me neither, to be honest. But that's what happened. One day, Mappie couldn't take it anymore and left the squirrel-tree. Well, and since then nobody ever saw her again.

— So suddenly?

— Yes. Crazy, isn't it?

— Mom turned into a bird. And left. She found another bird. And you never looked for her. Where is she now then?

— Hold on a second. You ask too much. Pappie, not I, never looked for her. He knew it would be no use. There's nothing you can do in such cases.

— Didn't mom love me?

— Very much. But…

— Your fairy-tale is silly.

— Maybe you're right.

— Why doesn't she come to see me?

— I guess she can't. She's…

— Where's mom?

— I don't know, darling.

— Will she come back to the squirrel-nest?

— To be honest, I don't think so. It's hard to come back once you've gone so far away. But life was good for Pappie and little Zappie, who grew up to be a pretty little girl who really enjoyed living with dad.

— Was that it?

— As far as I know, yes. It sounds like a slightly sad story but if you look at from some distance everyone was happy. Pappie had Zappie to play with now, Zappie had her daddy, Mappie could fly wherever she liked…

— What was his name?

— His name?

— Yes, the name of the parrot who took mom away. What was he called?

— Who cares? He was just an idiot anyway. But to be fair he used to know her from the old days, before we got to know her.

— Will I ever see her? Will she ever come to see me?

— That will happen one day. But we're doing pretty fine on our own too, aren't we? The only thing I can tell you with certainty is where your bed is. This I can tell.

— Is mom nasty?

— No, I don't want you to say this, it's not true. Let's go to bed now. I love you very much, isn't that enough for you? And the fairy-tale, OK, yes, it was silly. I just can't find a way to talk to you about all this.

I must be a pitiful sight because she stretches out her little arms as if she was trying to comfort me. Although it should be the other way round, damn it.

So I take in my arms and, although she's become quite heavy by now, I carry her to bed and kiss her goodnight and then I go back to the living room to chill out a bit and maybe to drink a cold beer. Or two.

And then I choose to listen to a song we always like listening to, *Goodbye Mr. Tears*, in the original Japanese version (*Namida Kun Sayonara*).

She always laughs when she listens to it. That's why I'm listening to it now;

to listen to her laughter.

Jazz slips out of her bed and comes to me.

— I love Mr. Tears, she says.

I smile, I take her in my arms and reply to her.

— I'd rather you call me Gregory.

About Fomite

A fomite is a medium capable of transmitting infectious organisms from one individual to another.

"The activity of art is based on the capacity of people to be infected by the feelings of others." Tolstoy, *What Is Art?*

Writing a review on Amazon, Good Reads, Shelfari, Library Thing or other social media sites for readers will help the progress of independent publishing. To submit a review, go to the book page on any of the sites and follow the links for reviews. Books from independent presses rely on reader to reader communications.

For more information or to order any of our books, visit http://www.fomitepress.com/FOMITE/Our_Books.html

More Titles from Fomite...

Novels

Joshua Amses — *During This, Our Nadir*
Joshua Amses — *Raven or Crow*
Joshua Amses — *The Moment Before an Injury*
Jaysinh Birjepatel — *The Good Muslim of Jackson Heights*
Jaysinh Birjepatel — *Nothing Beside Remains*
David Brizer — *Victor Rand*
Paula Closson Buck — *Summer on the Cold War Planet*
Marc Estrin — *Hyde*
Marc Estrin — *Speckled Vanitie*
Zdravka Evtimova — *Sinfonia Bulgarica*
Daniel Forbes — *Derail This Train Wreck*
Greg Guma — *Dons of Time*
Richard Hawley — *The Three Lives of Jonathan Force*
Lamar Herrin — *Father Figure*
Ron Jacobs — *All the Sinners Saints*

Fomite

Ron Jacobs — *Short Order Frame Up*
Ron Jacobs — *The Co-conspirator's Tale*
Scott Archer Jones — *A Rising Tide of People Swept Away*
Maggie Kast — *A Free Unsullied Land*
Darrell Kastin — *Shadowboxing with Bukowski*
Coleen Kearon — *Feminist on Fire*
Jan Englis Leary — *Thicker Than Blood*
Diane Lefer — *Confessions of a Carnivore*
Rob Lenihan — *Born Speaking Lies*
Ilan Mochari — *Zinsky the Obscure*
Andy Potok — *My Father's Keeper*
Robert Rosenberg — *Isles of the Blind*
Fred Skolnik — *Rafi's World*
Lynn Sloan — *Principles of Navigation*
L.E. Smith — *The Consequence of Gesture*
L.E. Smith — *Travers' Inferno*
Bob Sommer — *A Great Fullness*
Tom Walker — *A Day in the Life*
Susan V. Weiss —*My God, What Have We Done?*
Peter M. Wheelwright — *As It Is On Earth*
Suzie Wizowaty — *The Return of Jason Green*

Poetry

Antonello Borra — *Alfabestiario*
Antonello Borra — *AlphaBetaBestiaro*
James Connolly — *Picking Up the Bodies*
Greg Delanty — *Loosestrife*
Mason Drukman — *Drawing on Life*
J. C. Ellefson — *Foreign Tales of Exemplum and Woe*
Anna Faktorovich — *Improvisational Arguments*
Barry Goldensohn — *Snake in the Spine, Wolf in the Heart*
Barry Goldensohn — *The Hundred Yard Dash Man*
Barry Goldensohn — *The Listener Aspires to the Condition of Music*
R. L. Green When — *You Remember Deir Yassin*
Kate Magill — *Roadworthy Creature, Roadworthy Craft*
Tony Magistrale — *Entanglements*

Fomite

Sherry Olson — *Four-Way Stop*
Janice Miller Potter — *Meanwell*
Joseph D. Reich — *Connecting the Dots to Shangrila*
Joseph D. Reich — *The Hole That Runs Through Utopia*
Joseph D. Reich — *The Housing Market*
Joseph D. Reich — *The Derivation of Cowboys and Indians*
David Schein — *My Murder and Other Local News*
Scott T. Starbuck — *Industrial Oz*
Seth Steinzor — *Among the Lost*
Seth Steinzor — *To Join the Lost*
Susan Thomas — *The Empty Notebook Interrogates Itself*
Sharon Webster — *Everyone Lives Here*
Tony Whedon — *The Tres Riches Heures*
Tony Whedon — *The Falkland Quartet*

Stories

Jay Boyer — *Flight*
Michael Cocchiarale — *Still Time*
Neil Connelly — *In the Wake of Our Vows*
Catherine Zobal Dent — *Unfinished Stories of Girls*
Zdravka Evtimova — *Carts and Other Stories*
John Michael Flynn — *Off to the Next Wherever*
Elizabeth Genovise — *Where There Are Two or More*
Andrei Guriuanu — *Body of Work*
Derek Furr — *Semitones*
Derek Furr — *Suite for Three Voices*
Zeke Jarvis — *In A Family Way*
Marjorie Maddox — *What She Was Saying*
William Marquess — *Boom-shacka-lacka*
Gary Miller — *Museum of the Americas*
Jennifer Anne Moses — *Visiting Hours*
Martin Ott — *Interrogations*
Jack Pulaski — *Love's Labours*
Charles Rafferty — *Saturday Night at Magellan's*
Kathryn Roberts — *Companion Plants*
Ron Savage — *What We Do For Love*

Fomite

L.E. Smith — *Views Cost Extra*
Susan Thomas — *Among Angelic Orders*
Tom Walker — *Signed Confessions*
Silas Dent Zobal — *The Inconvenience of the Wings*

Odd Birds

Micheal Breiner — *the way none of this happened*
Gail Holst-Warhaft — *The Fall of Athens*
Roger Leboitz — *A Guide to the Western Slopes and the Outlying Area*
dug Nap— *Artsy Fartsy*
Delia Bell Robinson — *A Shirtwaist Story*
Peter Schumann — *Planet Kasper, Volumes One and Two*
Peter Schumann — *Bread & Sentences*
Peter Schumann — *Faust 3*

Plays

Stephen Goldberg — *Screwed and Other Plays*
Michele Markarian — *Unborn Children of America*